BENJAMIN H. LEVIN

Black
Triumvirate

A Novel of Haiti

THE CITADEL PRESS
Secaucus, New Jersey

First edition
Copyright © 1972 by Benjamin H. Levin
All rights reserved
Published by Citadel Press, Inc.
A subsidiary of Lyle Stuart, Inc.
120 Enterprise Ave., Secaucus, N.J. 07094
In Canada: George J. McLeod Limited
73 Bathurst St., Toronto 2B., Ontario
Manufactured in the United States of America
by The Colonial Press, Inc., Clinton, Mass.
ISBN 0-8065-0268-1

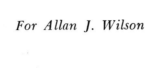

For Allan J. Wilson

Black Triumvirate

1

They lay side by side under the netting, and she knew a deep contentment as she stirred into wakefulness. Outside the latticed shutters a native rada drum throbbed in the heat of early noon. It was insistent; repetitious and insistent; muffled, yet insistent. The reverberations had been ignored in the crescendo of their love-making and their drowsing afterward, but now the boom-tete-boom, tete-tete-boom, boom-tete-boom ... was like a rhythmic heart that throbbed on a hill at the edge of Cap Français, pulsed across the Savane de la Fossette, and filled the whitewashed room with its unabated intonation.

She turned on her side and brushed Henri Christophe's ear with her fingers. A few beads of sweat glistened in her armpit where they clung like iridescent pearls on the crisply curled, black hair. She was fascinated by the convolutions of his ear, a sable brown in contrast to the ebony of his thick neck. His ear, as small and delicate as a woman's, was close to the side of his round head, and from its lobe, which he had pierced, hung a tiny nautilus shell.

Suddenly there was a roll of drums ... French drums ... and the boom from a single cannon burst from the direction of the Place d'Armes. The youth knew what it meant. He sprang from the bed and tore his cotton trousers from the wicker chair.

"Henri! You no go now!"

Lutétia sat upright in the bed, and the single sheet, slipping down, revealed her slightly distended belly and her outthrust breasts, as small as a girl's and as conical as those of a Senegalese before she has had her first child.

He was buttoning his cotton shirt. The French drums had drowned the throbbing of the native one as though they had devoured its sound.

"Henri! You stay some more!"

As though to insult her, he addressed her in patois without looking at her. "*Ou* not own Henri. Henri Christophe belong Coidovic."

She sprang from the bed and embraced him. "I buy this boy from Coidovic."

He ran his fingers down her naked back until his hands came to rest on the tan hills above her thighs. He pressed them together and laughed, "*Ou coiyou!** You not devour this boy. Drain him dry. This boy speak French good. This boy speak English! You get work for this boy inside the Auberge de la Couronne? You get this boy to

---

* Definitions of this and similar terms may be found in the Glossary at the end of the book.

[10]

wait on table? Not groom horses? This boy stink from horseshit. Smell!"

Her body quivered against his and she thrust herself against the genitals beneath his thin trousers. Suddenly the roll of the French drums ended and there was an ominous silence. He pushed her from him and burst, barefooted, through the doorway and into the blinding light of the noon sun. The Rue d'Anjou was deserted. The pebbled sidewalks in front of the two-story stone houses would be cooler, but he could run more quickly along the paving on either side of the street's middle kennel. The streets of Cap Français were crisscrossed at right angles, and as he hurried he glanced eastward toward the shopping centers of the Rue de Penthievre and the Rue du Vieux Gouvernement. There, despite the latest novelties from Paris, no one could be seen.

He reached the outskirts of the Place d'Armes and found the great square crammed with people, for the Provincial Assembly had declared the day a holiday. He could not sidle into the square, for he was Black, and it was forbidden for a Negro to thrust himself past a white, or even a mulatto. The Place d'Armes was shaded by rows of pear trees. As he edged closer he noticed a coconut palm. He hugged its girth, pressed his bare feet against its bole, and scrambled upward. In a moment he was under its crown of pinnated leaves and studied Cap Français from his vantage point.

It was a scene of beauty, bloodlust, horror. More than fifty ships rode at anchor within its harbor. Almost twenty barks, schooners, and brigs were moored to its quays. To the east, toward Monte Christi, he could see the battery

[11]

positions that had been built on the marshes. The houses of Le Cap, as most residents called Cap Français, were built four or five to a block and roofed with tiles from Anjou or Normandy. To the south he could see the church of Notre Dame, set within its tree-lined square like a truant stepchild of France having no kinship with Cap Français.

A slight breeze blew eastward from the little island of Tortuga and rustled the palm fronds. He looked into the Place d'Armes and studied the citizens who had gathered in front of a hastily built scaffold: wealthy Creoles, civil authorities, affluent planters . . . dressed in white and wearing broad-brimmed straw hats. Attached to their arms, sheltered from the torrid sun by opened parasols, were their wives and mistresses, attired as though attending a grand ball. Pressing immediately after were tradesmen, plantation managers, and *hôteliers*; while to one side, clustered together like a penned flock of birds, were a group of nuns from the Congregation of Notre Dame.

Aloof behind the circle of whites were two rows of mulattoes. The men were slender, tall, haughty. Their yellow-brown faces seemed filled with bitterness. Their women were dressed in voluminous skirts. They wore towering headdresses and large, fantastic earrings. Beyond the pear trees, in front of the carriages that lined the Rue d'Anjou, were *affranchis*, their raw-sienna faces somber, their woolly heads bare to the sun. Above them, on the filigreed wrought-iron balconies of the town's brothels, the Dominicaines—the *sang-mèlès* whores of Cap Français—were gathered to see the sight. Their domestics dispersed themselves among them. Most were tall, barefooted *griffones* whose sensual bodies were covered only by light cotton shifts which molded to their high breasts and powerful buttocks when they moved. Their red and yellow

[12]

headcloths were brilliant in the torrid sunlight, and their teeth glistened in their sable-brown faces as they enjoyed the spectacle beneath them.

Henri Christophe looked down at the scaffold in the Place d'Armes. The platform had been constructed on the opposite side of the square. The old one by decree was reserved for the execution of white criminals only. This new scaffold was what had come of the mulatto rebellion! Three weeks ago, while the outcome of the insurrection was still in doubt, a mulatto, dressed in a French coat, with a lace cravat at his throat, had the audacity to enter the Auberge de la Couronne and ask to be served. The Creoles had tied him to the tail of a horse and dragged him through the streets as an example!

There was a murmur at the edge of the square, and Henri glanced up the Rue du Conseil running northward, toward the jetties. The street was filling with Blacks, who were pattering down from the harbor. Barefooted and shirtless, they massed between the rows of white and yellow houses. Full-mouthed, strong-bodied, sweating and stinking of the heat of the sun, they craned their necks to see past the crowd in the square. The mulattoes watched them for a moment, wondering what their presence might portend. The whites glanced at them indifferently through the row of pear trees, then turned their attention back to the scaffold where the two captured insurrectionists awaited execution.

The rebels had insisted that freemen had political rights irrespective of their color! One was a short, stout quadroon. His name was Ogé, and Henri had seen him often. The other, whose name was Chavannes, had a metal collar and chain about his neck. The President of the Provincial Assembly climbed the few steps to the platform and began to read the indictment. It was in excellent French—a language foreign to many mulattoes and unknown to almost every Black.

> " . . . and to remain on the wheel
> as long as it will please God
> to preserve their lives."

As though his last words were a signal for the execution to begin, the accused were grasped and their clothes torn away. They stood exposed to the crowd. Stripping a black slave in public was a customary sight, but these men were mulattoes! The skin of educated, sensitive Ogé was like a white man's; the hair about his genitals was wispy and reddish in the sun. As he turned his head away, the executioner smashed an iron rod across his calves and he fell to his knees. Chavannes strained at his collar and chain. The rod came across his arms and cracked them. The executioner began to club the condemned men, methodically cracking their bones as they tumbled to the platform like sacks of copra, yet making certain he did not smash their heads. The whites watched in silence, the women shifting their parasols against the blistering sun. The mulattoes seemed dejected. Their women clung to their arms, straight-featured, thin-lipped, almost scornful.

Henri glanced up the Rue du Conseil. The massed Blacks had not stirred. He noticed Boukmann, a big-chested Jamaican Negro who was a gang driver on the Turpin plantation. Jean-François was at his side. He often saw them when they drove into town with their owners. He wondered why they were here and then remembered the town council had declared this a holiday. Cries of anguished pain, as though they came from a tormented animal, trembled in the air and tugged Henri's eyes back to the scaffold. They were lifting Ogé's broken body and tying him onto a wheel. Chavannes' cries gurgled in his throat as they tugged him up by the chain about his neck. The crowd grew restless as the naked bodies were left to blister in the sun. The *grands blancs*, most of them members of the Provincial Assembly, began to disperse. As the mulattoes made way for them, the Creole women lifted their parasols, gathered their skirts, and looked toward the waiting carriages in the Rue d'Anjou.

Henri followed their gaze and caught sight of Toussaint, the coachman from the Bréda plantation. He was seated on his box, his arms hugging his thin chest, his narrow, protruding jaw strangely simian. His pinched face was without emotion and yet, when his dark eyes caught a glint from the sun, Henri thought he could see the banked fires of a volcanic anger. It was said that Toussaint could read and write, that he could even recite passages from the white man's holy book. What use could a Black have for a white m___ god! Would a white god listen to a Black man's supplication? Avenge a Black man's torture?

The mulattoes were leaving, turning their backs upon the blistering bodies on the wheel—upon the expiring rebels who had insisted on mankind's equality. There was no longer any point in staying in the tree, and Henri descended, his feet splayed against the narrow bole, his arched back exposing a strip of dark skin between his shirt and trousers.

The executioner, a powerful Black, squatted on the platform where a rusty saber lay on the planks. His soiled cotton pants were wet with sweat and his naked chest and massive arms glistened in the tropic sunlight. He surveyed

[15]

the departing onlookers, his oily face expressionless, his thick, smoke-colored lips unparted, his wide nostrils dilated like an animal's snuffling the air for a scent. He lifted the saber, turned on his haunch, and prodded Ogé's thigh. The tortured body shuddered, a trickle of red oozed from the laceration and began to drip coins of blood onto the platform. Not yet . . . . The executioner had been told to wait until they expired. He glanced up at the red sun and replaced the saber.

Suddenly there was an animal scream from beneath a cluster of pear trees—a shrill treble that ended in an insane shriek. It was Défilée. Her raised arms trembled in the motionless air while her kerchief-turbaned head bobbed with a cadenced agitation. Henri knew her. Almost everyone in Cap Français knew her. A disowned slave, cast adrift, it was said by both the whites and the *gens de couleur* that she was demented; but the Blacks believed her to be a voodoo priestess. Seemingly ageless, tall and slender, she had the sharp features of the Creole who had sired her and the dark eyes and burnished sepia skin of her mother, a member of the serpent-worshiping Wydah tribe.

She moved rhythmically from side to side, and as Henri approached her he could see how her cotton shift, moist with sweat, clung to her breasts and outlined her raised nipples. One could well believe the legend that was whispered about her: The mistress of a white planter who had become infatuated with her, she had stealthily taken, for a lover, the ugliest Black in his cane field. In a frenzy, the planter had lopped off her ears and crudely cut away her labia majora. She had survived but was known from then

[16]

on as Défilée *la pauvre folle.* No one, other than Jean Jacques Dessalines, was ever seen with her.

As Henri thought this, he saw Dessalines cross the Place d'Armes in his hobbling gait, and rush to her side. He put his arms about her and comforted her. She still stared across the deserted square at the dying men, but her trembling ceased.

It was strange to see Dessalines comfort someone. Henri recalled the first time he had seen him—manacled and chained to a coffle, his dark body naked, his ugly bullet head swollen and streaked with red, a froth of blood on his thick lips, and his dark eyes ablaze with frenzied anger. . . .

The molten sun was now directly overhead, and Henri could hear the sound of the Angelus bell in the Place de Notre Dame. Two priests, their lean, ascetic faces tanned by the tropic sun, entered the square and approached the scaffold. They wore soiled wide-brimmed straw hats, thick-soled sandals, and their robes, patched and rusty-black, were belted with twisted rattan ropes. They were from the impoverished Church of St. Anne and had come out of curiosity, for it had been forbidden to grant the last rites to the rebels.

The executioner roused himself and stabbed at the men on the wheel. Getting no response, he rose, swung the heavy saber, and hacked off their heads with animal indifference. A shriek burst from Défilée, and Dessalines clamped a massive hand over her mouth and stifled her scream. The executioner jammed the severed heads onto pikestaves, held them aloft, and descended from the scaffold. Défilée reached between her breasts and brought

[17]

forth a voodoo talisman. It was a crudely carved serpent whose fangs were pierced by a necklace made of dried snake vertebrae. She shook it towards the scaffold and chanted:

"Solei' levé nan l'est;
Li couché lan Guinea
Li nans Guinea. . . ."

In the distance, on the ledges of the mountains, a few *tambours-travaille,* nonritual native drums, began to reverberate. They seemed near at hand though distant; hushed, yet distinct: tum-tete-tum . . . tete-tete-tum. . . . The sun was dipping toward the Windward Passage, west of Môle St. Nicolas. The drums grew more numerous and more insistent. Their throbbing seemed to ripple from the mountains south of Milot, from the plains of Grande Rivière, and from as far west as Gonaïves.

There was nothing left to witness in the Place d'Armes. Henri hurried from the square and sprinted in the direction of the Auberge de la Couronne.

2

Back in the cottage that Henri Christophe had left so abruptly, Lutétia Mongeon dressed herself languidly. She combed her dark tresses with the aid of a Florentine mirror, a gift from a white planter whose mistress she had been for three full years. There had been many others. There had even been Vincent Ogé. But now she was thirty-two—an age considered no longer young in the tropics. Remaining childless had helped her retain her semblance of youth, and a part ownership of the Auberge de la Couronne had lent her an authoritative dignity.

She thought of the stableboy, Henri Christophe. He always left her with a sense of fulfillment. And he had not been easily seduced. Could it be that the mulatto whores of Cap Français gave themselves to him? He was really no longer a boy but in his mid-twenties. Tall and handsome for a full-blooded Black; with a slender waist, powerful shoulders, short, curling hair, and large, dark eyes with whites not tainted with yellow like the Congos. His spirit was unbroken and he carried himself with pride and dignity. His features resembled those of the aristocrats of Africa who were found in the hot plains of the Soudan. Lutétia had learned that he had been born on the tiny British island of St. Christopher, from which he had most likely taken his name. She had been attracted to him when first she had seen him working as a stonemason, mixing the mortar, the muscles of his back and chest rippling in the sun. She had urged her partner, Coidovic, to buy him and had learned, to her amazement, that he spoke fluent French instead of the vulgar patois.

She would suggest to Coidovic that Henri serve at the tables. And she would eventually obtain his freedom. But not too soon. She wanted to ingrain a sense of obligation in him.

She lowered the mirror, studied the reflection of her swollen nipples on the smooth glass, and ran the palm of her hand over her slightly swollen abdomen. *Je suis enceinte,* she thought. *Oui!* I am with child. It has never happened before and now I am with child. It will be a boy, she daydreamed. He will look as aristocratic as Henri . . . but not as dark . . . and I shall call him Eugène. The Creole who had sired her had been named Eugène. She should buy a slave girl to help her in the last months, she thought. She could buy a young house slave for a few hundred livres. A girl would be happy with a length of cloth, a monthly bottle of *tafia,* and a ration of meat or salted fish that she could bring each day from the *auberge.* But Vincent Ogé had made slavery distasteful to Lutétia. Vincent should have remained in France where his equality had been accepted. He had been a fool to come back to Saint-Domingue, where all the gold he possessed could not buy him a single drink in la Couronne—a greater fool to think he could change the customs that would not permit the most affluent mulatto of the island to dress like the white French or allow his wife to ride into Le Cap in a carriage if she was tainted by a single drop of Negro blood!

The sound of rada drums broke in upon her thoughts. Their throbbing was now complicated by an angry under-rhythm that was insistent . . . unhurried . . . primitive in its relentlessness. She pattered to a window and opened the shutters where a screen of pepper trees shielded the cottage from the rays of the sun.

"*Adieu,* Vincent," she whispered as though her breath could carry to the Place d'Armes. "*Adieu.* . . . May the god Damballa be kind to your spirit. *Dormi pa' fumé,* Vincent. *Dormi pa' fumé.*"

3

Henri Christophe rushed into the garden behind the Auberge de la Couronne. The last guest had departed, and he could see candles being snuffed out behind the windows. The moon was heavy with deep, chrome yellow, the stars silvered the branches of the lemon trees, and the air was laden with the scent of jasmine. He removed his apron and white shirt, rolled them together, and thrust them into the low branches of a bougainvillaea. He hid behind the trunk of a lemon tree, his dark arms and chest lost in the shadows, and waited for Coidovic's daughter, Marie-Louise; for he had devised a scheme by which he might obtain his freedom. It was true that Lutétia Mongeon had transferred him from the stables, but his work as a waiter rankled him. He admired horses more than he did the *grands blancs* in the *auberge*, who laughed, drank, and exchanged confidences in his presence as though he did not exist. But he did exist. He did! Lutétia Mongeon had promised him his enfranchisement, but now she was big with child and no longer came to the *auberge*. And his visits to Boukmann's secret meetings filled him with a desperate impatience to be free. Still, it was not as though his latest scheme would cost him nothing. Marie-Louise, though intelligent, had the round, kinky-haired head and black, oily skin of the Congolese. Just turned thirteen, she was plump, unattractive, and without a single grace of movement. He had watched her closely in the *auberge* kitchen and knew that she had neither admirer nor lover. She would not be difficult to seduce, but would her father, a former slave himself, welcome him as a son-in-law? He watched a shadow emerge from a dark doorway and patter across the guinea grass with which Coidovic had seeded the garden.

"Marie," he whispered. "Marie-Louise. . . ." As she reached him, he could tell that she had rubbed her skin with crushed jasmine petals. He led her out of the garden, across the Rue Espagnole, and toward the edge of the Morne du Cap ravine. It was a secluded little plateau that was shadowed by palms whose slender boles inclined pisa-like to the sky. The air was filled with the fragrance of coffee blossoms, and the quiet was broken only by the rustle of fronds and the croaking of frogs. He sank to his knees and, as the girl turned to him, he was filled with misgivings. He was Coidovic's personal property. Coidovic could have him castrated and his balls flung to the goats. He could have his tongue ripped out, his ears filled with melted wax, and his body turned on a spit like a quarter of beef. No, Henri had not planned it well enough. He was too impatient for freedom—too impetuous! He looked up at Marie-Louise and suddenly felt uneasy in her presence, for she had been taught by the Jesuits and wore a crucifix about her neck. To his surprise she thrust him to the ground and flung her arms about him. Her round face was expressionless—a black shadow in the luminosity of the night—a shadow broken only by the flash of her teeth and the yellowish-white of her eyes. She covered his face with kisses, sucked at the lobe of his ear, caught the tiny nautilus shell between her teeth and snapped it in two. He was not aroused, for he had become accustomed to Lutétia's expert foreplay. But then her hand began to caress his thigh and came to rest between his legs. His phallus burst upward and strained against the thin cotton trousers.

"*Etes-vous fatigue?*" she whispered.

He shook his head. "*Vôtre* papa will flog me and sell me. Or rip out my entrails and feed them to the dogs!"

"Not if you marry me, Henri. Not if you marry me."

"Would your papa give this boy his freedom? I want to be *affranchi*. I want to be *affranchi* now!"

"*Oui. Ma maman* will make him do it."

"You can read and write, Marie-Louise. This boy cannot even scribble his name."

"I shall teach you. And do not speak patois to me. I have heard you speak *la langue français*. Even English. Come!" She rolled over on the grass and spread her bare legs apart. "I shall give you children, Henri Christophe. As many as you want. I am young and strong. I shall give you your first child."

She could give him his freedom, thought Christophe, as he settled himself on top of her, but not his first child. His first-born was in the womb of the mulatress, Lutétia Mongeon.

[24]

4

Henri Christophe glanced up at the Auberge de la Cou-
ronne as he rushed away. The grillwork of its balcony had
been freshly gilded, and the wrought iron was brilliant
where the moonlight pierced itself between the palm
fronds. He did not hug the shadows but hurried defiantly
across the Rue Espagnole—for he was no longer a slave.
Coidovic had granted his freedom, though he had post-
poned his marriage to Marie-Louise. She was too young
. . . another year would not matter. As an expression of
good faith Christophe no longer visited Lutétia Mongeon
and now proudly displayed a gold earring—a gift from
Marie-Louise.

He left the Rue Espagnole and took a shortcut across the
Place Clugny, a square that was bordered by fig trees.
Beneath their shade, on Sundays, hundreds of plantation

slaves would squat, bartering the produce from their kitchen gardens. It was dark and deserted now, and the drumbeats that drifted into it were ensnared by the gnarled branches of the fig trees. He was hurrying to a Boukmann meeting in the Bois Caiman, eight miles outside of Cap Français. He knew that Boukmann lied when he spread rumors that the King of France had proclaimed two holidays a week for the Blacks and was sending an army overseas to punish the planters for their cruelties. The *grands blancs*, in the *auberge*, spoke freely in Henri's presence, and the American and British ship captains were unaware that he understood them. The French King could not help the slaves. He was a prisoner in his own palace!

Marie-Louise insisted that secret gatherings should be of no interest to Christophe now that her father had given him his freedom. But they were! Was he a dog that he must run into a cul-de-sac with a bone—to worry it when out of sight? Slavery had become such a seething volcano on the island that the melancholy Eboes, impatient with the intervention of Damballa, were hanging themselves in batches.

As he reached the outskirts of the Lenormand plantation, the throbbing of the rada drums grew more distinct. There was no need to hush them, for in the dark no white would dare enter the alligator wood—a stretch of swamp and primeval jungle that was circled by huge mangroves, raised by their stiltlike roots above a monstrous undergrowth of ferns and orchids.

Henri stepped into the tangle of undergrowth and thrust his way past a great sablier tree and its thick girdle of strangling lianas. He was grasped by a dozen hands, his arms pinioned to his sides and a smoldering torch thrust into his face. He was recognized and heard his name whispered, echoed and reechoed: Henri Christophe . . . Henri Christophe . . . for he had become known to all the plantation *ateliers*. As he was released and the torch withdrawn, he could hear the scraping of vines and the patter of bare feet.

He pushed forward, in the direction of the throbbing drums, and entered a clearing—a circle of earth pounded flat by bare feet, made luminous by moonlight, lighted by resin torches, and fenced in by giant mapou trees whose smooth trunks were distorted by thickened spikes. Forms emerged from the dark-shadowed woods, found places within the circle, and crouched in silence. They shifted and changed positions as newcomers disturbed them. The stink of unwashed bodies and the heavy odor of animal grease drifted into the clearing as the latecomers thrust themselves into it. The new arrivals sweated and heaved in the shadows, for they had jogged from plantations that stretched across the Grande Rivière as far west as Ennery. They would have come from as far as Gonaïves, if they could, for Boukmann had promised them freedom and a plan for the destruction of the hated whites.

Extra torches were set ablaze and thrust into the earth at the edges of the clearing. Their fuliginous flames cast yellow and orange reflections on a cluster of wild cacao trees. Henri could now make out the faces of the Blacks who crouched at the edges of the compound. There were copper-colored Fulas, with straight hair and Caucasian features. One never saw them in town. Squatting in a group were almost twenty Aradas—proud and excellent agriculturists who tended their gardens with care and were seen every Sunday in the Clugny square. Their big-boned hands rested without movement on their bare knees. To

[27]

one side, standing erect as though too proud to crouch, were Bambaras—tall, insolent, and given to thieving. The Congos and Angolese—ebony-hued, their white teeth flashing in their round heads—mingled everywhere. Unlike the brazen Bambaras, they seemed contented with their lot, but they were not to be trusted. Henri noticed a dozen Senegalese, bunched together, some of them dressed in cotton shirts and nankeen trousers. Intelligent, proud of the Arabic strain in their ancestry, they were usually owned by the *grands blancs* and employed as postilions, coachmen, or household slaves. Why were they here? Had they stolen out of Cap Français because they, too, were aroused by the white man's intolerable insolence? As he glanced about him he realized that the Englishmen in the *auberge* did not lie when they spoke of a thousand ships that combed the coast of Africa, from Senegal to Mozambique, in order to fill their holds with slaves.

As more Blacks thrust themselves into the compound the smell of foliage was gone, and the air became tainted with the oily stink of sweating flesh. Christophe had become accustomed to the lighter scents of Cap Français, where clothes were beaten and washed on the jetties, and the public baths in the Place Luzerne were frequented by the whites. He felt a tinge of compassion for the Blacks who had been driven into the role of animals. The French Creoles would never free them! They had not imported one-half million Negroes for the purpose of making them French citizens in Saint-Domingue. He was startled as he noticed three emaciated Bambaras beneath the branches of a poisonous manchineel tree. A flickering torch cast an orange glow on their gaunt faces. Their thin necks were ringed with festering sores. They must have come from Sieur le Jeune's plantation. He punished his slaves by fastening iron collars so tightly about their necks that it was impossible for them to swallow, then had them dragged each day to the cane fields to do their share of work, and released them only when they were on the verge of death. Christophe knew Sieur le Jeune from the billiard room of the *auberge*, where he insisted that his discipline was mild compared to the Dupont plantation. There the punishment for running away was *brûler un peu de poudre au cul d'un nègre* . . . stuffing gunpowder into the slave's rectum and exploding it with a fuse.

Christophe's gaze continued to wander about the still-growing circle of Blacks. He recognized violent and quarrelsome Biassou . . . Jean-François, with his gross features . . . Jean Jannot. . . . Jean Jannot came from Savanette, near the Aubry plantation where the slaves had attempted an insurrection. To make an example of them, the manager of the plantation had chopped off fifty rebel heads and stuck them on pickets. Saint-Domingue had no carrion birds, and the heads were still there—shrinking in the sun—their sockets like the sightless eyes of zombies.

He noticed Toussaint. He was with a group of indolent, lanky Quiambas, and one could not tell if the slender Bréda coachman was standing or crouching. Toussaint had intimated that he would not come. He shrank from such a ferocious massacre as Boukmann planned. Yet here he was—a madras head kerchief tied about his crinkly hair, his widely dilated nostrils like little caverns above his thin, protuberant jaw.

As Christophe looked toward the farthest arc of the clearing, he caught sight of Dessalines, his arm around Défilée. He was naked to the waist, and in the torchlight, one could see on his left breast the glossy, tan weals that formed a letter *K*—a brand with which his first owner had marked him. When he turned, his back glistened with the crisscross scars and welts from innumerable lashings.

Dessalines glanced across the compound at Henri Christophe, and recognized him. The first compassionate gesture that he had known in his captivity had been Christophe's; and, though he had spurned it, he remembered. He had been brought from the coast of Guinea by a slave ship that had tacked its way into the harbor of Cap Français. He had spent five weeks in its dark, stinking hold, chained from wrist to ankle, driven into the bowel of the ship like an animal, and forced to lie on a wooden shelf that was half the width of his back while his chains were fastened to a ringbolt which even his great strength could not tear loose. . . .

Now, at last, he was close to freedom. Boukmann had promised it! Défilée had forecast it! Dessalines thought that Boukmann's plan for the massacre of all the whites in Saint-Domingue could be easily executed. He had learned that there were a half million slaves on the island. Once aroused, how could twenty or thirty thousand whites stand up against them? As for the cowardly mulattoes . . . he would shred the blanched flesh from their bones!

He glanced again at Henri Christophe. Why was he here? He was a town man. He had never labored in a cane field or sweated in the heat of the iron cauldrons in a boiling shed! His back was as smooth as a woman's, and he wore a gold ring in the lobe of one ear, like a fancy prostitute.

He recalled his first brutal beating. They had driven him into the blinding light of the quay, where he was linked to other Blacks . . . the women yoked with heavy forked poles, the children huddling amongst them, while the ones with ophthalmia were dragged away, bludgeoned, and cast into the harbor. They were herded to the Morne du Cap ravine where, at its edge near the Champ de Mars, stood the little church of Saint Anne, a simple oblong building with a peaked roof. He had not known that a Saint-Domingue law required newly arrived Negroes to be baptized before they were driven to the slave barracks beyond the city gates. He had seen a driver approach Henri Christophe, who was laying flagstones, point with his plaited lash to the *cailles* where Jesuits lived with their concubinary griffones and their bastard offspring, and command him to fetch a priest.

Dessalines had stared about him in the torrid sunlight. The yoked Black women wore shreds of cloth about their loins, but the men to whom he was chained were as naked as he, many with crusted stains on their legs from the flux. He noticed a few cannibal Mandingoes, their yellow teeth filed to sharp points; and at the end of the coffle, seemingly indifferent to their lot, were four Angolese who stank so strongly that they tainted the air about them.

Christophe returned with a priest, and the drivers began to herd the slaves into the church. Dessalines tore at his chains with ferocious violence. The dark interior of Saint Anne seemed to him like the hold of another ship, and he would rather die than leave the sunlight again. During the entire crossing there had been rumors that they were being taken across "the river of salt water" to be eaten by a race of white cannibals called *Koomi*. This must be the last leg of that journey!

Squat and powerfully built, Dessalines had lowered his head, swung his arms, and flung those about him to the ground. Christophe and the priest had watched in silence while the drivers clubbed him into submission—bludgeoned his back, his arms, his bullet head—and drove him into the church. The priest had scurried to the altar and rushed the celebration of the Eucharist, for the small church was now filled with an insufferable stench. Followed by a mulatto child who carried a basin of holy water, the priest hurried down the nave. With hasty swings of a battered aspergillum, he sprinkled the blessed water over the unbowed woolly heads while he intoned, between frequent shallow gasps, a Latin chant that would transform the Black savages into Christian converts.

The drivers, clenching little bags of camphor between their teeth, against the stench, began to prod the slaves from the church. Dessalines would not budge. He clutched his groin where a whip's stock had caught him an undefended blow, heaved the contents of his retching stomach, and doubled over from the spasms of his guts. The brutish drivers attributed his bowed head to stubborn defiance and clubbed him unmercifully until the Blacks to whom he was chained, in defense of their own backs, dragged him from the nave and out into the sunlight.

When Christophe saw him, Dessalines was on his knees, his lips a spongy pulp of red, one eye swollen shut and the other blinded by a rivulet of blood. Christophe had drifted to his side and offered him a sweat-stained strip of burlap. Crazed by the violence of his rage, Dessalines had torn at the bit of cloth and dashed it to the ground that was now spotted by his blood. He had struggled to his feet, lifted his arms as far as his chains would allow, and bellowed a roar of defiant anger that had reverberated through the torrid air and echoed from the green hills past Morne du Cap.

A spasm of lightning flashed in the sky and a clap of thunder broke in the distance, echoed in the hills, and rolled toward the clearing in the Bois Caiman. As the sound of the approaching squall swept from his mind the turbulent memory that Christophe's unblemished face and aristocratic bearing had evoked, Dessalines sprang into the compound, flung out his arms, and roared, "I, Dessalines, will disembowel every planter in Saint-Domingue and drape their entrails on the tchia-tchia trees. I will gouge out their eyes and feed them to the fishes!"

Boukmann, as though reminding the gathered Blacks that the insurrection was to be directed by him, rushed to Dessalines' side. In one hand he held a forbidden musket and in the other a thick lash made of plaited strips of bullock hide. There were scars on his chest and back—scars left by bone-deep lacerations that had been embedded with crushed pimento berries. A voodoo *ouanga* bag dangled from his neck. He flung out his arm, and the crack of the whip was like a pistol shot. "We cannot return to our native Guinea!" he cried in patois. "The cursed whites have brought so many of us here that we are like the seeds of the mocha plants. A thousand ships could not take all of us back to Senegal, Ghana, Zambesia, Somali, Katanga—to the hundred rivers and forests of our native land. And so we make this our Guinea. This land smell like Guinea! Look like Guinea! Is not this Bois Caiman like alligator swamp in Guinea? We shall burn the cane fields . . . smash the macerators . . . destroy the boiling sheds. . . . And we shall kill all the whites! *Les grands blancs! Les petits blancs!* Even the mustees and the mustefinos! We shall drive them into the sea! We shall run them into the hills and slaughter them! This land belongs to us. We shall kill *les blancs!* Kill them! Kill them! Who goes with me? Who goes with me?"

At first only a few voices cried, "*Moin pr allier!*" [I am

[33]

for going.] Then a hundred voices took up the cry, *"Moin pr allier!"*

As though Boukmann's harangue had enraged the drummers, they quickened their beat. The reverberations drowned out the replies, and the sounds of stamping, clapping, and a gibberish chanting began to fill the compound. An improvised altar was carried into the clearing, and gourds, filled with figs and cassava, were placed on either side of a crudely carved image of a serpent. A stuffed bag made of scarlet cloth, shaped like a water jug and surmounted by black feathers, was placed on a raised pile of stones.

A giant Negress stepped from the shadows, placed a barred cage on the ground, and withdrew a slender tree snake. Its writhing body glistened green, and its eyes were like sapphires in the torchlight, as she wound the snake about her neck and thrust its tail between her pendulous breasts. Two acolytes scattered a mixture of rum and flour on the hard-packed earth, as food for the sacred snake, and she lifted her arms and gyrated toward the center of the clearing. The drummers left the shadows and carried their tambours into the compound—a large *maman* drum made of cowhide, with a fringe of hair left on its sides, and two small goatskin drums whose cylinders were painted with mottled colors. As their rhythm grew frenetic, the snake began to slither upward.

The Negress twisted her neck and beat the air with her hands. The snake ceased its motion and nestled its sapphire-gemmed head against a dark cheek of the priestess. She flung her arms to the heavens and shrieked, "Damballa! Damballa! Damballa Oueddo!" She swept her hands toward the dark circle of trees, past the crouched blacks who had begun to rock and teeter on their bare feet, and cried to the god of the forests:

"Loco! Loco! Loco!"

She clenched her hands into fists and bent forward so her dark breasts hung like heavy gourds and the snake fell to the rum and flour-spattered earth. Then she pummeled her thighs and cried to the bloody, dreadful one whose voice is thunder: "Oguan Badagris! Oguan Badagris!"

The drummers reverberated their tambours in imitation of rolls of thunder. The priestess spun about with amazing velocity, faster and faster until a trembling seizure seemed to melt her very bones and she sank to the ground.

A bright moon, like a suspended orange cauldron, was rising over the mountains and shone into the clearing. Now that the tambours were silent, one could hear the bleating of a tethered goat behind the altar on which a lighted wick floated in half an oil-filled coconut shell. The flame was clear and blue in the windless air. Softly, a drummer began to beat the tall *maman* tambour with the heel of his right palm. The smaller tambours joined him, the drummers striking the taut goatskin with flat palms and bunched fingertips.

An old man, a *papaloi*, emerged from the shadows. He was barefooted, naked to the waist, and so emaciated that his rib cage could clearly be discerned. A red turban was wound about his head and he carried an açon, a gourd rattle, in his right hand. He circled the clearing and at every third step rattled the dried seeds in the gourd and sprang into the air as though he had stepped on a trampoline.

[35]

A young buck, a Wolof, tall and slender-legged, danced into the torch-lighted compound carrying a naked saber in his outstretched hands. As he followed the *papaloi*, his narrow, ebony face shone one moment in the moonlight and reflected the red glow from the torches the next. A priestess joined them, and Christophe saw that the *mama-loi* was Défilée. She was dressed in a scarlet robe and a feathered headdress. As she progressed about the clearing she spun in a Monter Voudou, a sort of dervish dance, and chanted:

> *"Damballa Oueddo, nous p'vini!"*
> [Oh, Serpent God, we come!]

The *papaloi* continued to circle the compound, and each time he bounced on the nonexistent trampoline he chanted:

> *"Sloei' levé nan l'est;*
> *Li couché lan Guinea."*

The tambours grew louder, more insistent, and the Blacks who crouched about the clearing answered:

> *"Li nans Guinea! Li nans Guinea!"*
> [He is in Guinea! He is in Guinea!]

The copper-colored Fulas thrust themselves into the compound, jounced on the balls of their feet, and chanted:

> *"Li nans Guinea! Li nans Guinea!"*

The Congos wove their woolly heads, clapped their big, yellow-palmed hands in cadence to the beat of the tambours, and chanted:

> *"Li nans Guinea! Li nans Guinea!"*

[36]

The *papaloi* was no longer a wizened old man but an ageless, tireless, frenzied dervish who sprang up and down, rattled his gourd, and cried in an effortless and inexhaustible singsong:

> *"Damballa Oueddo*
> *Ou couleuvre mois!"*

And the Fulas and the Congos called back, as though they understood the French words:

> *"Damballa, mois bien prêté*
> *Moins pas' river."*
> [I am ready but the road is barred.]

Défilée edged toward the altar, where she began a dance to the accompaniment of the tambours: tete-tete-tete boom! Tete-tete-tete boom! Three spluttering rumbles and an explosive note. With each percussive boom, holding herself as rigid as a lance, she leaped upward, as though from a springboard, and gyrated with incredible velocity. Dessalines dashed to her side.

Boukmann had removed his cotton trousers and, as though too fastidious to display his genitals, had tied a red bandanna about his loins. He reached behind the altar and dragged forth the bleating goat. Dessalines abandoned Défilée, rushed to the edge of the trees, and returned with a wooden trough. Immediately, a dozen empty calabashes were placed on the altar, their half spheres like dark cavernous mouths. At a gesture from the *papaloi*, the Wolof offered the saber to Boukmann. Dessalines grasped the goat's horns and held it over the trough, while the Wolof imprisoned its forelegs. Boukmann severed the goat's neck with a single swift motion, and its bleating ended in a

[37]

gurgle of sound that silenced the tambours. Blood gushed and spattered into the trough as the goat was shaken by violent spasms.

When the red rivulet subsided to a trickle, an aged Negress, with the deeply wrinkled face of an old prophetess, approached the altar, her thin, straight body twisting and turning as though curiously young. The strung vertebra of a snake was curled about one bare arm and she carried a pilon, a little wooden mortar, and poured its contents—a mixture of rum and gunpowder—into the trough. As the body of the goat was cast aside she dipped a calabash into the trough, swirled its contents, and tasted the dark liquid. Immediately she whirled about and implored a *mystère*, a spirit, to take possession of her—to enter her flesh and bones—and ride her. A seizure trembled her gaunt form and a single reiterated word rasped from her throat and escaped past the flecks of pink foam on her red-stained lips: "Guinea! Guinea! Guinea . . .!"

Boukmann whirled the saber above his head and bellowed, in the patois that was a mixture of French, Portuguese, and African, "Oguan Badagris, you who hold the key to the storm clouds, loose your thunder and lightning!"

He dipped a calabash into the trough and tasted the warm pungent blood. As though its flavor electrified him, he cried: "We shall kill the whites! Massacre them! We will shred the flesh from their bones so the thunder god can wash them into the earth!"

Figures leaped into the clearing and rushed to the trough crying, "*Moin! Moin!*"

They tasted the mixture of blood, rum, and gunpowder, relinquished the calabashes to outstretched hands, and began a dervishlike dance as though possessed. Their lips

[38]

bloodied, their teeth and eyeballs gleaming in the torch-light, they threw back their heads, as though their necks were broken, and whirled about with uncontained frenzy. Boukmann rushed to the edges of the clearing, pointed his Damballa snake staff to watching Senegalese, Aradas, and Bambaras and cried again and again: *"Bai li bweh! Bai li bweh!"* [Give him a drink!] He wanted everyone committed and pledged to the intended massacre.

The tambours reverberated with a wild, quickened rhythm as the Blacks, their faces now stained with blood, became a circle of frenetic dancers. Powerful Yorubas, Nagoes, Pawpaws, and even indolent Quiambas joined the dancers and were urged into frantic contortions as they pledged annihilation of the whites.

Boukmann noticed Toussaint, almost lost in the shadows of a mangrove. His outthrust jaw, with its protuberant teeth, was tightly clenched, and his dark eyes darted about as though disturbed by the turbulent frenzy of the scene. Boukmann rushed to him with a red-stained calabash and cried, "You do not pledge your vengeance, Toussaint? Drink!"

Toussaint reached out a gnarled black hand and raised the gourd to his lips. The acrid smell of the gunpowder that had been mixed with the rum and the goat's blood was strong in his nostrils. He exhaled sharply and intoned, "In nomine Patris, et Filii, et Spiritus sancti. Amen." He had learned that most Blacks were awed by his solemn pronouncement of Latin phrases. Boukmann was not. As he glared at him in anger, Toussaint threatened in patois, *"Pas brûler caille moin!* [Do not burn my house!] Do you hear, Boukmann? Do not burn my house!"

Défilée was behind the altar. She was cutting the scrotum from the goat.

5

On the night of August 22nd, eight days after the bloody rituals in the Bois Caiman, there was a great commotion in the Negro quarter of the Turpin plantation. The slaves armed themselves with machetes, and some hastily tied them to pikes in order to make bayonets. Boukmann raced about and exhorted them to kill and pillage. As a sign of leadership, he had dressed himself in a planter's straw hat, and had thrust his naked feet into a white man's boots. The slaves chattered excitedly in their African dialects, not knowing what was actually expected of them until Boukmann, lighting a resin torch, led them into a field of sugar cane and set it on fire. The glow illuminated a nearby workshed, and they rushed into it, smashed the circular coffee bean cutter, and overturned the sifters.

Lights appeared in the plantation manor, shadowed by

a veranda and a semicircle of palms. The Blacks, frightened by the thought of retributive punishment, began to mill about and huddle in the compound. Boukmann smashed a rum vat and urged them to drink the odorous mash. They thrust and wedged themselves there, and gulped the dark, sweet liquid until a musket shot startled them. The plantation manager was advancing toward them, his form outlined by the red glow from the burning cane field. A cart whip was curled about his neck. As they watched, frozen with fright, he raised a musket and fired at them. The Blacks cowered and sank to their knees in an attitude of submission. Suddenly Boukmann tore toward the manager, cleaved at him with his saber, and ran him through with the heavy blade. The Blacks watched, fascinated, as Boukmann hacked at the writhing body and cried: "Flambeaux! Flambeaux! Burn the house to the ground! No one must escape!"

The Blacks rushed to the blazing cane field and returned with smoldering cane haulm torches. Bursts of musket fire came from the fully aroused manor, but they did not deter the screaming Blacks, who now raced toward the veranda as though to avenge the brutality with which the whites had enslaved them.

"Hack off their heads!" roared Boukmann. "Tear out their balls! Spill their guts onto the earth they have enriched with our blood!"

When Toussaint arrived at the Turpin plantation, he found it in ruins. The manor was a rubble from which thick smoke, polluted by the taint of burnt flesh, spiraled into a sky illuminated by the still glowing cane field. He was riding a saddled horse that he had borrowed, without permission, from the Bréda plantation. He rose in the stirrups and glanced about. The compound and the slave shacks were deserted. Here and there a dark form lay motionless on the ground.

There was the sound of a horse's hooves on the palm-lined driveway that led to the smoldering manor, and a rider emerged from the shadows. It was Henri Christophe, riding bareback on a large gelding. Toussaint nodded in recognition, and Christophe pointed in the direction of the nearby Flavile plantation, where a red blaze, rising skyward, was reflected by turbulent billows of smoke. They turned their mounts and galloped toward the flames.

At the Flavile plantation, where Boukmann had led the Blacks, the owner, the manager, and the drivers and their families had hurriedly barricaded themselves in the plantation house that was flanked by a mill and storage sheds. Half-intoxicated with rum, harangued into a wild frenzy for freedom they had never tasted, the Blacks ignored the bursts of musket fire, scrambled across the deep verandas, broke through the windows, and smashed in the doors. Slaves from the thatched huts that lined the compound joined them as they massacred the whites and looted the rooms. They touched their torches to the furnishings and watched as flames shot upward and smoke belched forth. The blaze released a spirit of destruction and they hacked and mutilated the bodies of the whites, burst into closets, and smashed into all the rooms. By the time concern for their personal safety drove them out, some had adorned themselves with pantaloons, coats, hats, and even women's shifts and gowns. At the edges of the compound, rum vats were smashed. Sheds, warehouses, and mills were put to the torch, and all the fields were set ablaze.

When Christophe and Toussaint arrived, amidst the crackling of flames and the crash of falling timbers, Boukmann was urging the Blacks toward the Clément plantation. They gathered in a delirious horde, the women herding the little ones, the men chanting and dancing about as though possessed, many with hands and faces freshly smeared with blood. The sound of tambours burst through the Flavile conflagration with a crescendo of wild reverberations, and red patches on the nearby hills reflected the flames from the fields. Billows of smoke and a luminous haze obscured the moon as everyone rushed toward the Clément plantation.

Toussaint rode behind the marching blacks, his heart filled with misgivings. He had hoped that the slaves would not follow the violent Boukmann. He had even prayed! Prayed to the white man's god, for Toussaint was a devout Catholic. He had hoped to see the abolition of slavery, for he had witnessed its cruelties. He had been on plantations where the tongues of field slaves were torn out so they could not converse. He had been to plantations where the eyes of those too sick to work were gouged out before they were cast into ravines to die.

But the Blacks were not prepared for an insurrection! Once the towns were alerted, the slaves would be hacked down like stalks in a cane field! Toussaint's silent supplications seemed unanswered, for native drums were now reverberating from every hillside. It was not only Boukmann. It was Biassou, Jean-François, Dessalines, and others. . . .

Long before they reached the Clément plantation they could hear the crack of musket fire and see the glare from kindled fires. There was no way to stop or alter what Boukmann had begun. Toussaint spurred his horse past the dancing, ecstatic Blacks who filled the dusty road. A blaze crackled and swept across a dry cotton field and added its red glow to the crimsoned sky. The caramel of burnt sugar, the odor of roasting coffee, and the smell of burning tinder covered the scents of hibiscus and oleander as Toussaint dashed into the Clément compound. It was filled with the silhouettes of hurrying forms. The plantation house, set back among mango trees, was ablaze, and terror-laden shrieks and piercing cries of agony could be heard above the clangor of brazen bells and the reverberations of tambours. The sugar mill was consumed by roaring flames as whites were dragged from hiding places and slaughtered.

Toussaint noticed Christophe, who had reached the plantation sooner. He was straddling the gelding and observing the scene with seeming indifference. A saber rested across one dark arm, and his aristocratic face was expressionless in the reflected glare from the fires all about him.

Toussaint turned his gaze to Dessalines, who had armed himself with a bloodied machete. At his bare feet, drenched with blood, were the heads, arms, legs, and disemboweled bodies of whites. Plantation slaves, now in the glare from the fires, now in dark shadows, were dragging new victims to him where, despite their whimperings, screams, pleas, and agonized cries, he immediately hacked them to pieces.

Toussaint urged his horse to Christophe's side. "I do not approve!" he whispered, his protruding teeth reflecting flashes of red from the fires. "I do not approve! It is not yet time. The retributions will decimate us."

Christophe shrugged. Toussaint was almost fifty. Old

enough to be his father! The old never approved of violence. They felt themselves beckoned by the gnarled finger of death, even when at peace, and it was they who insisted that patience was a virtue. As for himself—he had not yet decided. He had not joined Boukmann, nor Dessalines, nor Biassou, nor anyone. He watched Dessalines slaughter the whites with cold unabated fury. To one side, sitting on the grass, her back resting against the slender bole of a palm, her fingers restlessly caressing her bare thighs, was Défilée. She was aware of nothing but Dessalines' furious hacking.

"Domini Christi," murmured Toussaint and rushed off in the direction of the Bréda plantation, where he had left his wife, Suzanne, and their sons. The owners had always treated him and his parents with kindness, and it was only just that he should warn them of the insurrection that would shortly reach them. He would offer them safe conduct to Le Cap if it cost him his life!

When he reached the Bréda estate, on the heights of Haut-du-Cap that overlooked Cap Français and the dark Caribbean, he found the plantation's one thousand slaves huddled in the compound. They had seen the reflection of the fires and heard the throbbing of the drums. The owners, the overseers, the drivers, and their families had all dashed off to Cap Français.

"And Suzanne?" Toussaint asked, searching among the uplifted faces for a glimpse of her.

"Gone. . . . Gone with them."

He hurried to a rise of ground that sloped toward the sea and looked down at Cap Français. Lights glowed within the town and twinkled from the ships' lanterns in the harbor. He knew that the Place d'Armes and the

[45]

Champ de Mars bristled with guns. Could so unarmed and unplanned a revolt terminate in anything but reprisals against the slaves? He had been born on the temperate Bréda plantation. Would it stay moderate after this? He had been raised so small and thin, as a child, that he had been nicknamed *fatras-bâton*, thrashing stick. Unfit for plantation work, too small and ugly for a household slave, he had been given, as a gift, to the Fathers of Charity at Cap Français. They had taught him French and Spanish, passages of Latin, and had raised him a devout Catholic, explaining to him that the soul within his dark body was white. He had wondered why the Jesuits concerned themselves with colors ... always speaking of the black of sin, the pink of angels, and the white of chastity. They had granted him his freedom; yet what could he do with a Black man's freedom in Cap Français? Or in all of Saint-Domingue? Go up into the high country, beyond Savanette, and live like an animal in the hills? He had taken his few possessions ... a lead crucifix, a worn missal, a much-mended shirt ... and drifted to the Bréda plantation.

He was aware of a rustling sound behind him, the rustling of bare feet raking through tall grass. The Bréda slaves were converging toward him, the women in sleeveless cotton shifts, the men in short, loose trousers, their dark bodies like zombies in the luminous night. They sagged to their knees as they reached him and implored, "Ca ou fais la, Papa Toussaint?" [What do we do now, Papa Toussaint?]

He looked down at the uplifted faces. He could tell them they were free. Free! But it would be a lie. To be free meant to be the master of one's destiny.

"Papa Toussaint! Papa Toussaint!"

Because of his education and his knowledge of herbs and potions that he had gleaned from the Jesuits, the slaves had always looked to him for guidance on the Bréda plantation. He glanced down at Cap Français, where the tile roofs glistened with patches of starlight and the cannons in the Champ de Mars thrust their bronze snouts at the dark sky. Father of God, how impregnable the town seemed! To what an impregnable white man's world his people had been bludgeoned and sold! "Stay here," he said. "Stay here until it is decided what should be done."

He regained his mount and rushed back in search of Boukmann, Dessalines, and Biassou.

6

In half a week almost every plantation in the Plaine du Nord was sacked and the entire North Province of Saint-Domingue seemed doomed. A hundred thousand slaves were in revolt!

Toussaint, who could not return to the Bréda plantation, and Christophe, who could not go back to Cap Français, watched as Boukmann led the Blacks from L'Acul to the village of Milot and circled back toward the sea. Hundreds of sugar, coffee, and cotton plantations ceased to exist. Clouds of smoke hovered in the humid air above sugar refineries, and at night, when the winds blew in from the sea, whirls of cane-straw sparks eddied and drifted across the land.

Delirious with freedom, intoxicated with rum, and thirsting for revenge, the slaves gave vent to ferocious violence wherever they found barricaded homes from which the whites had not yet fled. They grouped themselves into tribal circles of Angolese, Bambaras, Congos, Ashantis, Senegalese, Quiambas, and in the background, like camp followers, danced women and children, some of them mothers with nursing infants at their breasts, others with little ones straddled athwart their hips in slings of cloth tied over their left shoulders. As they approached Cap Français on the fourth night of the revolt, they found themselves trampling mutilated heads of Blacks along the roadsides. They were startled by the number of severed arms and legs. Many turned and ran back across the fields. They did not know that a cavalry detachment had sortied from the town each morning, and that every captured Negro had been hacked to pieces without being asked his attachment or intention.

Nor did they know that the town's mulattoes, to demonstrate that their "tainted" blood did not urge them to defect, had executed every Negro who had ventured into the streets of Cap Français. They had smashed into the homes of *affranchis* Negroes and massacred them. They had broken down the doors of the Auberge de la Couronne, and dragged the innkeeper Coidovic into the garden that he had carefully planted with rows of poinsettias. There they chopped off his fingers, forced him to swallow them, and then, as he choked on one, they had hacked off his head. Then they killed Marie-Louise's mother.

Boukmann dashed among the faltering slaves and harangued them not to turn back. "Le Cap will be ours in the morning!" he cried. "We will burn down the town as we did the plantations! We will force them into the sea. This is our Guinea! Our Guinea!"

"This is our Guinea!" cried the Blacks. "Our Guinea!" They left the road and filled the fields on either side. Toussaint drifted among them and all but wept at what he saw. They were field slaves who did not even speak the same tongue! Some were naked to the waist, while others had hastily dressed themselves in plundered garments or bedecked themselves with strips of colored cloth. Most were armed with machetes, mattocks, or ladles. Others held looted pistols or muskets though they had not the remotest notion of how to load or cock them!

Toussaint urged his horse to where Dessalines and Christophe sat their mounts. "You must help me convince Boukmann that the revolt is over," he said. "The whites will fortify themselves in all the coastal towns and we cannot force them out, for the sea will bring them all the reinforcements they will need. We must return to the plantations! We shall rebuild them. We have shown that we must be freed and we shall await their terms."

Dessalines lifted a blood-encrusted saber. "No!" he cried. "No! There are a hundred of us to a single white. We will massacre them!"

Boukmann and Biassou rushed abreast of Toussaint. "My mount has been trampling the flesh and bones of our brothers all along these fields," cried Boukmann. "The smell of their blood in my nostrils shrieks for vengeance!"

Toussaint glanced from one to the other and saw the unfaltering intent upon their faces. "If we must break into Le Cap," he advised quietly, "then we should advance to Pointe Picolet, capture its guns, and take the town from the underbelly of its harbor."

Boukmann studied Toussaint, the slender Bréda coachman who claimed he could communicate with the white man's god, read the white man's books, and understand the white man's thoughts. His wizened body seemed too small for the large bay on which he sat.

Westward, at the edge of the sea, Boukmann could discern Pointe Picolet and the dark outline of the fort that guarded the harbor. He turned and looked across the fields as he pondered Toussaint's advice. The Blacks had scattered, stretched themselves on the warm earth, and were dropping off to sleep. Their half-naked bodies blended with the dark shadows and their arms and legs were entwined with uninhibited intimacy, like twisted roots of fallen mangroves. "No!" Boukmann finally cried. "By the god Damballa, no! We burn Le Cap as we burned the plantations! We advance along this very road and smash down its gates! We die as slaves, in these fields, or enter Le Cap as free men!"

In four hours the sun rose across the bay, a molten ball of red that sucked the mists from the fields. Boukmann dashed about and roused the Blacks. With Jean-François and Biassou at his side he led the hungry, half-awake slaves to the edge of Cap Français and saw, in dismay, what had not been visible in the dark. A ditch had been dug all about the town and a palisade erected from la Carenage to the ravine. A breeze blowing in from the harbor wafted a stink of rotting flesh, and the morning light disclosed headless twisted bodies of Blacks, impaled on the palisade, their naked flesh so hacked apart that they seemed held together only by clotted rivulets of blood.

Boukmann reined his mount in front of the gates of Cap Français. There was no sound from beyond the palisade. The town seemed asleep in the morning sunlight. He swung his arm and urged the Blacks forward. They would smash down the gates and pour into the town. *"Fou!"* [Attack!] he cried. *"Fou!"* The gates swung open and dis-

[51]

closed two fieldpieces. They immediately discharged a round of grapeshot; and a volley of musket fire blazed from the palisade. A troop of light-horsemen, sabers aloft, charged out over the single roadway across the ditch. The Blacks scattered and fled. Many, unable to overcome the fears and submissions ingrained by years of brutal punishment, fell to their knees and lifted their arms in supplication. They were cut down like stalks in a cane field. The light-horsemen galloped among them, hacked at women, at children, at the bowed, remorseful heads of the men. The air was filled with cries of frenzied fright and anguish. The road and the bordering fields were soon covered with a debris of bleeding bodies as though the earth had vomited them from its tortured bowels.

Whites on foot, some with muskets, others with knives and bludgeons, now swarmed out of the town. They rushed amng the strewn Blacks; fired, hewed, and clubbed at the dead and dying. The light-horsemen galloped after fleeing Blacks, overtook them in the tall grass, and flushed them from the shelter of liana-tangled trees. The slaves scattered across the Plaine du Nord and raced toward the mountains beyond Milot.

It was late noon before they reached the flat, thorny desert of Bahonde, where they straggled past giant cactuses. There the blazing sun shone down, intense and relentless. They felt safe. The whites would never follow them there. When they reached the foothills of the mountains, they began to clamber over winding, rock-strewn paths. The air was still, and the dry pods of the tchia-tchia trees hung soundlessly from their branches. When the slaves had scaled to the first plateau, they flung themselves on the cool grass. The revolt was ended. All the tambours were silent. What would happen now? Would they be sought, even here, and massacred? Boukmann had been captured and his head impaled on a pike. The last stragglers had seen it—the eyes still open, as though they were staring, with unquenced malevolence in death, at the man who had hacked the head from its body.

When night came, the mountain paths that wound between towering pines were filled with clambering Blacks. Aroused by the thought of freedom, reinforcements were deserting the unburned plantations and streaming to the mountain slopes from as far east as the waters of the Grande Rivière and as far west as Gros Morne. They were barefoot and naked except for short cotton trousers. Their woolly heads were nests of burrs, twigs, and coffee-bean husks; and their lashed backs glistened with pale scars as they struggled upward. Women and children scrambled after them. The native drums, the tambours, had promised them freedom . . . *liberté*! The word itself meant little, but it had been whispered that they would not have to awaken to the crack of a whip and toil in the fields until dark. They could walk about or lie on the ground, as they pleased. That was what it meant to be free!

When they reached the plateau, laughter rose in their chests and gurgled in their throats. They rushed to a cluster of banana trees and stuffed their mouths with the sweet yellow fruit while moonlight filtered down on their dark bodies. Suddenly there was the throbbing of a rada-tambour. A *hungan* had carried it with him up the mountain path. They forgot their hunger, sped toward the sound of the drum, and reached a large clearing that was silvered with starlight. They broke branches from a stand of locust trees, tore away the twigs, and smote the tree trunks as though they were drums: thum-de-de-de-thum. Thum-de-de-thum. . . . They improvised patois words to

[53]

old chants while a dozen Congos pattered into the center of the clearing and began a strange, contortive dance. Wenches joined the dancers. In the morning they might be hunted, tortured, or slain . . . but tonight they were free! Shaking and shivering, with shuffling feet and flailing arms, they contorted themselves in cadence to a rhythm that grew faster and wilder. They exhorted each other into uncertain frenzies by rubbing their woolly heads together, staring into each other's eyes, and spitting into each other's faces. Without touching each other with their hands, they rubbed their bodies together, bending their knees and sinking and rising like spiraling black snakes. A thousand onlookers at the edge of the clearing shook and beat the air with their fists as though the plateau were an enormous drum.

Christophe was drawn to the clearing by the sound of the tambour, the thumping, and the chanting. He thrust past an almost solid circle of tireless, springing Blacks and found himself in the presence of Dessalines and Défilée. She had wound a red kerchief about her head and was dressed in a sleeveless, low-necked shift. An obnoxious scent hovered about her and exuded from an *ouanga* bag that hung from her neck. The *ouanga*, the size of a goose egg, was made of greasy cloth and filled with *merde-diable* (asafetida), dried pig-tree leaves, and snake bones. She stood with one arm draped affectionately about Dessalines' squat, ugly form as his bullet head nodded in cadence to the rhythm of the tambour and the shivering of the dancers.

Défilée insisted that she owned Dessalines . . . owned him as though she had bought him or had thrust him from her very womb . . . for she had nursed him back from death and given him his name—Jean Jacques. It was the

[54]

name of her former lover. Dessalines' mulatto owner, unable to tame his ferocious violence, had decided to rid himself of the ugly brute. He had flogged Dessalines until the bones shone white through the bloodied flesh, had ordered his ankles to be broken, his head and genitals to be smeared with burnt sugar, all his orifices to be filled with spoonfuls of ants, and his body cast into a gully. There Défilée had found him, bloodied, almost blinded, more dead than alive.

Christophe left the clearing and wandered past the locust trees. He noticed a shadow at the edge of a donkey path. It was Toussaint, standing by the side of his unsaddled mount. He was staring down at the foothills where countless Blacks were still funneling into the twisting mountain paths and clambering upward. The cold night air was filled with the fragrance of coffee blossoms, and out toward the sea, past the Plaine du Nord, dots of light, like earthbound stars, twinkled where Cap Français was entrenched behind its palisades.

Toussaint glanced up, and Christophe could not tell if he had been weeping or if his face was streaked with road dust. He swept a gnarled hand toward the distant harbor and confessed, "We need them, Henri. We need them! There are a half million of us on Saint-Domingue and yet we need the whites! They have the ships and the wealth. And knowledge. Knowledge! The white man's knowledge. Freedom is of no use to us in the hills. What can we do here, on a mountain? Boukmann was wrong. Dessalines is driven by violence. We must use the whites! Use them as a ladder while we struggle upward, rung by rung. Rung by rung! Do you hear me, Henri? It has become a white man's world and we must bide our time and use them!"

7

Christophe married Marie-Louise Coidovic in July.
When her parents were killed, she had escaped from the
looted Auberge de la Couronne and taken refuge among
the Jesuits, who found work for her in the women's section of Providence hospital. It had been a year since the
slave rebellion, and much had happened. France had executed her king and was at war with Britain, and the English had rushed a fleet to Saint-Domingue, where they had
blockaded its ports and captured Môle St. Nicolas on its
northwestern shore. Jean-François, Jannot, Biassou, and
others had formed guerrilla bands and were pillaging the
villages and looting the plantations; but Toussaint
remained in the hills, gathering supplies and biding his
time. He dreamed of equality for Blacks and would not be
diverted by acts of brigandage.

Christophe was drawn to Cap Français. He was a towns-man, and a year in the languid foothills and rocky defiles of the mountains was more than he could bear. He won-dered what had changed in Cap Français; reminisced of Sunday morning scenes in Place Clugny, evenings in crowded Place Montarcher, and laughter on the balconies of the calcimined houses that fronted the Rue d'Anjou. When he learned where Marie-Louise had taken sanc-tuary, he raced down from the hills and made his way across the Plaine du Nord in the night. He circled the still-standing palisades of Cap Français and clambered across the unguarded Morne du Cap ravine that was now tiered with rotting bodies of Blacks and filled with the flut-terings of a thousand bats. La Providence hospital seemed sentineled by the shadows in the Champ de Mars and, when he reached it, he pattered stealthily through its cor-ridors in the dark. He found Marie-Louise in a small, win-dowless cubicle. She was asleep on a palm-fiber pallet, and a flaming wick floating on coconut oil in a gourd on the floor cast a bluish light on half her face. He dropped to his knees, bent over her, and whispered, "Marie-Louise . . . Marie. . . ."

She opened her eyes and glanced up at him. Recogni-tion came quickly, her heavy, smoke-tinted lips parted, and she smiled. She rose, without a word, and began to roll up the pallet. It was as though she had expected him and was not surprised. She gave him the pallet and a half-filled gourd to carry. She had lost some of the plump-ness of puberty, but her hand was warm and soft as she led him from the cubicle. She guided him past the Providence chapel and the prison stockade that bordered the Rue Saint-Domingue. Beyond the Place du Gouvernement, she

[57]

led him into the now-deserted school that the congregation of Notre Dame had established. She took the pallet and spread it on the floor where starlight, piercing between the louvers of the shutters, dappled the palm fibers with luminescent coins.

"*Ou gagnin souf?*" [Are you thirsty?] she asked in Creole patois, forgetting for the moment that he spoke French well. "*Vini.*" [Come on.] "*Li empke douce.*" [It is sweet.]

She watched him drink thirstily from the gourd. He had grown heavier, and his nostrils were widely dilated as though they could not supply his chest with enough air. He offered the gourd to her but she shook her head, and only after he had set it down did she rush into his arms. For an instant she was on the verge of tears. Then she subdued them, and sank slowly with him to the pallet.

"*La auberge* is no more, Henri. *Mon Papa. . . . Mon maman. . . . You have heard, perhaps?*"

Christophe nodded. "You cannot remain in Le Cap with safety. The Republic of France is about to grant us our freedom. But what are we to the French, who are four thousand miles away and have never seen us? Toussaint says that the whites who have owned us are not ready to set us free, and Dessalines insists that the mulattoes will never accept us. When the decree for our freedom becomes official, the Creoles will massacre the Blacks who remain in Le Cap."

His words were slow and deliberate. His face was solemn, and the gold earring that she had given him still dangled from a lobe of one delicate ear. "You must come with me to the hills," he insisted. "There are any number of women in our camps. Even children."

[58]

She fingered the crucifix that hung at her throat and asked, "Would you marry me, Henri? You are already freed."

Laughter gurgled in his throat and bubbled from his lips as he thought of how he had gained that freedom. "But where?"

"In Saint Anne. Father Bernard still keeps his doors open to Blacks and conducts mass though the French forbid it."

He smiled broadly and rushed one hand under her cotton shift. To his surprise the triangle of crisp ringlets was locked tightly between her thighs. He thrust his arm upward until his hand found the firm rise of her breast, and its nipple distended itself, like a bursting bud, as his fingers caressed it. He wondered who had seduced whom on that little plateau at the edge of the Morne du Cap, and whispered, "I would have married you then, Marie-Louise. I never said I would not marry you."

She kissed him, and he sensed her body surge upward as she lifted herself in order to tug the shift from under her. She was like a small black mare—powerful, indefatigable—receiving him with an insatiable crescendo of violence, yet trembling and drifting to a repose of tenderness and caress. . . .

The crowing of cocks awakened Marie-Louise and Christophe and they rushed to the church of Saint Anne. In a compound at its back, priests were astir, readying themselves for their morning ablutions. One could see them through the open doorways of their straw-thatched huts. They were monks who had broken their vows or priests who had disgraced themselves in France and had

[59]

been sent to Saint-Domingue to do penance. Most of them lived openly with mulatto or griffe concubines. The sun was dispelling a shimmering mist that hovered over the tall grass, and it was beginning to bake the airless huts. Sepia-brown and fawn-colored little ones were being set out to crawl along wattle-and-mud walls or suck on short lengths of sticky sugar cane. Older children, in shabby cotton undershirts, unmindful of the ants that scurried over them, were already at play in the weedy lanes between the sparse coconut palms to which a few goats were tethered.

Marie-Louise hurried Christophe into the dim church, in search of Father Bernard. She had thrust a sprig of frangipani into the kinky hair above one ear and carried herself with obvious dignity. She left Christophe in the narthex of a narrow nave and entered a small anteroom with brazen familiarity. He had never been inside a church, though he had glanced into them and, as his eyes adjusted to the dimness, he stared about and satiated his curiosity. The low ceiling was a pale blue, studded with gilt stars. It was sagging, perhaps from the downpours of Saint-Domingue's rainy seasons, and was upheld by wooden columns that had been painted with a blue calcimine. There was no glass in the narrow windows, and light strayed in between the slats of dilapidated shutters and shone on paintings that were hung on the walls. One was a portrait of a kneeling man with flowing brown hair that fell in thick curls to his shoulders. A brass plaque on its frame labeled it *Louis, Roi de France*. Christophe could not read the inscription but recognized the fleurs-de-lis on the robe and wondered if it were a portrait of the executed King. A few mulattoes moved slowly up the nave, past rows of cane-seated chairs, toward the buff and gilt altar upon which slender bougies, set in tiny candelabra, burned with little, smokeless flames. Two barefooted Negresses shuffled softly to the stone floor of the chancel that contained a life-size figure of Christ—dressed in a red silk gown, his back bowed by a heavy wooden cross. They passed their large-jointed hands over the red-robed body and stroked the naked wax of the arms and legs with concerned tenderness. Inarticulate, it was as though they had come to assure themselves that He still existed. Upon leaving, they bowed to the very flagging of the floor. Christophe was unimpressed. What affinity could a Black have for a white god—other than slave for master?

Marie-Louise was gesturing to him from the threshold of the anteroom. Christophe recognized Father Bernard, for he had seen him often at the Auberge de la Couronne. The priest, though reluctant, married them with punctiliousness and a rush of Latin phrases:

"*Deus, qui tam excellenti mysterio*
conjugalem copulam consecrasti . . ."

Christophe was on his knees—a subservient posture! At his side, Marie-Louise was whispering, with bowed head, "Lord have mercy, Christ have mercy, Lord have mercy . . . ."

The priest was touching their heads, looking out past them as though there were no wall between the anteroom and the church itself.

"*. . . vivit et regnat Deus, per omnia*
saeculorum. Amen."

"You must go now. Hurry!" He led them to a door that opened into the courtyard of the church, and they stepped out into the brilliant sunlight.

[61]

To Marie-Louise's surprise, Christophe led her toward the Rue d'Anjou. He seemed to have no fear of being apprehended and carried himself with defiant arrogance. When they reached Lutétia Mongeon's cottage, he left Marie-Louise in the shade of the pepper trees and entered the cottage alone. Lutétia had awakened late and was dressing. She had grown slender, though her breasts were now as full as a sow's. Her bronze skin glistened with the early heat of the day and she stared at Christophe in amazement. "Henri!" she cried. "Henri!" Her smile was as provocative and inviting as ever, but before she could reach him he strode to a rattan pallet and lifted a child from the floor. He held it at arm's length and examined his first-born. Its skin was a cinnamon brown, its black hair was a tangle of swirls, and its eyes were large and attentive.

"This boy look like me, Lutétia," Christophe laughed. "This boy have my face."

She thrust her arms akimbo on her hips. "This boy named Eugène Armand," she said defiantly. "This boy have no runaway father! This boy have only mother like the white Domini Christi."

He grinned as he handed the child to her. "You raise this Eugène good, Lutétia. This boy is Eugène Christophe. I shall return for him."

She spat at him, but as he turned to leave she cried, "Henri! Henri . . . !" and pattered after him.

When he reached the pepper trees, he grasped Marie-Louise's hand and led her away without a backward glance.

They dashed past the Champ de Mars, where the spacious park was edged with palm trees, and circled back to

[62]

the ravine. They made their way to the mountains that rose beyond Milot and soon left the torrid sunlight at the base of its hills. Marie-Louise was startled by the repulsive cactuses that rose, spiked and hairy, to twice the height of a man on horseback. They pushed through a primeval jungle of giant ferns, orchids, mocha plants, scattered nutmeg trees, swarms of multicolored butterflies and, when almost exhausted, reached a rock-strewn path that wound up the mountainside. Christophe settled his arm about Marie-Louise's waist and urged her to clamber up the slope.

The first plateau was filled with slaves who had deserted their plantations. Donkeys were tethered in a wide circle within which squalid children scrambled about. Half-naked muscular bucks drowsed in the shade of hardy banana plants. Negresses, in soiled shifts, sat about on the bare ground. Some had adorned themselves with ragged pieces of colored cloth. As Christophe and Marie-Louise reached the plateau they came upon Blacks who had hacked their way from the Dondon plantation: sturdy, deep-chested Nagoes, their faces incised with tribal markings; Mandingoes, whose filed front teeth had been bludgeoned out; Angolese, whose cheeks were branded with the initials of their owners.

The flower-scented air was tainted with the heavy odor of animal sweat as Christophe led Marie-Louise across the plateau. She had never seen such varied Blacks. Ebony-hued Congos and thick-chested Ashantis sat on their haunches; Fulas, the hair shaved from their heads, milled about; insolent-looking Bambaras, their lashes and eyebrows singed by the fires they had stoked beneath copper boilers and iron half-spheres of molasses, sprawled in the shade. Their feet were caked with limestone dust and they had rubbed their bodies with rancid coconut oil to ward off mosquitoes and burrowing chigoes. When they came across a group of refuse Eboes, with jaundiced eyes and prognathous faces, like baboons, Marie-Louise recoiled from the sight and smell of them. She had led a sheltered life in Cap Français and had noticed only the proud Aradas, the intelligent Senegalese, and the griffes in the Clugny square. She had never imagined slaves like these!

Christophe sensed her revulsion. He put an arm about her and detained her. "These animals are your cousins, Marie-Louise. Toussaint says that their souls are white but I insist that their souls are as black as their skins. And I would not wish it otherwise. It is the blackness of their minds that I regret. Like the black of my own that cannot decipher a single letter of the alphabet or measure an ounce of gold. I, Henri Christophe, will whiten their minds, and then no one will concern themselves with the color of their skins. Toussaint will free them, but I shall fill their gourds with silver and watch them buy straw hats and cotton shirts. When they are no longer animals, they will even buy white women."

"And you, Henri?"

"No," he laughed. "I need no white whores, like old men feeding on lambies. But first you must help me whiten my mind. Teach me to read and write, Marie-Louise. Teach me—and some day I shall show these prolific Blacks how to spill their seed into *les coiyous* of a hundred thousand whites!"

8

In February, 1794, a decree in the French National Assembly abolished slavery in all its colonies. Toussaint was elated. Thousands of Blacks had flocked to "Papa Toussaint" in the hills, and he was convinced that he was destined to be their savior. He had but to lead them back to the plains, where he would resettle them on the plantations, as paid workers.

The Creoles and mulattoes in Saint-Domingue, distrustful of each other, the whites refusing to relinquish the aristocracy of their unblemished heritage, the mulattoes insisting upon social and political acceptance, had not considered the inarticulate slaves . . . the ebony cattle who were now freed. The decree of the National Assembly in France drew them together, made allies of them, for the whites saw themselves deprived of their slaves and the mulattoes refused to consider an equality with the "savage Africans" from whom they had stemmed. They alienated themselves from France and turned to England for aid—the England who had sold them these Africans. Better to invite the British than accept the freedom and equality of half a million barbaric Blacks!

France rushed an emissary to Saint-Domingue. She wished to retain her wealthiest colony, to keep it from falling into British hands, but she could spare neither ships nor men. She was not only at war with England but with Spain, Italy, Austria . . . with all Europe! The emissary tried not to show his disappointment at Toussaint's unprepossessing appearance—at this ludicrous Black who insisted, in excellent French, that he was the commander of all the loyal forces on the island. Toussaint had clad himself in a blue spencer with a red cape falling over his shoulders, eight rows of lace on his arms, a scarlet waistcoat, half boots, a round hat with a national cockade and yet, though he was flanked by Christophe and Dessalines, he presented a farcical figure.

The emissary had no choice. The Creoles, determined to preserve slavery in Saint-Domingue, had signed a treaty with England and offered their allegiance to His Britannic Majesty. The fortress of Môle Saint-Nicolas, with its two hundred cannons pointing out to sea, had capitulated without firing a shot. St. Marc, Verrettes, and Petite Rivière had welcomed the British. British troops had already landed at Jérémie. Nearly half a million placid slaves were still on the plantations and in the towns. They must not be freed!

The emissary offered Toussaint military aid in return for his allegiance. He would be sent uniforms, muskets, cannons, even French drillmasters. He would be given a commission in the French army, with the rank of *général de brigade*, and the freedom to appoint his own aides.

When Toussaint returned to his camp, after having accepted the emissary's proposal, he realized that France had flattered him in thinking he held a unified command. There were now a half dozen rebel armies, headed by as many commanders, scattered across the plains; and sansculottes, ferocious brigands who had hidden themselves in the hills and ravaged and pillaged the countryside. He took Dessalines and Christophe into his confidence and proposed, "I shall invite every commander who is partial to our cause to come and meet with us. I shall even welcome Rigaud and Pétion. They will come, for I shall inform them that I have the blessing of France and will shortly receive its military supplies."

"Those mulatto bastards!" cried Dessalines. "I shall hack their bleached heads from their arrogant necks!"

"No!" stormed Toussaint. "I insist on unity. And, I promise you, mulattoes will become the stepping stones between ourselves and whites."

Toussaint gave no thought to the political independence of Saint-Domingue. He detested the haughty French Creoles who had molded slavery into such a horror on the island, yet he respected the National Assembly, in Paris, that had proclaimed *liberté, égalité, et fraternité*. He had but one goal: freedom and acceptance for the Blacks.

When the morning of the meeting came, as though to overcome the unimposing appearance of his slight figure, Toussaint attired himself in an elegant uniform with gold epaulets and a black cordon embroidered with white fleurs-de-lis . . . gifts from the French emissary. A plumed hat, spurred top boots, and a huge cavalry sword completed his costume. He adjusted his narrow shoulders beneath the huge epaulets and thrust his scabbard behind a raised stirrup. He sat his horse between powerful Dessalines and aristocratic Christophe, whom he had appointed his aides, and awaited the arrival of his guests. Unlettered Dessalines was antagonistic to all who possessed a single drop of white blood in their veins, but his very ferocity made him indispensable. And Toussaint had discovered his Achilles heel—Dessalines could be tamed by flattery and kindness! Christophe had no formal education but was shrewd, devoted, and possessed an incomparable knowledge of towns, roads, and harbors. As for himself, his scholastic achievements, his concern for the slaves, and destiny itself had bestowed leadership upon him. As though to assure it, he appointed Moyse, a powerful full-blooded Black, as his bodyguard. Young and impetuous, Moyse had grown up on the Bréda plantation under Toussaint's tutelage, and still insisted upon calling him, though with affection, *"oncle."*

Rigaud and Pétion must have met on the plain, for they rode together into Toussaint's camp. André Rigaud commanded a detachment of mulatto regulars, stationed at St. Michel, and had come with a bodyguard of mulatto dragoons. His arrogance intimated that he would not serve under a Black. The son of a French nobleman and a native Negress, he was opposed to slavery, but insisted that mulattoes be accepted as a dominant caste.

Alexander Sabes Pétion, courageous and proud, had come with a single aide. The bastard son of a white French artist and a mulattress, he had been educated in France, had returned to Saint-Domingue and, like executed Vincent Ogé, was inspired by a desire for universal freedom.

Toussaint had corresponded with these men and, though there existed a disparity of color and social acceptance, they had three things in common: Their *langue maternelle* was French, their religion was Catholicism, and their resolve was the abolition of slavery.

Jean-François arrived, surrounded by a bodyguard of twelve mounted Negroes in natty uniforms with fleurs-de-lis insignia. His martial helmet sat clumsily on his thick, kinky hair, and its elegance was a contrast to his gross features. His tunic was covered with looted military decorations, crucifixes, and medallions. Biassou, ill-shaped and extremely ugly, rode at his side. They had their headquarters at the pillaged Gallifet plantation, at Grande Rivière, and both had become so corrupt that they did not hesitate to sell Negroes into slavery, to the Spaniards west of Dajabon—even the wives and children of their own soldiers.

Toussaint gave no indication of dismounting. He glanced up at the noon sun and said quietly, "Jannot has not arrived. And I do not think he intends to come; so we shall go to him. His camp is not far. *Suivez-moi.*"

Rigaud intended to protest Toussaint's assumed command, but as they filed from the camp he followed and urged his mount forward so he could ride abreast of Pétion. When they reached a clearing, near Poteau, they were assailed by a stink of rotting flesh. Jean Jannot, whose hatred of whites was so intense that it bordered on insanity, and stemmed from the utmost brutality with which he had been treated by the planter, Bullet, had decorated his camp with the severed heads of whites, thrust upon pikes.

The clearing was filled with his followers—unwashed Blacks who were dressed in rags or wore only loin cloths. About one in three had an old musket or a pistol, but no ammunition. A few were armed with machetes, iron-pointed sticks, or broken swords. A crude cage, made of pine saplings driven into the dark earth, imprisoned a dozen white women. They were naked, yoked in pairs, and their flesh was raw and blistered from the sun. Two priests, chained ankle to ankle, their cassocks half torn from their backs, were seated on the trampled grass in front of the cage. Toussaint recognized Fathers Sulpice and Delhaye, who had come to Saint-Domingue because of a genuine sympathy for the slaves. They were being held as hostages, or for ransom. To one side some draft horses, saddle horses, and donkeys were tethered in the shade of a few mango trees.

Jannot, aware of Toussaint and his party, mounted a magnificent saddle horse and met them in the center of the clearing. Toussaint drew away from Dessalines, Christophe, and Moyse. "Greetings, Jannot," he said. "I have brought you news. I, François Dominique Toussaint, have been appointed *général de brigade* by the government of France. Every officer and sans-culotte is now under my command." He could hear the tinkle of spurs and the pivoting of horses behind him. What had Rigaud and Pétion—even Jean-François—expected?

Jannot stared at Toussaint in amazement. He wondered at the epaulets and the military garb. He looked past Toussaint and smiled as he noticed the uncontained anger that showed in the faces of Rigaud, Jean-François, and Biassou. The news must be as unwelcome to them as it was unacceptable to him.

"I have pledged myself to the service of France, the liberty of my people, and the protection of all French citizens," said Toussaint. "There will be no brigands! From this day forth there will be no looting, no raping, and no more massacring of whites. We struggle for one thing: *liberté. Liberté!* But we must show the world that we are not savages. Henri! Break open the cage and unyoke the women. Unchain the priests!"

"No!" cried Jannot. "No!"

Toussaint drew his sword from its scabbard. He kicked his boot heels backward, and the new spurs pricked his mount into a little forward burst.

"In nomine Patris et Filii et Spiritus Sancti. Amen."

The strange words so puzzled Jannot that he did not comprehend Toussaint's raised arm until the sharp steel bit into his neck and severed his head from his shoulders. An excellent horseman, Toussaint swerved his mount in time to avoid the spurt of blood. To Biassou, who had raised himself in his stirrups, he said, unaffectedly, "A man who will not listen has no need for ears."

9

The incident at Poteau settled the matter of Toussaint's command. Even crude Biassou and vain Jean-François accepted the leadership of this wizened Black who was a web of contradictions: cunning despite his appearance of naïveté, violent despite his fastidiousness, and indefatigable despite his diminutive frame.

He established his headquarters at Tannerie and fortified it according to his own plan. A moat was dug around the entire town and a palisade was built behind the ditch. He loved to see his people at work and would ride out in the mornings to watch them. Their muscles would ripple, and sunlight would dance on their sweating backs as they felled mango saplings and hewed away the branches. Their voices were strong and full as they sang to the slow, untiring cadence of their work. He would dismount and walk among them, his heart bursting with pride and an encompassing love for them.

In March, impatient because almost all of his troops were still without weapons, Toussaint decided to raid the armory in British-held Port-de-Paix, directly across from the little island of Tortuga. He had learned that it was defended by fewer than three hundred British regulars and so, with Christophe and Dessalines at his side, he left Tannerie at the head of more than a thousand Blacks. He led them northward in forced marches along the Trois Rivières, whose banks were filled with red, yellow, and mauve bougainvillaea in full bloom. Laughing and jabbering among themselves, the Blacks were in high spirits as though they were on a holiday. When hungry, hundreds would leave their loose ranks in order to forage in the fields along the river banks.

They reached the outskirts of Port-de-Paix in early morning, unaware that sentinels had seen them and alerted the British. When they came to the main road, they were amazed to find British regulars lined up in tight columns in front of them, their spatterdashes contrastingly white against the brown earth, their red coats brilliant in the sunlight, their fixed bayonets glistening like shards of glass.

Toussaint reigned in his mount and glanced at the Blacks behind him. Many had only cudgels of mangrove roots. Most were armed only with machetes. The full-blooded Congos stood barehanded, as though they depended upon their strong backs and had placed their faith in the *ouangas* that hung about their necks—little bags filled with dry goat's dung and circled with cock feathers dipped in blood.

[73]

Impatient with Toussaint's hesitation, bursting with violent anger at the sight of the white faces that confronted them, Dessalines lifted his saber bellowing *"Fou! Fou!"* and spurred the Blacks forward. There was a volley of bullets all about him. The Blacks turned and ran, leaving half a hundred dead and wounded. "Slay them!" cried Dessalines as he stood his ground. "Slaughter each of them as you would a hog and listen to no cries for mercy!"

At the sound of Dessalines' furious voice the Blacks turned back and brandished their weapons with menacing lunges. The Nagoes and Mandingoes grouped together and flung themselves into demoniac contortions with horrible shrieks. The Congos thrust their *ouanga* bags toward the British and worked themselves into incantations with wild cries and howlings.

Angered by their senseless mouthings, Toussaint dashed among them and, like Dessalines, urged them to attack, for they could smash the British by their very numbers. They rushed forward, without any concerted purpose, and a second volley of musket fire tore into them. The impetus of their charge carried many of them to the British lines where, to Toussaint's horror, they thoughtlessly impaled themselves on the British bayonets or flung themselves to the ground as they reached them. He waved his arm and cried to them to turn back. Not a single Black had fired a musket. Not one ex-slave had struck a blow! The road was littered with dead and groaning Blacks as they deserted it and dashed into the fields. Toussaint wept as they retreated to Tannerie. The tears were in his heart, where they did not show, but he was weeping.

Back at Tannerie, Toussaint set to work to solve the

enigma of the defeat. His troops were not soldiers! They were ex-slaves, from dozens of different African tribes who were unable to communicate, even among themselves—the Bantu tongue, alone, had multitudinous dialects—and they should be sorted, like fruit in a marketplace. They must be trained! Disciplined and trained! Until they were a match for the whites he would instruct them to fight like cats—to hide in ravines, to escape into marshes, to rush down from hills to claw at the enemy and then scatter where they could not be followed.

Using fortified Tannerie as his headquarters, Toussaint led detachments of hand-picked Blacks over mountain ranges and across burned plains. His men had neither coats nor shirts. Some lacked even trousers. They fed themselves by foraging among papayas, coconut palms, and banana plants and preferred the arduous marches to remembered labor in cane fields and sugar mills under the whips of drivers; for Toussaint called them his "children" and raised his voice in song with them. With uncanny instinct, he taught them to be guérrilla fighters and armed them by raids upon enemy supplies. By unpredictable encounters in the eerie quiet of·night, in the mists of early morning, in the unbearable tropic heat of the noonday sun, he drove the British, unaccustomed to his tactics, from the Artibonite Valley to the sea.

He left the training of his main body of troops in the hands of Christophe, who seemed most proficient, and was astonished at the rapidity with which the Blacks learned to load their captured muskets, the adeptness with which they handled bayonets, and the accuracy with which they joyfully fired captured fieldpieces. Indefatigable, impassioned by a dream of freedom for his people, Toussaint stormed towns and villages and raised the tricolor of France in every settlement as he proclaimed the universal emancipation of the Blacks; for that was his hope as he looked westward toward Jamaica and northward to the Bahama Islands.

The French finally navigated two ships past the British blockade and landed their military aid at Poste Habert. They were advised that Toussaint had expended confiscated moneys for the purchase of military needs from American smugglers, and were amazed to learn that he now had a fully organized army of ten thousand trained and fearless Blacks. They wondered whether this ambitious "monkey in a headdress," as they spoke of him among themselves, was actually interested in recognition of Black equality. Was his true objective, rather self-aggrandizement? To remind Toussaint that his obligation was primarily to France, he was appointed chief aide to the Governor-General of the colony, with the title of Lieutenant-Governor. Lieutenant-Governor of Saint-Domingue! A Black Lieutenant-Governor! He was flattered, yet when alone he brooded. He was tortured by his inability to dispel the white's distrust of the mulatto and the mulatto's aversion for the Negro. Only Christophe seemed to understand what he was attempting to forge in Saint-Domingue. Toussaint was pleased when Christophe would address him, affectionately: "François Dominique. . . ." He treated Christophe as a son, for he admired his fine form, his aristocratic bearing, his keen mind. Besides, he was lonely for his own sons since he had, by special invitation, sent them to France to be educated.

10

By March of 1798 the British in Saint-Domingue held only the port of Môle St. Nicolas on the beautiful bay that widens into the Windward Passage across from Cuba. And in April of that year Toussaint, now dubbed L'Ouverture, made his triumphant entry into the capitulated colonial capital, Port-au-Prince, where the town's populace drew up in the streets to greet him. The fountains in the public squares were ornamented with garlands of flowers, and lanterns were strung among the branches of the orange trees that filled the air with a delicate fragrance.

A procession was hastily formed at the steps of the Government Palace, and sent to meet "the defenders of French liberty" and "the liberator of the Blacks." First came two acolytes carrying a gilded cross; then choir boys, swinging censers in slow-moving arcs, their deeply tanned faces freshly scrubbed; then the clergy, perspiring in their vestments; then the town's leading citizens and humbled planters who had sought refuge in Port-au-Prince.

Three French Creole women, their parasols lifted to shield them from the intense rays of the sun, sat in an elegant carriage in front of the Government Palace. As Toussaint, Dessalines, and Christophe drew abreast of them they set aside their parasols, filled their arms with enormous bouquets of jasmine, gathered the trains of their silk gowns, and stepped from the carriage. With forced smiles of false recognition, one stepped toward Toussaint, one toward Christophe, another toward Dessalines, and offered them the fragrant bouquets. Dessalines glanced past the steps of the Government Palace, where a line of dragoons had lifted their swords in a salute. Behind them a crowd of whites craned their necks and jostled each other for a better vantage point. A number of haughty mulattoes had wedged themselves among the whites. Shielded from the sun by wide-brimmed straw hats, as though to preserve the paleness of their acceptability, their faces seemed to express indifference and disdain. Behind them shuffled the Blacks—mute and patient as oxen.

The bastards! thought Dessalines as anger boiled in his chest. The bastards! The town of Port-au-Prince may have freed their Blacks but they still herd them like cattle!

He felt a soft touch on his hand where it rested on his booted knee. It was the Creole. She smiled as she offered him the bouquet. His mind raced back to an incident in his past. He did not know why, for he had not thought of it in years. It was with just such a smile that Bullet's wife had watched the planter stuff his ass hole with ants when he had tortured him! He flung the cluster of jasmine into

[78]

the street, fashioned a hasty glob of bile and sputum, and would have spat it into the Creole's face but that a voice at his side suddenly cried, "Jean Jacques! Jean Jacques! *Ca ou fais!*" It was Toussaint, leaning toward him from the saddle.

Toussaint dismounted at the steps of the palace. As thin and unprepossessing as ever, it was difficult to presume him a conquering hero. His kinky hair was graying at the temples and when he smiled one could see dark gaps where a glancing blow from a spent cannonball had carried away two teeth. His military hat was overhung with costly blue and white plumes, and yet under it, as though for comfort, he had knotted a yellow madras kerchief about his head. His coat was lavishly decorated with gold braid, and his epaulets were too wide for his narrow shoulders.

When he reached the top of the steps, four officials rushed out and raised a baldachin over his head. He stepped from under its shade, glanced about, faced the milling Blacks behind the whites and mulattoes and said, "God, not man, deserves a baldachin, for He alone is immortal. Who knows if what I have accomplished will be undone after I am dead? There are different kinds of slavery. There is the bondage of the body that dies under the white man's lash. There is also the slavery of the mind that cannot free itself without the white man's tutelage."

He turned and, as though addressing Dessalines, predicted, "The Blacks must tolerate the whites or they will not liberate their minds. The whites must accept the Blacks or someday they will rise in such numbers that they will devour them! And now we must all work together to restore prosperity to Saint-Domingue."

There was no single acclamation. White, pink, yellow,

tan, and Black found offense in Toussaint's words. How could the Blacks forgive the bleached and bastard race that had enslaved them? And though the Creole *sang-mêlés* had banked the fires of retribution that burned within them, they felt that they would never accept the full-blooded Blacks ... the African animals that Toussaint insisted were now their poltical and social equals!

Toussaint entered the Government Palace, where a banquet had been arranged for him and his officers. The tables were laden with *pâtés de foie gras* that were made with goose livers and rested upon cushions of mushrooms. There were glazed hams, stuffed tongues, salads, and creams. This would be no novelty for Christophe, who had served in the Auberge de la Couronne, but for Moyse, Dessalines, and the others. . . . He would observe how they conducted themselves.

Toussaint was seated at the side of a French Creole, whose dark hair was elegantly coiffured and whose lips were faintly tinted with carmine. Her white neck turned, swanlike, as she surveyed those about her and then, as though impatient with the lack of formality, she introduced herself to Toussaint in a languorous, drawly voice as Madame Prophéte, the wife of the former mayor of Port-au-Prince—but recently widowed. She extended a slender hand and Toussaint, though not rising, raised it to his lips and kissed it. She did not withdraw her hand but let it linger in his, a strange contrast against his wrinkled, black skin, while she studied him for a long moment as though searching for the answer to an enigma.

Her gown was very décolleté. Reaching down between the fullness of her half-exposed breasts she extracted a small, folded memorandum and handed it to Toussaint.

He was aware of a delicate fragrance as he unfolded it. The note was from a British official, in their last stronghold, at Môle St. Nicolas. England was prepared to evacuate the entire island and recognize François Dominique Toussaint as King of Saint-Domingue—even protect him from the French—in return for a commercial treaty.

Toussaint glanced about. It was the first time he had seen whites, Blacks, and mulattoes seated together at a table. The Blacks were smiling broadly, the mulattoes seemed diffident, the whites brooding and ill at ease. He had no objection to trading with England, if it could be done discreetly, but he had not thought of founding a kingdom. His first wish was to integrate and unify the people. The French Republic was too powerful to provoke, and he was not impressed by the title of King.

He turned to the smiling Madame Prophéte. White women were not like his guileless wife, Suzanne; or Henri's Marie-Louise, of whom he had grown quite fond. White women were shrewd and not to be trusted. "*Mais non*," he whispered. "I assure you, I have no desire to wear a crown."

11

On October 3, 1798, the last of the British troops withdrew from Môle St. Nicolas, and the English occupation of Saint-Domingue came to an ignominious end. In the five years that they had tried to wrest the "Pearl of the Antilles" from Toussaint, they had expended 20,000,000 pounds and lost 40,000 men—more of whom had perished of tropic fevers and disastrous dysentery than had been killed in actual combat.

Toussaint lost no time in dividing his authority. He appointed Dessalines Governor of the South Province and, aware of his limitations, offered him the assistance of a wealthy, well-educated young mulatto by the name of Dupuy. He unhesitatingly chose Christophe to govern Pointe Picolet and Cap Français, for Christophe's soldiers were now matchlessly trained and the best dressed of

Toussaint's troops. Christophe commanded a personal bodyguard of 150 cavalrymen and two demi-brigades of infantry—some 3,000 men—which included a battalion of white troops that had been abandoned in the colony by France. In order to prepare a triumphant welcome for Toussaint, in Cap Français, Christophe chartered the American brig *Rebecca* to ship fresh provisions from Santo Domingo. With Marie-Louise now constantly at his side, he refurnished the Governor's mansion and supervised the decorations in the Place d'Armes, where lanterns were strung from the pear trees and a brass twelve-pounder was lifted onto a newly constructed platform. This was Christophe's element. Though without the appearance of vanity, he loved grandeur and pomposity.

On November 22nd, at the end of the rainy season, escorted by a guard of honor dressed in the elegant sky-blue uniforms of Swiss Guards and preceded by trumpeters in scarlet-plumed helmets taken from the British, Toussaint made his entry into Cap Français and passed under a triumphal arch that Christophe had erected in the Rue d'Anjou. The Place d'Armes was bursting with a crowd of whites, mulattoes, and Blacks that commingled now like the colors of a tapestry, filled the square, and spilled over as far as the Rue Notre Dame. Knowing Toussaint's reverence for the church, that he went nowhere without a breviary in his saddlebag, Christophe had invited the clergy. Priests from Notre Dame, which had finally, though hesitantly, opened its doors to Blacks, were on the decorated platform. Below were a group of monks from la Providence—a most varied lot, for some were beardless, some bearded; some were tonsured, some unshorn; some in gray tunics, others in rust-brown robes;

and, while most had adorned themselves with crucifixes and rosaries, a few held aloft little tricolor banners of France.

Dessalines had defied Défilée and married. To this ceremonial occasion he had brought his wife, Claire Heureuse—a sable-colored griffone—young, buxom, and intelligent. She had been attracted to him, perversely, by the violence of his nature and the brutish ugliness of his face. As though he wished to impress Toussaint that he was not averse to culture, his new consort, Claire, could read and write both Spanish and French; and Dessalines seemed docile and subdued in her presence. She was seated beside Marie-Louise, whose classically Negroid features were a polished ebony in contrast to the matte tones of her own face, and she scanned the crowd, with trepidation, for a glimpse of Défilée. She had burned every twist of hair that clung to her comb and carefully buried the parings from her fingernails, for she had been told that Défilée, despite her gift of a dried hummingbird, was preparing a voodoo curse; and this morning she had awakened with a touch of dengue!

Christophe hurried to the twelve-pounder as Toussaint and his guard of honor entered the square. The cannon's snout was pointed at the blue sky, above the close-by harbor, and when he pressed a lighted flambeau to its touchhole it boomed a startling salute. For an instant the crowd was hushed, as though frightened by its potential, and then, without the accompaniment of a single flute or drum, broke into the *Marseillaise*—the trebles of the whites drowned out by the deep, uninhibited voices of the Blacks:

> *Allons, enfants de la Patrie,*
> *Le jour de Gloire est arrivé!* . . . .

The harbor guns on Pointe Picolet boomed their salvos, and the Blacks, unable to contain themselves, sprang up and down and chanted: "Papa Toussaint! Papa Toussaint, ou mâit!"

Toussaint helped his wife, obese in contrast to his slight form, climb the steps to the platform. Her dark, perspiring face was serene, and only a slight redness that veined the yellow of her eyes, disclosed that she had discovered, that very morning, that Toussaint had taken a young mulattress for a mistress. Unlike his generals, Toussaint had shed his grandiloquent military attire and dressed himself in the traditional planter's uniform of white jacket and breeches, with a madras kerchief about his head.

He lifted his spindly arms, extended them in an attitude of benediction, and addressed the crowd. He expressed his hopes and ambitions in French and his commands in the patois that even the ex-slaves could now understand. "There is no more war. We are now at peace. . . ." He was going into semiretirement at Ennery, a few miles from the port of Gonaïves, and all who had labored on plantations, before the war, must return to them. "We must make Saint-Domingue prosperous once again, as an example to the world, but now the prosperity will be for us and not for those who unrightfully owned us!" The Blacks who had followed their Papa Toussaint with fanatic devotion, magnetically drawn to him by his dynamic puissance, bellowed their acclamation.

Toussaint repaid his generals with gifts of confiscated plantations, proclaimed himself Governor-General of Saint-Domingue, and chose Jean Jacques Dessalines to be his successor. Impatient Dessalines followed him to Ennery and urged him to declare the island independent—to cast off not only the shackles of the government of France but the influence of whites and mulattoes and create a completely Negro state.

Toussaint shook his head. He had gained liberty and equality for every Negro on Saint-Domingue. Was that not enough? He was trying hard to tread a middle ground—to give offense to no one and restore prosperity to the desolated country. "We must tread softly," he advised Dessalines. "By practicing Catholicism we shall stamp fetishes and superstitions from the minds of our Blacks, and by insisting that we are still a colony, we shall enjoy the security of a French possession. Would you expect coffee berries to ripen without sun, or cacao pods to yield their nibs for the asking?"

"I insist upon independence and alienation from all whites, who are still our enemies," cried Dessalines, "and you prattle of coffee berries and cacao pods!"

Prodded by Dessalines and ill-tempered Moyse, who regretted the loss of an eye in a skirmish at the edge of Gros Morne, Toussaint finally agreed to declare Saint-Dominigue independent. As members were chosen to draft a constitution, Toussaint, in deference to the Creoles, insisted that Borgella, a native white who was familiar with foreign governments, be elected President of the Assembly.

The draft of the constitution was completed on July 7th, and publicly proclaimed on the following day at Cap Français. In order to avoid the heat of the day, the ceremony took place immediately after sunrise at the Place d'Armes. The tolling of bells and a roll of drums awakened the citizens at 3 o'clock in the morning. An hour later the garrison stood massed in the square, surrounded by a great concourse of citizenry—whites, Blacks, mulattoes, griffes, and the *gens de couleur* that generations of miscegenation had produced. Every house that faced the Place d'Armes displayed a now irrelevant tricolor of France, while balconies were crowded and heads and shoulders thrust themselves from every opened window. A wooden structure, from which speakers were to address the populace, was decorated with bunting, palm fronds, and garlands of hibiscuses.

At five in the morning civil, military, and ecclesiastical authorities arrived in a solemn and impressive procession. Toussaint wore the dress uniform of a general. After much deliberation, he had decided not to remove his French medal for valor. He had permitted the constitution to be drafted without the approval of the French government, but wished to maintain at least a pretense of loyalty to France.

Télémaque, a venerable Negro, now mayor of Cap Français, was the first to speak. He was followed by Borgella, who read the proclamation in French, although most of the citizens who had crowded into the Place d'Armes understood few of its words.

Toussaint rose and was greeted with deafening cheers. To the amazement of everyone, he finished his short address by crying, *"Vivent à jamais a République Français et la Constitution Coloniale!"* [Long live the French Republic and the Colonial Constitution!] He insisted on straddling a tall fence. Bells tolled, cannons boomed, and cheer after cheer rang out, for everyone was finally liberated. The whites were free of France, the mulattoes were free of discrimination, and the Blacks were free. . . . Free!

[87]

The ceremony at the Place d'Armes was followed by a Te Deum at the church of Notre Dame and a banquet at the Government Palace. As the day progressed, Toussaint's elation was dampened, for Christophe leaned toward him and whispered soberly, "François Dominique, the constitution is premature. It is against every principle that you have taught me. I shall support you in whatever you attempt, Ouverture, but we are not ready to govern ourselves. Are we about to caparison dray horses, or harness donkeys with elegant trappings?"

12

In the first year of the nineteenth century, France found herself at peace for the first time in a decade. French Creoles in Paris, who had never adjusted to the confiscation of their abandoned plantations in Saint-Domingue, urged Napoleon to reclaim the island—that tropic jewel whose plains and hillsides had filled the holds of a thousand ships with coffee, sugar, indigo, cacao seeds—and was now governed by a wizened Black!

Napoleon's wife, Josephine, a Creole from Martinique, had fallen heir to a vast Saint-Domingue plantation near Léogane, and cautious Toussaint had the Beauharnais lands cultivated at government expense and the revenues sent to her with precise and attentive regularity. But how could the revenue from a plantation compare to the opulence of the island? The wealth and energy of France depended on rich colonies, and Saint-Domingue, her most

[89]

treasured overseas resource, had slipped away while she was occupied elsewhere.

Bursting with unbridled energy, now that the European wars were over, Napoleon decided to retake Saint-Domingue and ordered preparations for one of the greatest expeditions that France had ever dispatched from her shores. He assured the Military Council that France would not, like England, piddle men and supplies into Saint-Domingue, for five years, only to end the occupation in an ignominious withdrawal. Immediacy was a word that he, himself, had coined! He envisioned a fleet of more than a hundred ships of war that would carry, along with military goods, 22,000 men—veterans from the armies that had conquered Italy and Austria—to be followed, immediately, by a second 20,000!

Not accustomed to doing things by halves, he enlisted the aid of Euroean monarchies, pointing out that a republican government in Saint-Domingue—a Negro republic dominated by a half million ex-slaves—meant the eventual rebellion and loss of every slave colony in the West Indies from the Honduras to the Windward Islands. As though he was unaware that Great Britain had offered to accept Toussaint as King of Saint-Domingue, he predicted: "Unless this scheming Toussaint is overthrown, the scepter of the New World will sooner or later pass into the hands of the Blacks!"

England, fearing the loss of her slave trade, promised to send supplies from Jamaica, and Spain committed herself to furnishing the same from Cuba. Holland agreed to co-operate in transporting the army, and a fleet of eighty-six war vessels and transports was assembled in the harbors of Brest, Orient, Rochefort, Toulon, Havre, Cadiz, and

Flushing. Admiral Villaret-Joyeuse was placed in command of the fleet and was assisted by seven Vice-Admirals—five French, one Spanish, and one Dutch. Napoleon planned to roll across Black Toussaint's island like a tidal wave! The world would see that everything he planned was absolute, and slaves would learn they could not wrest their freedom without the acquiescence of the sovereign land that owned them!

So that nothing might be left to chance, Napoleon decided that Toussaint's sons, sixteen-year-old Isaac and twenty-one-year-old Placide, should accompany the expedition, as hostages. They had spent the last six years in France, attending the Colonial Institute, a government school in Paris, that had been founded for the education of the sons of distinguished mulattoes and Negroes. He had been advised that the older boy, Placide Séraphin Clère, had a penchant for a military career, influenced perhaps by the success of his father, but laughable nonetheless. He had ordered the boys placed in the care of Abbé Coisnon, who managed the Colonial Institute, and had held him personally responsible for them. There had never been any doubt in his mind that he would find a way to maneuver these two inconsequential pawns against the "black knight"—Toussaint. As hostages, the boys would insure the success of the invasion.

Napoleon appointed his brother-in-law, Charles Victor Emmanuel Leclerc as Captain-General of the expedition; and insisted that his wife Pauline accompany him. Pauline might be his favorite sister, but Napoleon admitted that she was pampered, vacuous, and indiscreet—and he did not want jealous Charles speculating upon her infidelities while at the head of an expedition 4,000 miles from home.

[91]

He directed that they take their three-year-old son, Dermide, with them. The child might occupy Pauline's idle time and remind her of her marital obligations.

As an afterthought, Napoleon also sent his younger brother, Jérôme. Charles Leclerc was barely thirty, and though he had distinguished himself in Italy, on the Rhine, and in Portugal, he had permitted Pauline to weld a ring through his effeminate nose, and Napoleon mistrusted a man who allowed his decisions to be swayed by a wife. He entrusted Jérôme Bonaparte with Leclerc's instructions—and thus assured himself of regular and unbiased reports.

On January 29, 1802, the French armada was sighted off Cape Samaná, on the eastern coast of the island. As it tacked its way past Monte Christi, Toussaint, Dessalines, and Christophe rushed to catch a glimpse of it. They met on a rise of ground past Fort Dauphin and stared out at the blue sea where billowing sails drifted on the horizon like a tremendous skein of geese. They were unaware that Keverseau, with two frigates and 1,500 men, was approaching Santo Domingo; and that Generals Boudet and de LaCroix, with almost 4,000 army regulars, were on their way to Port-au-Prince.

Christophe studied the fleet through a battered brass telescope and passed the glass to Toussaint. After a long moment he lowered his thin arms and, still looking seaward, cried, *"Mon Dieu!* We must perish, for all France is about to invade us!"

"Never!" cried Dessalines fiercely. "Never! We will attack the landing parties, one by one, and annihilate them! There is your white treachery, Toussaint L'Ouverture. The treachery of the white world against the

Black. I will spill their blood into the ravines! I will cut out their livers and cast them to the fishes!"

Toussaint shook his graying head. He had permitted many whites and mulattoes to retain their political offices, and Saint-Domingue had had three years of peace and freedom. Now this! "I say no, Jean. No! They will overwhelm us. We must retreat to the mountains and plan our strategy. Time is on our side, for we are already at home, whereas an entire ocean separates them from their needs."

Dessalines drew his sword from its scabbard with a single impetuous motion. He had metamorphosed from the chrysalis of a slave to an unrestrained and ferocious officer, and it hurt his pride not to make an immediate use of the arms and trained men under his command. Yet he had the greatest veneration for "Papa Toussaint," this protuberant-jawed, wizened old Black whose life he could snuff out with a single powerful hand. To him, Toussaint L'Ouverture was the epitome of culture and statecraft. *Un grand homme*—a man who had rejected a crown so there would be no single obsequious phrase or gesture demanded of the Blacks in Saint-Domingue. He sheathed his sword as Christophe watched with seeming indifference.

"You will go to Fort Dauphin," said Toussaint quietly, "and defend it if you can. Henri will return to Cap Français. I shall go back to Ennery and from there to the mountains that rise behind Milot. We shall not engage the enemy but harass them—harass them—harass them! We will abandon what we cannot defend, and as we retreat we shall burn the towns and lay waste the countryside—scorch the very earth—so the invaders will find only ruins and ashes wherever they pursue us. We must remember, at all times, that we are not expendable. Only the living can be free. We do not know who owns the dead."

[93]

13

*Leclerc reached Cap Français in the evening, with four-*teen ships of the line and nine frigates. As soon as the promontory at the western end of the bay was sighted, he ordered the vessels to come to rest in the open sea, permitted his flagship *L'Ocean* to drift as close to the harbor as possible, without endangering her, and secluded himself in his cabin in order to study the explicit instructions that his brother-in-law, Napoleon, expected him to execute. Leclerc was dapper, fair-haired, small of stature; and, though his troops referred to him as "the blond Bonaparte," he looked more like a genteel dandy than a soldier. Even the twist of hair that he cultivated on his cheeks seemed to bolster his vanity rather than his authority. He read Napoleon's orders with trepidation, guessed that Jérôme was fully aware of them, and sensed the impatience with which the entire expedition had been assembled and dispatched. Napoleon had divided his instructions into phases:

First Phase:

You will negotiate with Toussaint and promise him anything so as to enable you to occupy the coastal towns and gain a foothold in the country.

Second Phase:

Toussaint and the Black generals are to be flattered, loaded with honors, and allowed to keep their ranks. But the Black troops must be disbanded!

Third Phase:

You will charge Toussaint to come to Cap Français where, without scandal or injury but with honor and consideration, he must be put on board a frigate and sent to France. At the same time, if possible, arrest Christophe and Dessalines. Hunt them down! If this period lasts 15 days, all is well; if longer you will have been duped.

Fourth Phase:

If, after 15 days, Toussaint and his Negro generals have not surrendered, proclaim them traitors and enemies of the French people; and begin a war to the death! Start the troops and give them no rest until you have their heads. If

Toussaint, Dessalines, or Christophe are taken in arms, they should be tried before a court-martial and shot within 24 hours.

All the whites who have dealt with Toussaint shall be sent directly to Guiana.

You will reorganize the gendarmerie and suffer no Black above the rank of captain to remain on the island.

White women who have prostituted themselves to Negroes, whatever their rank, are to be deported.

No instruction *of any kind* shall exist in Saint-Domingue.

Slavery is to be restored and anyone who discusses the rights of Negroes (on any pretext) is to be sent back to France!

Leclerc had entertained no doubt as to the success of the expedition but now, as he pondered Napoleon's instructions and timetable, he was touched by misgiving.

On the morning after *L'Océan* anchored in the bay, Pauline Leclerc left her cabin and strolled onto the deck. The sun had set so quickly the day before that she had not even caught sight of Pointe Picolet. She could feel the heat rising all about her as she crossed to the rail. The translucent blue-green sea shimmered, as though they were becalmed, and a white foam swirled gently over a coral reef. Above her, the sailors were furling the useless sails. She had been seasick, intermittently, for almost three weeks, but now the sight of land stirred both her appetite and her curiosity. In the distance, beyond the palm-fringed shore, rose a great chain of mountains—majestic and mysterious. Jade-green, primitive forests covered their slopes, and above the timber line, bare and formidable, huge boulders and massive gray slabs of rock jutted their craggy shoulders into the very clouds. At the water's edge, strange and exciting, sprawled the town that must be Cap Français.

There was the sound of footsteps, and Pauline saw that General Boyer had joined her. He carried a telescope under one arm with unaffected nonchalance, greeted her courteously but briefly, and scanned the harbor. He studied how effectively the guns on Pointe Picolet guarded the harbor and noticed that all the marker buoys had been removed from the channel. Anchored alongside a jetty, at the foot of the Rue du Conseil, was a two-masted square-rigged ship, and past the Cale Royale two American schooners drifted carefully in the blue-green water.

Pauline observed General Boyer as he studied the island through the telescope, as though unaware of her presence. One could not deny that he was handsome, but she resented his self-assurance and was still infuriated by the audacity with which he had carried her from her home. She had been excited, at first, by the thought of accompanying the expedition. She had wed Leclerc five years ago, when she had been seventeen, but after Dermide was born the marriage had palled and she no longer found Charles stimulating. She had looked upon the expedition as a lark, had spent weeks in selecting a limitless wardrobe and a profuse collection of elegant furniture and *objets d'art* and in inspecting the luxurious cabin that was being furnished for her on *L'Océan*. She had rushed about and engaged a staff of decorators, musicians, actors, and dancers—for she had envisioned a protracted stay in Saint-Domingue. Her brother might declare Charles its king . . . and she would be its queen! But at a last moment she had a change of heart and refused to go. She had found that her friends were amused by her readiness to leave Paris. Leclerc insisted, pleaded, cajoled. She would not want for company. There would be Rochambeau, whom she admired, Boudet, whom she praised, de LaCroix, Hardy, Claparède . . . all of whom she knew well. And Napoleon had decided to send her brother, Jérôme.

"Jérôme? Jérôme? My dear Charles," Pauline had taunted, "if Napoleon is sending Jérôme, don't you realize that it is only so he may spy upon you? My dear brother has accepted your family tie, but not your ability!"

Three days before the fleet sailed a young officer had rushed into her mansion in the Rue de Courcelles, presented himself as General Boyer, and insisted on seeing Madame Leclerc. The hour was late but he asserted that his visit was urgent and refused to remove his snow-flecked cloak. Pauline had retired early and received him in her boudoir. She noticed with mounting irritation that he was not disconcerted by the marks that his wet boots left on the Aubusson rug. His handsome face was unsmiling and his voice quite stern as he presented his compliments and offered her a wax-sealed envelope. He studied her as she read the lengthy letter from her husband. Her eyes were blue, like her elder brother's, but her long hair was flaxen. She had a smooth wide brow, a thin nose, and a voluptuous mouth whose corners were now tugged down by anger. She was petite—he remembered her as being taller when they had met momentarily at a ball—and then noted that she was barefooted, the arches of her small feet lost in the soft, deep pile of the carpet. She pattered to the fireplace, tossed the letter into its flames, turned to him, and smiled.

"General Boyer, are you aware of the letter's insolence?"

The faintest trace of a smile hovered about his lips. "*Oui, Madame.*"

She permitted her dressing gown to slide down one shoulder, as though unaware that it exposed the rise of a pink breast curving as smoothly as the arc of a cherub's cheek. "And do you think I will leave *émouvant* France to live in exile among Black savages and snakes?"

He inclined his head and smiled.

"I will not go! I suffer from *mal de mer*. I am not a Creole, like my *belle-soeur*, and I shall die of *ennui* on such a barbaric island.

"Then may I extend my apologies when I insist that you must. I but carry out the command of my superior officer. I suggest that you dress warmly, for the weather leaves much to be desired." He strode to a chair, dropped into it, and adjusted himself to its comfort as though he intended to wait there while she dressed.

She slipped the dressing gown from her and let it fall, as though defying his suggestion. The firelight outlined her exquisite form.

Boyer was unabashed. His dark eyes observed her as though the female figure was no novelty to him and he often engaged in its appraisal. In a voice that seemed untouched by the slightest emotion he said, "My instructions are to escort you if you come willingly; and to bring you by force if necessary."

"Napoleon would have you in chains if you dared! I have but to scream . . ."

"Then you shall not scream." He sprang from the chair and clapped a gloved hand across her mouth. Then he flung her onto the bed, rolled her in its quilted coverlet, and dashed with her from the room and out to his coach waiting at the door.

Her thoughts were interrupted as Boyer offered his telescope. She looked toward the island, one eye squinting against the sun, and smiled as she saw she had not come to a barbaric wasteland but a civilized town whose streets were lined with dwellings, many having walls calcimined with pleasing colors—pale blue, brilliant yellow, coral pink—warm pastel tints that reflected the brilliant sunlight. She could see natives quite clearly along the quay. The men were dressed in white pantaloons and loose jackets that resembled short smocks. Some seemed no darker than Corsicans, others were as black as teakwood. The women wore thin cotton dresses and short aprons, their heads covered by colorful madras kerchiefs, beautifully tied. Nearly all had necklaces of coral beads and pendulous earrings. They were tall, lithe, and seemed rather pleasing despite their indolent bearing and dark, irregular features.

General Boyer circled an arm about her, as though to steady himself against the rail, and directed the telescope to a small palace whose circular approach was shaded by graceful palms.

"Why it flies the tricolor of France!" she exclaimed.

"Of course. That is the Government Palace. Saint-Domingue is still, after all, a French colony. You are now looking at Place Montarcher. The building to the right, decorated with bunting, is the Théâtre Français. And now, if you turn toward the ravine...." His hand felt warm across her back as he guided her. "The tall building with the cross on its belfry is an Ursuline convent. So you see, we have not come to a land of snakes and savages as you presumed. Behind the convent, where you cannot observe them from here, are the botanical gardens. They are pervaded with the tropic flora of this primitive island—luxuriant, variegated, and sensuous beyond description. I look forward to escorting you there."

He had evidently been to Saint-Domingue before. He seemed familiar with Cap Français. She fell into his arms as though the anchored vessel had tossed her there, and offered her lips. He kissed her, unconcerned as to whether or not they were observed, and was not surprised when she suddenly darted her moist tongue between his teeth.

"That is for bringing me," she said, and was immediately angered by his self-assured smile. "And this is for the insolent manner in which you brought me!" she added, and ground her heel into his soft boot.

At noon Leclerc sent a young ensign, named Lebrun, to request a pilot and advise Christophe to prepare the town for his reception. Christophe had been awaiting an emissary and watched as a boat left the flagship and was rowed to a shale-strewn beach in the shadow of Pointe Picolet, as though to spy on the fortress.

By the time the small boat was tugged, pushed, and maneuvered onto the beach so that Lebrun would not have to step into the water, Christophe, with an escort of several officers, was at the scene. He greeted Lebrun with somber courtesy, and the ensign, young and arrogant, was astonished by Christophe's excellent French and the dignity of his appearance, for he was magnificently garbed in the full-dress regalia of a general of France! To add to Lebrun's disquietude, as they mounted the steep slope where a carriage awaited them, Christophe paused and pointed to a battery of cannon that had been positioned on a ledge overlooking the bay. "If you have come to spy on our fortifications," said Christophe, "than add these to your tally. I assure you, Cap Français is impregnable."

As they rode to the Government Palace, Lebrun was impressed by the well-kept gardens, the wide streets, the tree-shaded homes, and the sparkling fountains in the public squares. A troop of cavalrymen cantered over the Rue Espagnole and joined them. Lebrun could not avert his eyes from the smartly dressed officers and proud, powerful Blacks who comprised Christophe's personal bodyguard. When he was led into a reception room, he was further discomfited to see liveried servants standing at attention before each carved, gilded door. Christophe saw to his guest's comfort with the charm and ease that his early training at the Auberge de la Couronne had made possible and ordered glasses and a decanter of wine to be brought. Lebrun was amazed. He had imagined a desolated country whose government offices had been usurped by Black savages. Christophe left him little time for reflection but asked, amost immediately, for his credentials and his dispatch.

"Captain-General Leclerc expects Cap Français to be delivered at once. I am to. . . ."

Christophe's dark face was instantly distorted by violent anger. Lebrun erred in lifting his hand to a pocket where the sealed directive rested; and as though he would have nothing to do with the verbal orders of a lowly ensign, Christophe rushed to him, tore away the envelope, and thrust it into the keeping of a mulatto officer at his side. Lebrun grasped the hilt of his sword, but as his gaze swept the reception room he realized the folly of drawing it from its scabbard. He guessed that Christophe might be illiterate as the mulatto tore open the dispatch and read aloud:

" . . . You will furnish a pilot for my
vessels and suitable quarters for the
squadron on board. . . ."

Christophe refused to hear more. He defied them to attempt a landing at Cap Français! He turned to Lebrun. "I cannot consider any proposal without orders from Governor-General Toussaint. It is evident that you have not come in peace and I spare your life only to show that we are not savages. Now go. Go! Before I have a change of heart."

Christophe dashed from the reception room and ordered his military guard to stand at readiness. He directed powder and shot to be stacked at the batteries on the quay. Iron grates and sacks of coal were hauled to the fort, where they would provide the cannon with red-hot shot, to be fired into the frigates, should they attempt to enter the harbor. He reviewed the garrison at the Place d'Armes and instructed the soldiers to fashion lances tipped with tow. He was determined to burn Cap Français rather than surrender it—a decision prodded by a rumor of Napoleon's instructions and Leclerc's subservient intention to restore slavery in Saint-Domingue. "Would you rather lose your homes or your freedom?" he cried to the garrison. "They have come to tear the muskets from your hands and lash your backs into submission. Fort Picolet is our signal post. Should it be forced to fire a single shot we will ignite the town. I promise you, their victory shall be ashes! As long as I, Henri Christophe, am alive they shall not enslave us. We must have the fortitude to leave them nothing but ruins for spoils!"

When Christophe returned to the Government Palace he found a deputation of citizens, led by Mayor Télémaque, awaiting him. They had learned of Christophe's intention to burn the town and begged him to comply with Leclerc's demands. Saint-Domingue was still a French colony; they were all French citizens . . . .

Black Télémaque had never known slavery, for he had been born of freed parents. The others were Creoles and mulattoes. Christophe drove them out. It was a military decision, and there was much to do. There were American vessels in the harbor that should be advised to leave . . . the town's population to be evacuated . . . his own family to be cared for . . . .

Ensign Lebrun was back the next day. He was rowed directly to the quay where, to his surprise, he was placed under a military guard, escorted to the Government Palace, and detained in an anteroom while Leclerc's message was read to Christophe:

Liberty and Equality
Army of Saint-Domingue
Headquarters on board *L'Océan*
13th Pluviose,
10th year of the Republic.

[104]

I learn with indignation, Citizen-General, that you refuse to receive the squadron of the French army that I command, under the pretext that you have received no orders from the Governor-General.

I give you notice that if you have not in the course of this day surrendered Fort Picolet with all the batteries on the coast, tomorrow at daybreak, 15,000 troops shall be disembarked. 4,000 men are at this moment landing at Fort Dauphin and 8,000 more at Fort Republicain. I hold you responsible for what may happen and salute you.

General of the Army of Saint-
Domingue and Captain-General
of the Colony.

Leclerc

Lebrun sweated in the anteroom while he waited for Christophe's reply. He had secretly brought handbills for the townsfolk that read:

Whatever your origin or your color, you are all free and equal before God and man. Welcome the French and rejoice to see your friends and your brothers from Europe. We bring you peace.

Whoever dares to act independently of the Captain-General will be a traitor to his country, and the anger of the Republic will devour him as fire eats up dried sugar cane!

He had left the false handbills in the boat and hoped they had not been discovered. If things did not go well, he might be returned to *L'Océan* with his head in a sack. After an hour that seemed interminably long, he was

[105]

handed Christophe's reply. It was without an envelope and lacked the authority of a seal:

Headquarters at Cap Français
13th Pluviose.

I have dispatched one of my aides to Governor L'Ouverture to inform him of your arrival. Until his reply reaches me, I cannot permit you to disembark. If you put into force your threats of hostility, I shall resist you, and you shall not enter Cap Français till it be reduced to ashes.

I have the honor to salute you.

H. Christophe

The following morning Christophe watched from the tile roof of the Government Palace as Leclerc's fleet dispersed. Leclerc boarded the frigate *Uranie* and, leaving the large men-of-war at the edge of the harbor, led the frigates and corvettes eastward along the coast. By late noon news reached Christophe that they were disembarking at Port Margot, but twenty miles away. Torn between violent anger and bitter despair, he ordered soldiers to go from door to door and warn the citizens to abandon Cap Français.

Though Leclerc could not believe that Christophe would carry out his threat to burn the town, the Creoles stuffed their carriages with personal possessions and fled. They had intended to welcome the French—they had suffered enough from a forced equality with illiterate and *grossier* Blacks—but how could one wait for "liberators" in a burning town? Mulattoes burdened themselves with their wardrobes . . . large-hipped Negresses balanced towering loads on their brightly turbaned heads . . . big-chested, full-mouthed Blacks deserted the warehouses along the quays . . . and soon an exodus of multicolored humanity trod upward along the winding road that led to Haut-du-Cap. Some crammed their belongings into the little ferryboat that linked Cap Français to the Petite-Anse road, across the Haut-du-Cap River. Others, impatient, swam across and toweled themselves with wet hands. Past L'Acul, at the foot of the mountains that brood behind Milot, they halted and made camp.

The next day, news arrived that at Fort Dauphin Rochambeau had cannonaded his way ashore and massacred every prisoner! Christophe issued *lances à feu* with which to set fire to the town. As he entered the tree-shaded square in front of the Government Palace, he found it filled with weeping Negro women, children, and old men who had not yet left Cap Français. They had been assembled by the mayor in a last attempt to soften Christophe's heart, and waved aloft the handbills that Lebrun had smuggled to them.

"You fools!" cried Christophe. "The French have returned to enslave you! Are your memories so short that you have forgotten the whips and the chains? The slave ships that anchored along our quays? And you, Télémaque, if you don't wish their ashes commingled with the town's, lead them to the hills!"

He left the square and hurried to his home, in the Rue Royale. It was now abandoned by both his family and his servants. As he passed the Place de Notre Dame he glanced up at the belfry of the church and thought: "Ring! Damn you, ring! You would sound the tocsin for the French. Is there no tocsin for the Blacks!"

When he reached his home he found soldiers squatting

on the floors, sitting at ease on the elegant settees, gaping at the tapestries, and pulling aside the rich hangings in order to stare outside. They had brought barrels of tar, as he had directed, and snapped to attention as they became aware of his presence. He had acquired one of the town's most imposing mansions and had furnished it with a grandeur and ostentation that had become dear to his heart and second nature to his being. He looked about at the treasures that he had accumulated while Marie-Louise had marveled at his preferences—bric-a-brac, statuary, gilded mirrors, paintings.... And none of it was loot! All had been purchased with profit from plantations that he had rented from the state. He mounted the circular stairway, strode from room to room, and stared at curtains, bedding, and dressers as though saying farewell. He lingered longest in the nursery. Both his daughters, Améthiste and Athénaire, had prattled their first words there.

As the sun began to cast lengthening shadows in the bay, a man-of-war weighed anchor and tacked carefully into the harbor. Fort Picolet fired a warning shot across its bow and immediately received a broadside in return. A heightened cannonading boomed from the harbor and echoed back from the mountains. Christophe snatched a torch from a soldier and set fire to the furnishings. As the Blacks hesitated, he cried, "Burn it! Burn it! *Brûler caille moin!*" and dashed from room to room. Flames blazed from the draperies, scorched the tapestries, smoldered the carpets, scaled the paneled walls, and licked at the frescoed ceilings.

When the spreading fire and billowing smoke forced them outdoors, Christophe galloped through the town and directed its burning. Except for the military, a few shopkeepers who would not leave their wares, and idlers who seemed intent on looting, Cap Français was now deserted. Westward, toward Môle St. Nicolas, the sun dipped below the horizon, and sudden darkness, characteristic of the latitude, enveloped the countryside.

Christophe sped about and directed his men. The public buildings were the first to be sacrificed. Within moments flames burst skyward from the warehouses along the quay, the barracks past the Champ de Mars, the Government Palace, the theatre in Place Montarcher. In gold-braided uniform, with widespread epaulets, his raised sword reflecting the red flames, Christophe's big form was as terrifying as his voice as he galloped through the streets of doomed Cap Français. Shops were broken into, and private dwellings were entered and set to the torch. Here and there a desperate mulatto or Creole tradesman tried to protect his property and was beaten or killed. Within two hours the city was a boundless, blazing pyre with flames shooting through the roofs of houses and illuminating the crisping fronds of the palm trees in parks and courtyards. As buildings collapsed, showers of sparks and cinders were blown skyward as though from the throat of a massive bellows. Suddenly the powder magazine in the Champ de Mars exploded with an echoing boom and a rush of wind that filled the sky with a swirl of burning debris. As though it were the signal for his departure, Christophe ordered his men from the doomed town.

When they reached the road that led to L'Acul, Christophe was dismayed by the great number who, angered by the burning of the town and the loss of their personal possessions, lined the edges of the fields and shook their fists at him, shouting curses and invectives. He led his men to

[109]

the mountains behind Milot, and there they camped for the night.

In the morning the realization that they were again at war filled him with bitterness and distress. A drowsy quiet pervaded the hills and the rich green valleys but far below, in the distance, the ruins of Cap Français still smoldered. He must look for Marie-Louise and the little ones. She would become a camp follower once again—worse off than before—because he was now a general without an army. He could count on no more than a regiment. Former slaves, turned peasant farmers, would have no further use for rebellion as though the white world had accepted them as blood brothers. He must join Dessalines and Toussaint, wherever they might be!

14

On *February 5th, Leclerc left Port Margot at the head of* 10,000 troops and 1,200 grenadiers in full dress and bearskins, with flags and banners limp in the windless air and horses and men sweating in the noonday sun. He had been advised to march the men in early morning but had delayed until noon because he needed his sleep. He had been awake most of the night, observing the illuminated sky in the direction of Cap Français. He was unaware that Pauline had watched the conflagration from the deck of *L'Océan* and been filled with rage and despair as she witnessed the destruction of the town. She had confided to General Boyer that she intended to rename it Petite Versailles.

Leclerc's exhausted troops reached Cap Français only to find the gutted town smoking and filled with debris. There was no drinking water, and there was little shade to shield them from the blistering sun. Of the 2,000 houses, only 60 had escaped the ravages of the flames. In the Place de Notre Dame, though the soot-blackened stone walls of the church were intact, the roof had collapsed, leaving its nave open to the sky. The government buildings were in ruins. An odor of scorched flesh tainted the air and half-burnt corpses of animals and men could be seen trapped in the rubble that filled the streets. Drenched in sweat, the troops broke rank; the grenadiers shucked their bearskins and the enlisted men opened their tunics. When someone discovered a trickle of water from a debris-filled fountain, there was a wild stampede to reach it.

In the evening a violent thunderstorm broke over Cap Français, for the island was on the verge of its rainy season. Now that the middle kennels of the streets were filled with rubble, the town soon became a quagmire. Leclerc, dismayed by the devastation all about him, marched his scattered troops to the Champ de Mars, where there was neither shelter from the rain nor relief from the oozing mud.

Along the Rue Espagnole and the Rue d'Anjou, whites and mulattoes were drifting back from the hills. They carried their belongings with them but now had no place to put them. They rushed to their homes, wept openly at the sight of their destruction, and rummaged, in despair, among the ruins. Cries of "Batard noir!" [Black bastards!] were spat from every mouth. They had intended to welcome the French. They had a greater regard for them than for the Blacks who had usurped an equality which they had grudgingly tolerated. Now they would take up arms against the Blacks! Never again would they permit them a voice in the government of Saint-Domingue!

Christophe joined Toussaint and Dessalines at Grande Rivière, and learned that the French had taken possession of every coastal town from Fort Liberté on the east to Môle St. Nicolas on the west. Short of supplies, forced to abandon his artillery, Toussaint had stretched his thin line of defense across the Plaine du Nord. From there he led his columns in the night, raided the French outposts, and was gone before dawn. He seemed tired but undaunted, as he welcomed Christophe and his smartly attired regiment. "A people who are determined to be free cannot be enslaved," he insisted. "The hills are still ours; and beyond them the mountains. Should they push us into them, we shall burn everything in our line of march. The mercenary French will conquer nothing but mango trees and ruins!"

Jérôme prodded his brother-in-law to set out after the Black generals, but Leclerc, a stickler for military detail, refused to leave Cap Français until he officially declared Toussaint, Dessalines, and Christophe rebels. He had lost three junior officers and almost sixty sentries! On the fourth day, the French troops assembled in the Champ de Mars, as though on dress parade, and sweated in the sun while Leclerc affixed his signature and seal to the official document. At last, at high noon, with drums beating and limp flags at the head of their columns, Leclerc led them over the Rue Espagnole, past rubble-filled Place Montarcher, and out of the town.

As Leclerc's troops advanced across the Plaine du Nord, they met with no resistance other than a persistent and demoralizing series of ambuscades. Time and again the Blacks would rise from the side of the road, as though the very earth had spawned them, deliver a devastating volley, and then disappear into a stand of trees or a deep gulley.

The skirmishes were not to Dessalines' liking, but Toussaint insisted that they must not engage in a pitched battle. "We are whittling them!" he would cry. "We are whittling them! Every day they leave at least a hundred dead on the sides of the road, and their wagons are filling with wounded."

By the 20th of February all of the north plain and most of the western provinces were firmly in Leclerc's hands, yet he knew he had won nothing. The rainy season was in full force and his soggy columns were at a standstill. Horses were unable to cross swollen mountain streams, cannon were abandoned in bogged roads, and foot soldiers were halted by the violence of the tempestuous storms. His brother-in-law had expected him to conquer the island in fifteen days. Fifteen days! It had been almost three weeks since he had come to this God-forsaken, mosquito-infested marsh, and he had not won a decisive battle or captured a single Black general. Napoleon was mad! There was not even a franc's worth of loot on this damned island! Did Toussaint mean to lay waste the entire country? He decided to return to Cap Français and carry out, belatedly, the *First Phase* of his instruction:

> "You will negotiate with Toussaint
> and promise him anything. . . ."

15

B*ack in Cap Français, Pauline Leclerc awaited the* return of her victorious husband. What was keeping him? Her brother had promised that the entire island would be subdued in fifteen days! They were rebuilding a gutted mansion for her temporary occupancy, on a promontory that overlooked the wide bay, but it was far from ready for the elaborate furnishings that were still stored in the hold of *L'Océan*. Her entertainers, her decorators, and her personal servants were constantly shifted from room to room amidst the sound of hammering and the smell of wet plaster.

She found the days exhaustingly tedious with Leclerc away and Boyer absent. Her only constant companion was General Humbert, a member of the former nobility of France whose Creole family had owned an extensive plantation in Saint-Domingue; but he was almost twice her age, intolerably dull and insipid. She had insisted that at least one room be completely restored, and she reclined there now on a sofa, shielded to some extent by latticed shutters from the sunlight and the torrid heat. She had dressed herself in a loose morning gown and Humbert, as though presuming the role of protector, had seated himself at her feet. He was overwhelmed by her voluptuous mouth, her air of languor and the fairness of her skin. She swung one leg in a little arc above him, indolently, and permitted its slipper to fall directly into his lap. He smiled and, grasping it with the ardor with which a dog might retrieve a flung stick, raised her foot and kissed its toes before he replaced the slipper. She seemed unaware of the gesture.

"What is keeping Charles? This interminable rain has been so depressing, I thank God for a sunny day. Napoleon said it would take only a few days to conquer these Black savages. If only the theatre were rebuilt. Or even the Government Palace. . . ."

"I assure you, Madame Lerclerc, these Blacks have escaped to the hills only because they have been frightened. Actually, they are as docile as cows and as stupid as oxen. And where could they go? Saint-Domingue is an island surrounded by water. When the plantation lands are restored to their rightful owners and slavery returned to its old footing. . . ."

"Enough. Enough! I shall die of *ennui* before then. Or waste away from this incessant and terrible heat." She kicked her slipper from her foot, and it dropped, once again, into his lap. He turned to replace it and noticed, with the skip of a heartbeat, that she had raised her gown above one knee. Her skin was as pale as alabaster, and the satin, moistened by her body, fell in little folds between her legs. Had she nothing on beneath? He guided his hand upward, over the soft flesh beneath the loose gown, and she said, "Please! It's so hot!... I have been told that the rains are about to end. Do you think we could hold a soirée? Are there enough Creole women that we could invite?"

His thoughts were stirred by the scent of her perspiring body and the soft flesh he had touched. "I could arrange a *calinda*," he said. "You have never seen anything so provocative, Pauline. It is a native dance that stokes the passions and transforms everyone into an animal in rut. The drums, the licentious contortions...."

She leaned toward him and kissed him on the mouth. "You will arrange it," she said.

She had not minded his calling her Pauline! His blood quickened as he rose to embrace her. She caught his underlip between her teeth and bit it sharply. A trickle of blood spilled from it and stained his chin. She settled back among the cushions, as though unaware of his hurt, and said softly, "You will see to the dancers and the guests. I would like to observe this *calinda*."

Two days after the end of the rainy season Leclerc marched his footsore army back to Cap Français. The dead had been abandoned in ditches, the commissarial wagons were filled with wounded, and a penitent sun heated the puddles in the roads and sucked at mists that hovered in the fields. When he reached the town he was disquieted by Pauline's excitation and the bustle in the half-restored mansion. What was there to celebrate? He had gained no

[117]

victory and captured no single Black officer. And his losses
.... His losses! They had begun to plague him. He would
awaken in the night, horrified by the thought that the
Blacks could have cut his throat as noiselessly as they had
severed the jugular veins of his sentries!

Pauline immediately attached herself to General Boyer.
He had returned deeply tanned and hardly recognizable,
for he had permitted a dark mustache to sprout on his
upper lip where it enhanced the albescent color of his
wide-spaced teeth.

"All this *remue-ménage* for a *calinda*," he laughed.
"Humbert is an old fool! I assure you, Pauline, a *calinda*
is as commonplace here as a minuet in Paris."

Pauline refused to be dissuaded. The mansion was not
completely refurbished but its garden was quickly decorated. Lanterns were hung from bougainvillaea vines,
candelabra were set on wood-and-plaster pedestals, marble
statues were hauled to the edges of garden paths, and settees and chairs were spaced along a circular clearing. A
hedge of lemon trees shadowed the thick grass, and starlight glittered on the pebbled walks as Pauline made a
last-minute inspection. From the height of the garden one
could see as far west as the island of Tortuga, where
lights began to wink along its shore. In the wide bay, the
lanterns on the warships became visible. In the harbor the
darkening water was spattered with starlight all the way to
Pointe Picolet. Humbert was leading the performers into
the garden. Most of them were griffes, a few were sepia-
toned mulattoes. The women were most likely Dominicaines who had returned to Cap Français. They had not
only brought their drums and their dried rattle gourds,
but their own resin-tipped flambeaux. She must hurry and
dress. . . . She was aware of her constant tardiness.

[118]

When Pauline returned to the garden, the *calinda* was already in progress. Creole women, dressed in their salvaged finery, had scattered themselves on the chairs and settees. Mulatresses, with brilliant kerchiefs, gilt earrings, white bone bracelets, and necklaces of coral beads, were seated on the grass all about the clearing. French officers in full-dress uniforms, despite the humidity of the night, stood behind the flambeaux and watched, with growing interest, the dance of creation . . . the primitive ritual of sexual selection. It was no novelty for the Creoles, yet they found themselves swaying to the beat of the drums and the rattle of the calabashes.

Everyone seemed intrigued, and no one greeted Pauline as she observed the little orchestra that was seated on the grass at the edge of the clearing. It consisted of two drums—one tall and one short—made of hollowed logs with goatskin or sheepskin stretched over the openings. A young griffe sat astride each drum and beat upon the taut skin with the tips of his fingers and the ball of his hand. One drummer's beat was fast, the other slow . . . and the percussions of the drums had a strange rhythmic sound that was filled with a hypnotic throbbing.

A half dozen griffones sat in a semicircle behind the drummers. They had decorated their frizzy hair with white flowers from the calaba tree, and they shook their rattle gourds in time to their nodding heads and a weird chant, without beginning or end, seemingly discordant, yet cadent as though it obeyed some primitive law of harmony.

The dancers—Dominicaines and young griffes—were in the center of the clearing. Their feet were naked and their arms akimbo as they faced each other in two rows. They swayed slowly, in rhythm with the throbbing of the drums. First the shoulders, then the hips, finally the entire body swayed, twitched, and shook as the chanting and the rattle of the gourds, with their cha-cha-cha . . . cha-cha-cha . . . cha-cha-cha cadence, urged them on. They advanced toward each other, stopped to engage in violent contortions; then twitched and shook as they advanced again. When they finally reached each other they stood face to face—Dominicaines and griffes—unsmiling, eye probing into eye, inviting yet taunting each other with obscene gestures and provocative gyrations of belly and hip. They broke into pairs that circled, drew together, and rubbed bellies and thighs as they sank and rose, twitched and shook to the incessant rattle of the gourds and the wildly accelerated, pulsing percussions of the drums.

Pauline watched the tireless young griffes as they gyrated in the shadows, trembled in a patch of starlight, or writhed as they sank and rose in the red glow from the flambeaux. Lithe and provocative, they were like erect young animals dressed in short pantaloons and sleeveless shirts. Brown-skinned, midway between Black and mulatto, they seemed to have inherited the lascivious proclivities of the one without accepting the ambitions of the other.

The French officers were fascinated by the twitching and shaking Dominicaines in loose, low-cut, sleeveless shifts that swirled about their naked legs. Their faces, softened by African contours, yet outlined by Caucasian angles that sharpened both septum and jaw, seemed molded by violent passions.

The drums were suddenly hushed and the rattle of the gourds drifted off to a prolonged and inaudible cha . . . cha . . . cha . . . as General Boyer reached them. He was herding a half-dozen full-blooded Blacks, thrusting them forward. One of them turned and cried, *"Zaffai neg pas z'affai Blanc!"* [Negroes' affairs are not for whites!]

"Ca li fait plaisi" [he seems to like it], he answered in patois and dropped three gold coins into the Black's hand. He had brought the Blacks to perform the *loiloichi*, the African fertility dance. All this fuss for a simple *calinda*! If Pauline wanted to witness an authentic African dance . . . well then, let her see one. *"Lever ou, tout suite,"* he ordered the *calinda* drummers. *"Tout suite!"* And as they rose, he ordered the Blacks to take their places.

Pauline had never seen such Blacks! There was no shading between their ebony bodies, their round faces, and their woolly heads. If it were not for the torchlight that highlighted their cheekbones, one would discern nothing but the flamingo-pink of their mouths and the yellow of their eyes. They bent their dark faces over the rada drums, as though they were invoking them, and caressed them with the tips of their fingers. The Negresses had brought their own gourds and, as they began to rattle them, in cadence, they sounded exactly like the trembling branches of a tchia-tchia tree when the wind is strong. The drums, so taut and resonant that merely to brush them set off throbbing vibrations, settled into a rhythmic sound that rose and fell as it urged the rattle of the gourds to support it: tchia-tchia-tchia-boom! tchia-tchia-tchia-boom! As an unintelligible chant joined the percussion of the drums and the tchia-tchia of the gourds, a slender buck and a *nung gal gullah* [a young girl] burst into the clearing. He was naked to the waist—a dark form of quivering, rippling muscle and flashing teeth. The girl's legs as well as her feet were bare, and as she trembled before the flam-

[121]

beaux one could notice that she had nothing on beneath her loose shift.

They faced each other, their foreheads burnished by the glow from the resin torches, and vibrated their bodies in cadence with the pulsing of the drums, the rattle of the gourds, and the weird and high-pitched chant. The buck raised his arms, and his palms were an iridescent yellow as he faced them forward. The girl quivered and stepped toward him in an attitude of surrender. They approached each other as though they were magnetically drawn together by the snakelike, sibilant intonations of the chant, the throbbing of the drums and the rattle of the gourds that took possession of their bodies and urged them on. As they reached each other they sank, rose, and swayed with a flexibility that thrust their pelvises toward each other—tempting, arousing, almost touching, only to recoil . . . offering and hesitating, gyrating as though their flesh were joined, yet retreating as though to whip themselves into a greater sexual frenzy. Trembling, quivering, and vibrating, they approached each other as though in a seizure that refused to culminate in an embrace. Their bodies, now almost stationary, quivered and trembled to the cadence of the drums. They threw back their heads in a simulated paroxysm of ecstasy. Shaking their arms as they sank and rose, they rubbed their bellies against each other with an incredible velocity. As the throbbing of the drums quickened, they began to thrust and recoil, thrust and recoil—as though copulating and bursting into a powerful orgasm. They seemed possessed by the necromancy of the drums and the runaway tchia-tchia rattle of the gourds.

The blood throbbed and quickened in the veins of all who observed them, and a scent of animal rut, primitive and urgent, hovered in the clearing. Suddenly the girl clasped the buck as though to draw him into her very womb. Her hands clawed at his back, her fingernails leaving crimsoned trails of denudated flesh. She clutched his cotton trousers, ripping them down, and as she sank to her knees in a frenzied trembling, her pink mouth sought the origin of his thrusting. Now he sank as she rose, tearing the shift from her, pressing his head between her conical breasts, slithering down her vibrating, pulsing form like a blind animal nuzzling and searching for the source that had aroused his frenetic frenzy. Suddenly, as the drums and the rattles burst into a furious crescendo of sound, he rose and embraced her with a fierce paroxysm of uncontained motion that sprang from his very loins. . . .

Pauline glanced about in search of Boyer. Only a moment ago she had noticed him at the side of a slender griffone. With a throb of her heart that needed no quickening, she felt a hand slip into hers and followed where it led. As they left the shadowed walk she realized, with a twinge of regret, that she was being guided by General Humbert. She hesitated and then, overcome by the urgency of her moistened need and the throbbing in her temples, she dashed with him into an unlighted corridor.

Leclerc, detained by the quartering of his troops in the half-repaired Champ de Mars, arrived late at the festooned garden. He was embittered by the failure of his campaign, angered by the rains that had swollen the rivers and turned the roads into quagmires, and exasperated by the sun that had waited until his return to fill each day with its brilliant light. He had hoped that Pauline's welcome would dispel his despondency—only to find all of her

[123]

interest taken up with preparations for an African dance! Last night he had insisted upon his consort's privilege only to have her declaim: "Please, Charles. It's so hot. . . ." He had been away for almost a month! She might be Napoleon's sister but she was also his wife! He had left the bedroom, returned with a mulatress, stationed her beneath the tester of the bed, and ordered her to fan them. Pauline had lain motionless, the backs of her hands on the pillow where her flaxen hair was spread in moist ringlets. He had cajoled, fondled, and caressed without arousing her. Surely she was not so fastidious as to mind the presence of the mulatress who witnessed his fumbling efforts as though she were a disinterested mute. In desperation, he flung himself upon her and pinioned her hands to the pillow as though expecting a vehement protestation. In the midst of his turbulence she had exclaimed, with martyrish passivity, "Haven't you finished yet . . . Charles?"

Now, as he listened to the throbbing of the drums, the tchia-tchia of the gourds, and watched the sensual and lascivious *loiloichi*, he thought of Pauline and last night's humiliation. He must find her, for it seemed incredible that her blood was not quickened nor her desire aroused by this carnal animalism and this aphrodisiac rhythm whose cadence aroused an erotic echo in his loins. He pushed through the circle of watching Dominicaines, griffones, officers, and Creoles and burst through the first open door in search of her. He dashed from room to room, entered her boudoir—though it was incredible that she would be there—and found her in bed. She was not alone. Tropic moonlight shone through an open window and splashed its brilliance upon the naked bodies as they heaved and trembled in a frenzied imitation of the Blacks.

[124]

He stood rooted to the spot. They must have heard him dash into the room, for he had clattered against a chair. A vein in his temple throbbed as though it would burst. He pulled his sword from its scabbard, only his arm moving, and in that moment Pauline rolled from under the viper he thought was Boyer, sat up in bed, brushed back her hair that glistened with sweat, and cried with the indignation of a child, "Really.... Really, Charles..., how dare you!"

16

Time was running out for Leclerc. Anger against Pauline boiled and bubbled in his heart, and the sight of his complacent officers filled him with rancor. He wondered if they were aware that he had been cuckolded by General Humbert, whom he had ordered back to France. He was homesick and saddened by a frightful and persistent premonition; and, as Napoleon had advised, began to draft a declaration for the restoration of the plantations and the return of slavery. News of his intentions leaked into the countryside, was spread by native drums in the night and echoed from the hills in the heat of the day.

Thousands of cultivators, who had not known slavery for almost four years, left the plantations and rushed to the mountains to join "papa Toussaint." Christophe formed them into regiments, drilled them with severe discipline and, while Toussaint, his saddle padded with feather cushions, dashed across the plains and valleys in order to reenlist his peace-scattered "rebels," impatient Dessalines galloped through the hills and exhorted: "Take courage! Take courage! *Les batards blancs* shall never enslave us again. We now have guns, *habilité*, and have tasted freedom. They shall never enslave us!"

From the promontory in Cap Français, where Pauline's rebuilt mansion was now constantly filled with festivities, Leclerc watched with growing alarm as the campfires in the hills spread all the way from Les Trois Rivières to the heights behind Fort Dauphin. It was ridiculous to sit and sweat while time raced by and Jérôme occupied himself in drafting secret reports to Napoleon. He had five separate armies under his command, and his brother-in-law, though mistaken, had evaluated that it should take no more than fifteen days to subjugate this damnable island. He would remain for months in this strangely erotic land if he and his generals did not leave the coastal towns and force the rebels from the hills. Hesitant to leave Pauline, he ordered General Rochambeau to proceed northward from Port-au-Prince, and Generals Hardy, de LaCroix, and Bourke to march eastward from St. Marc.

Rochambeau, second in command, reluctantly left Port-au-Prince where, although stocky, big-nosed, and possessed of a violent temperament, he had gathered a harem of widowed or abandoned Creoles. Pompous and cocksure, knowing the terrain well—having once lived on the island—he led 5,000 of Napoleon's veterans toward the hills, where he intended to make an example of the "niggers" whom he loathed with an overwhelming passion.

[127]

When he reached the Artibonite Valley, he ordered an inspection of the troops. The heavy wagons, shielded from the sun by sailcloth, had already spent the horses; the field-pieces, drawn by oxen, were covered with films of white dust; and stains of sweat darkened the soldiers' uniforms and spread from beneath their knapsacks. Rochambeau rose in his stirrups and cried. "This will be like a holiday for you. We go to exterminate rebellious Black slaves— savages who will not dare look you in the face and will flee in every direction. Pursue them as you would wild animals and exterminate them, for these *sauvages* have neither thought nor feeling!"

Toussaint insisted upon intercepting Rochambeau. Dessalines was dispatched to St. Marc. Christophe was ordered to remain in the Plaine du Nord, south of Cap Français. But he, Toussaint, would take on veteran, pig-eyed Rochambeau himself. He would prove to this arrogant and pompous aristocrat that the color of a man's skin is no reflection upon the astuteness of his mind and display to him the valor of those who defend their freedom.

Toussaint had fewer than 5,000 men. Two thousand of them were only cultivators who had been hastily armed and drilled by Christophe, but he had 1,500 grenadiers of the guard and 400 well-mounted dragoons. He marched them to the Ravine à Couluèvre, a mountain pass through which Rochambeau would be certain to advance. He hid his foot soldiers behind boulders, trees, and shrubs and stationed his dragoons where they could gallop down and seal the pass at the sound of a first volley.

Rochambeau, with his uncomplimentary opinion of the Blacks, gave no thought to an ambuscade as he led his veterans through the mountain pass. Then the quiet of the drowsing noon was shattered by a volley of musketry that echoed from every side. The French spun about and sought the source of the devastating attack. They noticed only mangroves, sablier trees, and a tremendous outcropping of rock from whose height a stream trickled and cascaded past bushes, creepers, and velvet-green moss. A second volley tore into them without their having caught sight of the enemy. They retreated hastily, only to find the pass now sealed by dragoons. They were doubly confused because the Blacks on horseback were dressed in French uniforms, and a French banner rose from a stirrup, in full sight.

Suddenly thousands of Blacks, screaming and howling, charged down from the hills. Penned in the pass, many of Napoleon's veterans dropped their muskets and threw up their arms so they would not be butchered by these awesome, big-chested, full-blooded Blacks who were rushing toward them. The rest, abandoning the fieldpieces and the commissarial wagons, broke, ran and thrust themselves by the force of their very numbers past the dragoons who hacked at them unmercifully with their sabers. By the time the battered remnant of Rochambeau's army reached the Lacroix River, followed and harassed by the tireless Blacks, the French were so fatigued that many of them shucked their knapsacks in order to swim across the narrow stream.

Crestfallen, enraged by his defeat at the hands of the Blacks whose strategy he had not foreseen, Rochambeau shrank from returning to Port-au-Prince. He decided to join Hardy, de LaCroix, and Bourke, help capture the Black-held fortress of Crete-à-Pierrot, and thus participate in a victory.

Dessalines reached the fortress before the French and

found it under command of a full-blooded Black by the name of Magny, an officer of Toussaint's bodyguard. Toussaint himself had planned the *guerre à mort* of the fortress's defense, and its valiant officer welcomed Dessalines with effusive jubilation. Dessalines shook his bullet head and stubbornly refused to cage himself and his men within the confines of a walled camp. He had suffered from claustrophobia ever since his entombment in the hold of the slave ship and would meet the traitorous and bastard French only under an open sky! He rushed his men to the woods and the hills behind the fortress.

When Rochambeau reached Crete-à-Pierrot, he found his compatriots preparing to take the fortress by assault. They had more than 12,000 veterans and had trained all their fieldpieces on the fortress that guarded the road to St. Marc. Despite assurances that his reinforcement was not needed, Rochambeau insisted that he must participate in the destruction of this stronghold that was defiantly held by the damnable Blacks who had become a festering thorn in his pride! Suddenly, as he began to station his fatigued men in strategic positions, Dessalines' fully armed Blacks swooped down from the hills and raced across the fields in full view. They were like gadflies about to attack an elephant. They clattered and rattled, clanged and clamored as they danced at the edge of the French lines without any seeming regard for the slaughter they invited. They shrieked and taunted as the French were formed into solid ranks and then, at a last moment, without having fired a shot, they turned and ran. The French charged, their bayonets glistening in the sun. The Blacks, as fleet as gazelles, outdistanced them and suddenly disappeared as if by magic. They had jumped into a deep trench, especially dug by Magny, and the fortress discharged all its guns. From the trench, Dessalines' Blacks fired volley after volley at the retreating French. The number of dead and wounded left on the field was astounding.

Rochambeau's anger was apoplectic. As though he had assumed command, he turned his horse and ordered a fresh assault. De LaCroix spurred to his side and tried to dissuade him. Blind with rage, Rochambeau swung his saber at him. Now that he knew of the ditch he would reach it and cross it. He would send the grenadiers first. "Charge!" he bellowed. "Charge!"

The Blacks were fearless. They held their fire until horses and men were almost upon them, and then the guns from the fortress and a tremendous volley from the trench mauled and scattered Napoleon's veterans. The horses that reached the ditch were impaled upon lances; the men who rushed valiantly into it were swallowed by it.

The French retreated, their ears filled with the high-pitched animal screams of the terrified and wounded horses. The astonished generals met in the field while the men scattered, flung themselves on the ground, or sought whatever shade they could find to shield them from the blistering sun that was dehydrating their heavily clothed bodies.

It was decided to lay siege to the fortress. They bivouacked and prepared the artillery to pound the fortress in the morning. It was all most incomprehensible to Rochambeau. He remembered the slaves as they had been on his last visit to Saint-Domingue ... subservient in the households, docile and tractable in the fields. What had changed them?

As the sun was about to set and innumerable wounded crawled back to their lines, a flag was unfurled on a fortress turret. It was the tricolor of France! The French veterans thought it raised in derision, and then they heard their own *Marseillaise* being sung. The voices were deep and resonant; the words were clear:

> *"Allons, enfants de la Patrie,*
> *Le jour de Gloire est arrivé! . . ."*

They had been sent 4,000 miles, to a strange land, only to find an enemy that sang their own *chant de gloire*. They had been told that they were bringing liberty to this French colony. Liberty for whom? *For whom?*

Day after torrid day the French artillery pounded the fortress while the men sweated in the fields. In the dark of night, Dessalines led bewildering and frightening sorties into the very heart of the French camp. Soundless in their bare feet, their naked bodies reflectionless, the Blacks were indiscernible shadows in the tall grass and under the very bellies of the tethered horses and oxen with which they seemed to have some strange affinity. They quietly bludgeoned the heads of sentries, cut the throats of sleeping men, set fire to the wagons, demoralized Napoleon's veterans and filled their hearts with fear.

The French formed a tight circle about the fortress. Protective fires were built at sunset, and detachments were detailed to patrol the fields. The generals speculated on how long it would take the besieged to find themselves without water or provisions. Surely a Black could not hibernate like a bear, or sustain himself inanimately like a lizard!

[132]

At the end of three weeks it was decided that food—at least water—was being smuggled into the fortress, in some inexplicable manner, by means of the trench from which a suffocating stench was now wafted when the night wind shifted. A line of infantrymen was ordered into the ditch along its entire length. The foot soldiers wound lengths of cloth, torn from their rotting tunics, about their mouths and nostrils, for the trench was not only like an immense heated cauldron but filled with bursting, bloated corpses of men and horses. Some of the French veterans had fought in Italy and Austria; others had sweltered along the banks of the Nile and watched as their numbers had been decimated by plagues, in the shadows of the pyramids. But they had won great victories for France! Many of them had been decorated for valor. But what were they doing here? So far from home? Why? No actual enemy . . . no foreseeable conquest. . . . This was not even a war. This unbearably foul and stinking trench was hell!

Dark came and the tropic night was as hushed as though man had never been created. The heat of the day had exhausted the camp, which had been free of Dessalines' sorties for almost a week. Had everyone in the fortress died? Was there no single Black left alive behind those thick, silent walls?

Suddenly there was a tremendous blaze of light. A rush of ignited gunpowder swept through the trench and a crimsoned boom erupted shattered bodies, agonizing screams, and a debris of bloodied fragments of flesh and bone. The heavy fortress doors swung open, the Blacks poured out and, even before Dessalines could reach them, they heroically cut their way through the aroused French battalions.

17

*B**ack at Cap Français, Leclerc's bitterness was diverted* by the precocious antics of little Dermide, and his anger was placated by the now-attentive Pauline, whom he forgave everything and denied nothing. Unable to contain his impatience upon receiving no word from his Generals, he left a detachment of picked veterans to guard Cap Français and led his rested army out of the town and across the Plaine du Nord.

Despite the oppressive heat, his spirits grew brighter as he approached Milot. The rainy season was over and now, at last, he envisioned the complete subjugation of this damnable island. He had studied his maps well. Hardy, de LaCroix, and Bourke would now be marching westward from St. Marc. Rochambeau was most likely sweeping northward from Port-au-Prince. He would travel southward, past Milot. They would encircle the Blacks and force them into the Savanette marshes, and that would be the end of it.

When he by-passed Milot his confidence was dispelled, for he found that the roads had been made impassable by felled trees and burned bridges. He struggled southward only to discover that Toussaint, without revealing himself, was always a day's march ahead of him. When the way led through mountain passes, huge boulders detached themselves from the slopes and crashed into his marching columns. He fared no better on the open plains, where men, horses, and cannon were trapped in cunningly disguised pits, and he dreaded passing through a woods, for the Blacks would occupy it, on both sides of the narrow road, and carry out a relentless series of ambuscades. By the time he reached the Cannof River he decided to go no further. Where in God's name was Rochambeau? Where were de La Croix, Bourke, and the others! He did not know that the single fortress at Crete-à-Pierrot had detained them for weeks. Nor did he realize that Blacks were joining Toussaint's ranks by the thousands. They had learned the meaning of freedom in the last four years and refused to be enslaved again. They had contrived their own patois, developed an affinity for the island, and no longer considered themselves Eboes, Fulas, Aradas, Congos, Bambaras, Senegalese ... but Blacks with attachments and destinies of their own. They would not be enslaved!

Leclerc camped in a field and waited for news of his Generals. The waiting was more frightening than the marching. Sentries were slain without a sound, and horses were run off in the night. At daybreak the Blacks would appear on the perimeter of the field as though the very earth had spawned them in the night. They would dance and taunt and threaten until Leclerc would order a detachment of dragoons to disperse them. The hesitant horsemen would be engulfed and swallowed by the very numbers of the enemy. As though they were insensible to pain or death itself, the Blacks would drag the saber-wielding French from their rearing mounts and disembowel them with their machetes. Musket fire had little effect on them. They were like hydras that sprang from the earth, redoubled, after each volley; and soon learned to stay out of range.

After two sweltering weeks, Leclerc left the field. Without having engaged in a single pitched battle, he had lost almost a thousand men, as well as horses and supplies. He had marched from Cap Français at the head of a proud French army, with unfurled banners and drums beating. Now, exhausted by the blazing sun, tormented by ants, mosquitoes, and chiggers, incessantly mauled and harassed by the Blacks, he was heading back with three bedraggled, demoralized brigades. Christophe joined Toussaint and, as they pursued the retreating Leclerc, their forces recaptured St. Michel, St. Raphael, Dondon, and Marmelade, where Toussaint set up his new headquarters.

When Leclerc finally reached Cap Français he was alarmed by dispatches from Rochambeau and de LaCroix. They had lost over 4,000 men! And the number of sick and wounded was staggering. Half of his army was dead or dying! Damn these unpredictable, Black savage bastards! He had been told they were as stupid as orang-utans and as placid as oxen. If he could not conquer them on the field, then he would subjugate them with an engine of terror. He would remain in the fortified coastal towns and decimate them until they surrendered! Detachments were sent into the surrounding countryside, and hundreds of pacifistic Blacks, women and children, and vagrant cultivators were encircled and marched to the Morne du Cap ravine. There they were shot, bayoneted, hacked to death, and tumbled into it. In Cap Français itself, every Black who was not a domestic or engaged in required labor was herded into the Place d'Armes or the Place de Notre Dame. Docile and unprotesting, they were paraded to the quais and forced into the holds of the frigates and corvettes. When the vessels drifted to within sight of the island of Tortuga, they were slaughtered and cast into the sea.

As news of the atrocities reached the Black generals, Dessalines became frenzied with anger. He smashed along the outskirts of St. Marc and massacred not only whites but mulattoes, griffes, quadroons, and even octoroons—maintaining that, if they were tainted by a single drop of white blood, they were enemies! It was all Toussaint could do to restrain him from rashly attacking any and every superior French force.

Aging Toussaint wept at the staggering loss of civilian lives. He had promised his Blacks freedom from slavery, but Leclerc was inflicting them with death. He was annihilating them! Not only at Cap Français but at Port-de-Paix, at Môle St. Nicolas, at Mont Rouis, at Petit Goave. . . . How could he scatter his forces, or expend them upon attacking heavily fortified towns? And then, at the psychological moment, he received the proffer of an armistice from Leclerc. It was brought by Abbé Coisnon, who had tutored his sons at the Colonial Institute. He read Lecerlc's terms with great care:

> . . . I offer amnesty to all the Black generals. The rumor that I favor the restoration of slavery is a

falsehood! It is my intention to procure the liberty and equality of the population of this colony, and the war is being forced upon me. As a guarantee of my intentions, the Black generals will retain their commissions and enter the service of the French army. I ask only that you relinquish your own command, and for this I shall return your sons and give you my personal guarantee, upon my honor, that I shall effect the freedom and security of all Negroes.

General of the Army of Saint-
Domingue and Captain-General
of the Colony.

Leclerc

Toussaint met with his Generals. He had decided to negotiate with the French in order to end the slaughter of his people. He was influenced by Abbé Coisnon and trusted the honor of a General of France.

Christophe deferred to Toussaint's decision, but Dessalines was wild. "Your trust is unfounded!" he bellowed. "You are being swayed by the return of your sons and by false promises!"

"No!" cried Toussaint. "It is only I who surrender my command. You shall retain yours and we can accomplish more by strategy than we have by force, for you will enter Le Cap like a Trojan Horse. You will have access to the armory, the quais, even the ships!"

Neither Christophe nor Dessalines had ever heard of a Trojan Horse and they were unimpressed by Leclerc's terms that Toussaint held in his hand. Christophe glanced quietly from Toussaint to Dessalines.

Dessalines was pacing the room, in his awkward gait, for

[138]

his broken ankles had never been properly set. Finally he turned and submitted, "I follow your orders, L'Ouverture, but I spit on white honor! Let Henri Christophe go first. If, at the end of a week, his neck still supports his head, I, too, shall enter Le Cap."

Toussaint was grateful. He was sickened by the incessant slaughter and hungered for a glimpse of his sons. He sank to his knees, extracted a crucifix that hung beneath his tunic, and offered up a prayer of thanks, whispering, "Hail Mary, full of grace, the Lord is with thee. . . ."

Dessalines rushed to him, tore the crucifix from his fingers, and dashed it against the wall. "To whom do you pray, old man? To a white god who watches with unconcern as the Blacks are slaughtered? I shall go to Le Cap, François Dominique, but I shall go with a sword in my hand. And when I pray, I shall pray to the god Damballa to strike every French ship in the harbor with bolts of lightning!"

Christophe believed in the sincerity of the French, and Toussaint convinced him it would be an unnecessary waste of lives and property to continue the war when the same end could be achieved by "inferred submission." He released almost a thousand white hostages, dismissed the cultivators who had joined his force, and permitted most of his followers to disband. Early in May, with obvious pride and dignity, he rode into Cap Français at the head of 1,200 regulars.

Most of the town was in ruins, and its streets were choked with rubble. Some of the people lived in tents, while others had constructed shelters within gutted buildings whose walls, being of hewn stone, still stood though their roofs and floors were gone. The entire length of the

[139]

Rue Espagnole, however, had been cleared of debris and was bedecked with twigs of scarlet poinsettia and branches of bougainvillaea. Arches, wound with frangipanis and hibiscuses, had been erected over the street crossings and, as they approached the waterfront, French foot soldiers in parade uniform lined the Rue Espagnole. Captain-General Leclerc and his officers received Christophe on the broad terrace of Pauline's rebuilt mansion, while every gun in the harbor fired a salute.

Leclerc was startled by the elegance of Christophe's uniform and his aristocratic bearing. He had expected to see another wizened, Black Toussaint. *"Bienvenu,"* he said and extended a fragile hand.

Christophe relinquished his sword hilt as though reluctantly and took Leclerc's pale hand in his sable one. A slight pressure intimated that he could crush Leclerc's fingers with ease. To Leclerc's amazement he said, in excellent French, his throaty voice giving the vowels an impressive inflection, "Forgive me, General, if I impose upon your hospitality. Were my home still standing, I assure you, I would welcome you there."

Leclerc was disconcerted by Christophe's audacity. This Black, though courteous to a fault, acted as though he were the victor.

Toussaint's secretary and aide-de-camp, a mulatto named Couppé, traveled back and forth to Cap Français to work out acceptable terms for the truce. Toussaint insisted he must retain his command. Leclerc countered that he could retain his staff and reside where he pleased, but that he must retire from active service. He pledged, once again, that the liberty of Negroes and mulattoes would not be infringed upon and that their rights as citizens would be respected. He suggested a meeting at Mornets, eight miles from Cap Français, in order to settle all their differences.

Toussaint decided to call on Leclerc at Cap Français because there he could not refuse him a visit with his sons. He took with him his staff and an escort of 400 dragoons under command of Colonel Morisset. News of his approach reached the town, and crowds assembled in the streets to see him pass. Though the whites and almost all the mulattoes remained silent, Blacks who had drifted back, as though their freedom was already assured, cheered him with deep, resonant cries of "Toussaint! *Bienvenu, papa Toussaint!*"

Colonel Robillard, a Negro officer who still served under Christophe, came riding up, saluted Toussaint and, pressing close so that the flanks of their horses almost touched, whispered, "I have been sent by General Christophe. He has alerted the loyal troops and awaits your orders."

Toussaint glanced at the ruins on every side as though he had heard no single word. When they reached the debris-filled Place Royale he answered in an undertone, "My respects to General Christophe but I have no orders for him. Advise him not to be concerned."

Leclerc was lunching with Vice-Admiral Maigon on board the flagship. When he was informed of Toussaint's approach, he ordered the warships and the guns on Pointe Picolet to fire a salute. Then he sent word to Generals Debelle and Hardy to receive the Black commander with full military honors. He had been advised that Blacks loved nothing so much as a show of pomposity and an intimation of importance. He could afford to extend both, for at last—at long last—things were going well. Dignified Christophe seemed complacent, and now Toussaint, too, would soon be eating out of his hand.

Toussaint was escorted to a former convent school at the edge of Rue du Haut du Cap—a large building that had escaped the flames and been converted into a temporary Government House. As Toussaint and his escorts rode up, commands rang out and the French guards presented arms. Morisset's dragoons ranged themselves opposite the building and remained in the saddle, swords drawn, faces grim, as Toussaint and his staff entered it.

Toussaint and his officers were ushered into a reception hall dominated by a full-length portrait of Captain-General Leclerc. A collation was served with military dignity, during which the French officers could not keep their eyes from the members of Toussaint's staff. With the exception of frail-seeming Toussaint, the full-blooded Blacks appeared powerful brutes who could smash in their heads with one blow or crush them in their arms. Though they expressed defiance in neither word nor gesture, their proximity alone was frightening!

After awhile Leclerc himself, slight and vivacious, came bustling into the reception hall. He was in a General's undress uniform, as though to lend an air of informality to the meeting. Rushing to Toussaint, he seized his hand with a show of cordiality and linked his arm through his as though to show all present that he bore him no animosity—that the meeting was in friendship and he intended to keep every promise to which he had committed the French. Toussaint remained cold and distant even when

[142]

ebullient Leclerc praised his sons and spoke of them as though he knew them well. When a hastily prepared dinner was announced, Toussaint was seated in the place of honor, on Leclerc's right, but he remained reticent and moody as though his thoughts were given over, at a last moment, to the possibility of betrayal.

"We could have come to terms long before," informed Leclerc, "but General Dessalines has always worried me. Can I rely upon him to obey orders?"

"General Dessalines may have faults, but I assure you, he understands military discipline."

"You may, of course, retain your personal staff; but Colonel Morisset and his dragoons are now in the service of France and will remain here."

Toussaint looked to Morisset. Above a tight-fitting military collar that spanned his thick neck, the Black officer's face was expressionless. It showed neither alarm nor his devotion to "papa Toussaint." There was not even a silent reproach for his General's decision, though he did not agree with it.

Tempting viands and choice wines were pressed upon Toussaint but, having been forewarned by barely audible rada-tambours in the early hours of the morning, he partook of nothing except a piece of cheese and a glass of water. Leclerc's voice droned on as though he was stimulated by the forthcoming results of the meeting. "As a sign of good faith you will, of course, retire to your plantation at Ennery. As soon as you have settled there, your sons will be sent to you." He finally ran out of words. There was no need for him to say more. It had all been decided in their correspondence.

He studied the silent Toussaint. It seemed incredible

[143]

that this wizened old Black, in a French uniform that was too big for him, with his simianlike face that contained neither arrogance nor self-confidence, could have wreaked such havoc on his veterans and routed the armies of France! It had been temporary. It could not have lasted! To impress upon quiescent Toussaint that his submission was a foregone certainty, he said, "Tell me, General, if the war would have continued, where would you have obtained more arms and supplies?"

A glint of defiance sprang into Toussaint's dark eyes. "I would have taken them from you!"

18

When Toussaint *returned to his plantation, a few miles* from the port of Gonaïves, to join his wife and await his sons, he was startled by the sight of a French garrison that had been rushed there. A crowd of Negro cultivators assembled to greet him but there was no acclaim. Their faces were mournful and every pair of eyes seemed to reproach him. Then a voice cried, "Papa Toussaint ... Papa Toussaint ... have you forsaken us?" Other voices joined the query.

He lifted his arms to them. "No, my children. No! Your brothers are still under arms. Their officers are still at their posts and I have not renounced your freedom." His eyes filled with tears as he turned away.

Two weeks later, in order to validate the terms of Toussaint's truce, Dessalines rode down from the mountains and entered the burned city of Cap Français. There was a bustle of excitement all along the quays, for a reinforcement of 4,000 French troops had arrived from Flushing and Le Havre. The ships' holds were bursting with wine, flour, uniforms, and muskets. In answer to Leclerc's advisers, France had sent 20,000 capes and coats to keep the men warm at night and 20,000 high-crowned hats to protect them from sunstroke by day. Ecstatic Leclerc sent General Hardy to receive Dessalines and advise him that he was to be appointed commander of the district of St. Marc. He wanted this contumelious and blood-drenched Black stationed as far from Cap Français as possible without arousing suspicion. Strategically, Dessalines would thus be placed halfway between himself and Rochambeau at Port-au-Prince.

Dessalines glared defiantly at the crowd of whites and mulattoes that lined the Rue Espagnole. As Hardy, at the head of a cavalry detachment, clattered over the cobblestones to greet him, Dessalines turned his broad back rudely toward him and kept his head averted. He had sworn that he would never again look into a white man's face! Hardy was angered and troubled. One of Dessalines' aides accepted the orders and read them aloud. Without speaking a single word, Dessalines spun his horse about and led his Blacks southward toward the port of St. Marc, on the island's eastern bay.

As the rebuilding of Cap Français began, some of its old gaiety filtered back. Now that the hostilities were over, French soldiers were pressed into the service of restoring government buildings and Providence hospital, for hundreds of newly arrived French were succumbing to a strange malady—a tropic fever from which they did not seem to recover. The quickly enervated and exhausted French were no match for the tireless, big-chested, heavily muscled, full-blooded Blacks as they worked among the rubble and toted burnt beams to the cadence of an endless chant that bubbled up from the depths of their lungs and murmured from their thick, smoke-hued lips that refused to be seared by the blistering, tropic sun. "*Ils sont animals!*" the French would whisper to each other. Yet they could not suppress entirely the admiration with which they regarded these inexhaustible, half-naked, dark-skinned brutes.

Leclerc was overjoyed. He admitted that the Negroes were being negotiated with rather than subdued, but he had crushed their organized resistance! He would follow his brother-in-law's explicit instructions—but with patient care. One phase at a time. Meanwhile he would assure himself that Toussaint remained at Ennery, for he had given up his hostages . . . Toussaint's two sons. He accused Toussaint of encouraging guerrilla leaders who had concealed themselves in the hills, and sent 500 picked men, under command of Colonel Pesquidon, to join the French garrison and patrol the plantation.

The Government Palace was quickly restored, and Pauline found a fleeting interest in furnishing it with the contents of the many crates she had brought with her in the flagship *L'Océan.* Her boudoir was decorated in blue satin and her bedroom in white and gold. Figurines, in provocative poses and various stages of disrobing, were set on tables and pedestals, while a descending flight of cupids held back the gold-trimmed curtains that drooped from

[147]

the tester of her bed that faced a large Florentine mirror. In these rooms, darkened by latticed shutters, she reclined most of the day complaining of the heat, regretting she was not in Paris, and receiving guests. Among them was Fréron, one of her earliest lovers (from whom Napoleon had "saved" her by a forced marriage to Leclerc), who had arrived with the latest reinforcements.

Inflamed by Leclerc's jealousy, actually relishing his futile protestations, Pauline recovered some of her spirits and supervised the construction of a vast cage in the court-yard of the Government Palace. Slender palms, squat fig trees, pear trees, and even young sablier trees were hauled intact, replanted, and roofed with netting from the marine stores. Scarlet poinsettias, frangipani shrubs, and bougain-villaea were bedded. Parrots, parakeets, and monkeys were set loose in the cage, and a complete menagerie was ordered from the Paris Jardin des Plants. Despite her activity, she could not dispel the remembrance of the *loiloichi* performance from her mind. She would awaken in the tropic night, filled with sensual need, hearing in the distance the rattle of tchia-tchia gourds, the incessant throbbing of drums. Then she would see in her mind's eye once again the slender buck nuzzling the *nung gal gullah*, his dark form quivering as he whipped himself into a frenzy of sexual release. Damn Boyer! Damn his insolent and arbitrary hide for having made her aware of the erotic excitation of an uninhibited, muscular Black! If Boyer were here, instead of in Port-au-Prince, she would tear his very balls from their pouch!

Unable to obtain performers who would execute the lubricious *loiloichi* in her garden cage, Pauline had to content herself with the less libidinous *calinda* for her outdoor soirées. In the meanwhile, Leclerc insisted that she go home to Paris with little Dermide. He was too late, for Pauline had fallen under the spell of the island—the lassitude of its days and the aphrodisiac urgency of its cool nights. By day there was the dark green of its foliage, the opal blue of its sea. At night there was the boundless, star-spattered splendor of its sky, where an enormous, low-hung, orange moon shone down and quickened the blood.

"Home?" she cried. "But this is my home now, Charles! Even little Dermide loves it here. Look how tanned he has become."

"And I insist that you must return to Paris!"

She cast a rancorous gaze upon Leclerc. "*Eh, bien,*" she pouted, as though submitting to his demand. "But I must have 100,000 francs."

"*Mon Dieu,* Pauline! You know I have no such sum."

"Then you shall obtain it . . . somehow . . . for I will not leave without it. Do you think I receive no gossip from home? Murat has become Napoleon's *enfant gâté* now that I am here; and he showers her with favors that were formerly mine."

"Pauline . . . I cannot raise a hundred thousand francs!"

"And I will not go to the Tuileries dressed as a beggar!"

Exasperated by Pauline's refusal to go home and goaded by her infidelities, Leclerc abandoned his design to subjugate the island slowly and, despite his better judgment, began the immediate execution of Napoleon's "Third Phase" as best he could. The sooner he would enslave these barbarous Blacks and subdue this damnable island, the sooner he could return to France! He ordered General

Brunet, commander of the French troops at Gonaïves, to arrest Toussaint by deceit. The frigate *Creole* would be secretly dispatched from Cap Français, under cover of darkness, and anchor in the Gulf of Gonaïves. They would arrange for signal lanterns.

On the afternoon of June 7th, Toussaint was asked to meet with General Brunet at his headquarters on the Georges plantation. Brunet said he wished to discuss some salient points relating to the disposal of more Black troops and their return to their former plantations as cultivators.

Toussaint's sons, who had been permitted to join the family at Ennery when they were released from hostage, watched as their father dressed for his meeting with Brunet. Upon their homecoming, they had been disappointed by his planter's clothes. He kept a madras kerchief tied about his graying head, and he now habitually gathered his crinkly hair into a little pigtail. His sons were disillusioned, too, by his slight stature, his slender form, and his simianlike, aging face. Now, as he attired himself in the uniform of his rank—with gold epaulets, sword, and scabbard buckled at his side, cockaded hat adorned with heavy gold braid—he assumed the stature that they had imagined. They were impressed by the white guard of honor, a squadron of grenadiers under Major Ferrari, that arrived to escort him to the Georges plantation. They formed themselves on each side of Toussaint and his aide-de-camp, César, as they cantered from Ennery.

It was early evening before they reached Brunet's headquarters. Toussaint was received with courtesy and led directly to the general's study. It was strangely deserted. A large map of Saint-Domingue was tacked on a wall, and Toussaint studied it with great interest. He had not realized that the Artibonite River ran almost to the very border of the French colony.

Suddenly there was a rush of feet, and a squad of soldiers, with fixed bayonets, burst in through the door. They formed a tight ring about Toussaint and forced his aide against a wall. With the point of a bayonet pressed against his heart, Toussaint was forced to relinquish his sword. The French had lured him into a trap by deceit and false "words of honor"!

As his wrists were shackled, he protested against the indignity and demanded to see General Brunet. With complete indifference, as though the color of Toussaint's skin negated the authority of his uniform, the soldiers formed a cordon about him and marched him from the study to where a carriage and an escort of dragoons were waiting. Major Ferrari seated himself opposite Toussaint and averted his face as the vehicle drove off. Despite the fast-settling darkness, Toussaint noticed that detachments of soldiers had been stationed at short intervals all along the road.

It was almost midnight when the carriage and its escort reached the little town of Gonaïves, on the wide western gulf of the island. They were met by a squadron of cavalry and led, through back roads, to the harbor where Toussaint was rowed to the waiting frigate *Creole*. She immediately unfurled her sails and set out for Cap Français.

Native tambours quickly informed the entire countryside of what had befallen "papa Toussaint." Along every road, from the Georges plantation to Gonaïves, although unobserved themselves, the Blacks had watched the progress of the carriage that had rushed Toussaint to the waiting frigate. The French failed to interpret the quickened,

[151]

angry cadence of the drums. As their unending reverberations echoed from the hills that ringed Poteau and the
mountains behind Milot, they were like a relay of sound
that accused and insisted, threatened and insisted, insisted
. . . until the convolutions of one's ears were filled with the
spiraling echoes of their reverberations and the mind
longed for the cessation of their turbulent, soniferous
throbbing.

When the *Creole* reached Cap Français, Toussaint was
immediately transferred to the warship *Hero*. There his
wife, his sons, and members of his personal staff, who had
been taken into custody, already awaited him. He was led
below, to wait until dark. Even here, Toussaint had not
been unobserved and, as the sun set, he heard a fresh
throbbing of drums despite the lapping of the incoming
tide against the quays. Then the *Hero* weighed anchor
and followed a single pilot light that would guide her out
of the harbor.

Toussaint's heart was bursting for a last glimpse of his
native land—the towering mountains of Saint-Domingue
where he first conceived freedom for his people—but his
captors had circled his manacles about one of his bunk
posts. He had never known shackles . . . even when he had
been a slave! Now, because of a white man's treachery and
deceit, he was being taken to France in chains!

19

*In June, six months after Leclerc's arrival in Saint-*Domingue, prompted by Jérôme Bonaparte's reports, impatient Napoleon reestablished the slave trade. Leclerc was filled with apprehension. It was not the time! Added to the arrest and deportation of Toussaint earlier in the month, the prospect of a return to slavery would alert the entire colony! He quickly wrote to Napoleon:

> For a week past there have been illicit gatherings in the plains and even in the towns. They plot to massacre the Europeans! Only today one of Toussaint's mistresses has been arrested. She came here for the purpose of assassinating me!

If Leclerc expected his brother-in-law to sympathize with his insecurity, he was mistaken. Napoleon congratulated him on his success in duping Toussaint and wrote, emphatically:

> ... we await with impatience the arrival of Christophe and Dessalines.

Christophe and Dessalines! As though they could be taken without bloodshed, after Toussaint's betrayal.

Leclerc ordered the disarming of all former slaves. There surely were at least 20,000 muskets in their possession. The disarming had to be accomplished quickly, for he had already written to Napoleon as though it were a *fait accompli*:

> A few brigands have taken refuge in the mountains, but they are isolated and dare not approach our posts. When my reinforcements arrive I shall complete my assignment here, and Saint-Domingue will be French for all time.

It was an exceptionally hot summer, and Saint-Domingue sweltered in the humid heat. Leclerc decided to send Christophe to disarm the south provinces while French officers and enlisted men rested near the seacoast. Unlike Dessalines, Christophe seemed trustworthy and loyal to France; his faithfulness appeared ensured by his love of pomposity and the apparent stability of his command. Free from guile, as most Blacks were, he believed in the sincerity of the French; and had placed his seven-year-old son, Ferdinand, in care of General Boudet, so that he could enjoy the privileges of a French education, in France.

Weeks drifted by while Leclerc waited impatiently for news from Christophe. He had left Cap Français with a complement of fully armed and splendidly attired Blacks.

[154]

After more than a month, just when doubts and the possibility of desertion began to gnaw at Leclerc, Christophe returned from the hills and the Artibonite plains ... but without a single retrieved musket!

Leclerc ordered an escort of grenadiers and rushed to the restored Auberge de la Couronne that Christophe had converted into a private home. He found a scene of domestic tranquillity, for Christophe was spending his homecoming in the courtyard with his wife and children.

Christophe had developed a poise of authority. He was aware that he was sturdy, handsome, and that his voice, when not raised in anger, was as pleasing to the ear as his face was attractive to the eye. He arose from his chair, received his guest with polished, almost pedantic manners, and introduced Marie-Louise and the little girls without hesitation.

He smiled as Leclerc questioned him, on the verge of anger, concerning the unrecovered guns. Unruffled, he whispered to Marie-Louise, and she left and returned with a worn ledger. He nodded and, as though they had rehearsed the foreseeable confrontation, she read slowly and distinctly from the ledger's pages: "Twenty-two thousand, four hundred and thirty-seven muskets; eighteen 12-pounders; seventy-six 5-pounders. . . ." Her voice was undemonstrative and her round, sable-brown face seemed to contain no single sentiment of emotion—although but ten minutes ago she had expressed a premonition that Christophe, swayed by his regard for learning, had erred in sending little Ferdinand to France.

"But where?" cried Leclerc. "Where are they? When will you bring them to Cap Français?"

"As soon as I can commandeer enough horses and men. Right now I have them safe, Captain-General. I assure you, every musket and every gun is being well guarded."

The little girls looked up at Leclerc with disarming smiles. The parts in their hair crisscrossed each other and their heads were covered with carefully braided, slender little pigtails.

Christophe was assuring him that the guns were being well guarded. The treacherous, lying Black bastard! He was shrewder than he had thought.

Early in October the frigate *Cocade* arrived at Cap Français and brought the disturbing news that slavery had been restored in Guadeloupe and Martinique. Napoleon, impatient with Leclerc's "fumbling" subjugation of Saint-Domingue, had sent a separate expedition for the conquest of those islands. Guadeloupe had been quickly and thoroughly subdued and, with Napoleon's refusal to recognize any distinction between brown and black, mulattoes had been put up for sale on that island!

Dessalines' volcanic anger erupted with uncontained fury. First the betrayal of Toussaint . . . now the restoration of slavery on the Windward Islands! How long would it be before the bastard French would renounce their promises and welcome slave ships into the harbors of Saint-Domingue? He abandoned his command at St. Marc, gathered a few horsemen about him, careened from plantation to plantation, and urged the Blacks to discard their farm tools and gather their hidden weapons.

"This land is ours! Ours!" he cried. "The bastard whites own it no more than they own the seas or the sky. We did not ask to be brought here, but now that we are here we shall be our own masters. The French have lied to us! They wish to enslave us again! But there shall be no

[156]

single slave in Saint-Domingue while I, Dessalines, have a breath in my body. We shall ambush the roads and cast the dead into the springs. We shall destroy everything, burn everything, so that those who would force us back into slavery may have before their eyes that image of hell which they would have us endure."

The Blacks gathered in every field along the Petite Rivière, grouped themselves into marching columns, and followed Dessalines. They had tasted freedom and would not relinquish it. Their recollections of slavery were still too vivid! Suddenly, as they reached a rise of ground, they looked down into a valley that was filled with a thousand mulatto troops. They did not know that Alexander Sabes Pétion, tormented by an abhorrence of slavery as deep-rooted as Dessalines', had defected from the French and brought his entire command from le Haut-du-Cap. As Dessalines watched, Pétion left his troops and urged his horse up the rise of ground. He was slender and taciturn, his military bearing the product of the French academy that had educated him. Dessalines spurred his mount and dashed down to meet him halfway. To Dessalines' surprise, Pétion gave him a military salute. "Greetings," he said. "I have come to offer you my brigade and serve under your command, for mulattoes and Blacks are now faced with a common enemy—slavery! It is an enemy against which I have dedicated my life."

Dessalines was but half convinced. "You have lost faith in the French. But what of your many friendships with whites?"

Pétion looked into Dessalines' brute face. He could discern nothing but untutored cunning and uncurbed violence in the heavy, scarred countenance, and yet he said,

"The Blacks are now my brothers. How can I believe in the sincerity of whites when I have not even the friendship of my own father—for the single reason that I have African blood in my veins?"

For a long moment Dessalines glanced up at the blue sky where a nebula of white clouds embraced each other in an endless coherence. On the rise of ground the Blacks waited with patient docility. In the valley the mulattoes shielded themselves as best they could from the blistering sun. Finally he extended a grudging hand. "*Eh, bien.* I accept you as a blood brother, Alex. Do not give me reason to regret it."

"There is a large cache of arms and ammunition at Crete-à-Pierrot," said Pétion. "We should encounter no difficulty in taking the fortress. And then, as an artilleryman, I suggest we lay siege to St. Marc."

A wide anticipatory smile fashioned itself on Dessalines' face. "*Venez!*" he cried to his Blacks as he turned on his mount. "*Venez!*"

At Cap Français, Christophe was secretly supervising the defection of his officers and men. In the dark of night, in little bands of ten or twelve, they would steal out of the town and hurry to the St. Michel plantation on the road that ran southeastward from Cap Français to la Petite Anse. He entrusted his wife and children to their care, for he intended to establish his headquarters there. Nine years ago Marie-Louise had followed him about as a camp follower, uncomplaining, and had given birth to Ferdinand in a field, like an animal! But now he was a general with enough cached weapons to arm 20,000 men!

No one was aware of the exodus of Christophe's Blacks,

for the streets of Cap Français were no longer patrolled nor its gates guarded. The town had been struck by a pestilence! The French called it the "Siamese sickness," and though there were no casualties among the Blacks, long immune to the disease, more than a hundred French troops died each day. In the marshes along the bay and in the quagmires of the Savane de la Fossette, mosquitoes hovered like mists and swarmed into the town with the first breath of night air. To conceal his losses, Leclerc forbade military funerals. Carts, preceded by drummers, lumbered through the streets at midnight, collected the dead who were left on the doorsteps of their billets, trundled them out of town, beyond la Fossette Cemetery, and dumped them into hastily dug common graves. Apprehensive and alarmed, Leclerc wrote to Napoleon:

> You will never subdue Saint-Domingue without an army of 12,000 acclimated troops . . . and you will not have this army until you have sent 70,000 men.
> The month of Fructidor cost me more than 4,000. Today they tell me that the sickness may continue until the end of Brumaire. If that is so, and it continues with the same intensity, the colony is lost. The troops that arrived a month ago no longer exist!

In the middle of October, less than three weeks after the *Cocade* had dropped anchor with its disturbing news, Christophe, at the head of a column of Blacks, stormed out of Cap Français, presumably to join forces with Dessalines and Pétion. Leclerc, at his wit's end, sent for Rochambeau.

Not trusting the roads, Rochambeau took the longer sea route and sailed around Môle St. Nicolas in order to meet with Leclerc. When he reached Cap Français, he was appalled by Leclerc's wasted form. The man was driving himself to his death!

Grown lank from worry, with a spreading hatred of everyone and everything about him, Leclerc was embittered by the sight of Rochambeau in his polished red boots and his uniform *à la hussar*. Nothing seemed to affect this cocksure, big-nosed pompous fool. Bursting with energy, Rochambeau strode up and down and cried, "Didn't I warn you against that bastard, Dessalines, that cowardly Christophe, and that traitorous Pétion? Mulatto and Black—they are all alike. There are none to be trusted. Every Black in Saint-Domingue has been tainted by the mood of rebellion and should be slaughtered like the worthless savage he is. There must be no half measures, Charles. They have become violent animals who must be exterminated! We shall repopulate the island with fresh cargoes from the Guinea coast."

Leclerc stared at Rochambeau with tired, red-veined eyes. His skin appeared jaundiced; he had awakened with a sense of malaise and a headache that would not subside. He listened to Rochambeau and thought of courteous, aristocratic Christophe as he had seen him in the courtyard of la Auberge de la Couronne. His wife had read the sums from the ledger without hesitation and in excellent French. The children, although Black, had seemed intelligent, well groomed, affectionate.

"A half million fresh slaves?" he challenged. "Have you determined the cost, Donatien?"

"Make your choice, Charles. We must exterminate these animals or they will exterminate us. You must send immediately for more troops. I insist on another ten battalions!"

Leclerc regretted that he had sent for Rochambeau. The meeting had accomplished nothing. Still suffering from an enervative malaise, he worked with his secretary, Norvins, in his bedroom, where a desk had been slipped under a mosquito netting. Troubled by Christophe's defection and the spread of the "Siamese sickness," he wrote to Napoleon, forgetting that his brother-in-law had expressed a similar strategy:

> Here is my opinion of the country. We must destroy all the Negroes in the mountains; men and women—retaining only children under twelve years of age. . . .
>
> If you are to be master of Saint-Domingue you must, without a day's delay send me 12,000 men. . . .

While he waited for reinforcements, Leclerc decided to subdue the island with the instrument of terror. It had worked against Toussaint. Why should it not work against Christophe . . . even violent Dessalines? He began to empty Cap Français of Blacks. Hundreds were taken aboard the ships in the harbor, manacled wrist to wrist, and forced to jump overboard in deep water. When the store of manacles was depleted the Negroes were crammed into the ships' holds, the hatches battened down, and sulfur candles burned until they were suffocated.

The sea cast up the bloated bodies of the Blacks. They bobbed along the quays and burst and stank in the sun where the tides washed them up on the marsh flats. A military surgeon suggested to Leclerc that the bodies on the beach might further spread the pestilence that was decimating the whites as though the gods of Africa were revenging themselves upon the French. Would it not be more prophylactic to bury them?

At daybreak, by Leclerc's order, the compounds were emptied and a tremendous gang of Blacks—men, women, and children—were herded to a field behind the Champ de Mars to be executed. Jesuit priests, aware of the intended massacre so close to St. Anne, hurried their morning ablutions in order to witness the spectacle. Across the blue-green water, eastward toward Monte Christi, the sun rose like a molten red sphere and shimmered the dew in the field. The adult Blacks were forced to dig a long, deep trench while the children watched. As the mounds of dark, moist soil were formed higher and higher along the sides of the pit, the deep expirations of the Blacks grew in resonance and fashioned themselves into a slow rhythmic cadence—a chant that was filled with Eboe melancholy as though they had resigned themselves to whatever destiny the gods had devised for them.

The French, prodded into impatience by the rising heat of the day, made apprehensive by the weird, unintelligible, unending, and unhurried chant, were suddenly alarmed by the sound of native drums that began to reverberate from across the Morne du Cap ravine. They began to execute the Blacks—shooting them in the back so they would pitch into the trench. It was incredible! There was no single outcry of protest or pain. Not even the whimper of a child! Animals would have turned and fled! Despite the sound of the gunfire behind them and the sight of bodies sinking to their knees and tumbling into the common grave, no single Black dropped his shovel until he, himself, was pitched into the trench by the burst of a musket ball ripping through his flesh.

The priests left and turned their steps toward la Providence hospital where the sick filled its rooms and corridors, and the dying were stretched on outdoor pallets in the shade of mango trees. Young mulattresses, pressed into the service, were taking care of those who had died in the night. They wrapped them in sheets and struggled with them into the courtyard where creaking carts would gather them up, after dark. Jesuits hurried past the fever-stricken enlisted men. They avoided their frightened, beseeching eyes as they offered up incantations for souls in purgatory, their Latin phrases as much a gibberish to the dying men as the patois they had not yet mastered. At officers' cots, the priests lagged long enough to offer a supplication to Our Lady of the Seven Sorrows and pressed old quartos and sacred relics to fever-stricken lips so they could kiss them and thus be made receptive to a miracle.

Sick, frightened, haunted by the multitudinous deaths he was senselessly inflicting upon the unprotesting Blacks, too proud to ask his brother-in-law, Napoleon, to recall him, Leclerc decided to send Pauline and little Dermide to the islet of Tortuga across from Port-de-Paix. There they would be free of the persistent stench that drifted into Cap Français from the marshy flats, and would run almost no risk of contagion.

Pauline refused to go! Several of the youngest and most gallant officers, who had arrived with the fresh troops, had attached themselves to her. She had just begun, at last, to enjoy herself and rid herself of that enervating boredom that was worse than the fever. Leclerc had not the strength to threaten or plead; though he knew quite well what lured her into remaining in pestilence-ridden Cap Français. Almost all his officers had turned dissolute. Startled by the ravages of the plague, they sought out mulatto women and griffones, whom they cajoled, bribed, or threatened in order to drink and whore with them. They sought to brush from their minds, with a continual swirl of amusement, the inevitability of their own deaths. Every night the gaiety of a cotillion in a barracks hall would be temporarily wilted by a young officer, stricken by the fever, suddenly slumping down through the brown arms that embraced him. For a few moments the fiddles, the horns, and the bassoon would be hushed—everyone's blood would be chilled by the apparition of death while the officer was being removed—and then the reckless abandon of the night would be resumed. This is what Pauline had begun to frequent—sucked into the insatiable, dissolute vortex of such nights in the barracks.

Leclerc sent General Debelle to plead with Pauline. It was midday but she was still abed, reclining on a mountain of cushions. Debelle had always been most attentive. Now he was abrupt with her. Did he disapprove of her escapades? Was he then so fastidious? His dark eyes were lackluster and she could not tell if his plump face was perspiring with the rising heat of the day or if he, himself, was touched by the fever. Standing at her bedside, he read from a long list of figures as though she would be swayed by what they implied: "The plague has stricken 20,000 of our soldiers, 9,000 sailors, 1,500 officers, 700 doctors. . . . *Seven hundred doctors!*"

She was unimpressed.

The next morning, when Pauline learned that General Debelle had died in the night, she packed her treasures and permitted herself to be escorted to a vessel that would transport her and little Dermide to Tortuga.

On November 1st, Leclerc himself lay on his deathbed.

[164]

He cursed Toussaint ... Dessalines ... Christophe ... the island of Saint-Domingue and the ill-fated expedition. He was only thirty years old! He did not want to die on this plague-ridden island, 4,000 miles from home, surrounded on all sides by these Black animals. He had appealed to Napoleon for fresh troops with monotonous regularity. Now he dictated a letter to him:

Disease has made such frightful ravages among my troops that I fear to engage the Blacks who have broken out into a new insurrection. I am trying to terrorize these Negroes into submission but they laugh at death. If you wish to preserve Saint-Domingue, send a new army. If you abandon us to ourselves ... this colony is lost. Once lost, you will never regain it!

Leclerc wrote to Pauline that he was sick, perhaps dying, but she refused to visit him. She had not known that a military hospital for wounded officers had been established on the island of Tortuga. She had settled herself, with her retinue, on the Labattut plantation; found the islet surprisingly free of the plague and its inhabitants little concerned with the insurrection on Saint-Domingue. Tortuga was idyllic! Its daytime hours were filled with the sound of the sea and the rustle of palm fronds; its night breezes bore the scent of orange blossoms. Young officers addressed her as *Madame la Générale,* and she invited them to share her couch within a bower of frangipani and flaming immortelles. From that vantage point they could observe scantily clad Negroes twist and torment themselves in the lascivious abandon of their native dances. What could she do for Charles if she returned to Cap Français? Hold his hand? Fall sick herself?

[165]

On November 28th, she received an official dispatch that Charles Victor Emmanuel Leclerc had sunk into unconsciousness during the night and died in the morning. Charles Victor Emmanuel. . . . *Emmanuel*, beloved of God!

A seemingly grief-stricken Pauline was escorted back to Cap Français. When she saw Leclerc, rigidly displayed in a cedar coffin, she was astounded at his wasted form. He bore as little resemblance to the dashing officer she had married as a phantom in a distorted mirror. She was touched by remorse, and sank to her knees and prayed aloud:

> "O Immaculate Heart of Mary, Mother of Jesus, inspire me to grieve sincerely for the sins that weigh heavily upon the souls of men. O Immaculate Heart of Mary, you who suffered, and shared with Him each pain caused and inflicted by our sins, intercede for us. . . ."

A young officer insisted that she accept a red velvet cushion to kneel upon. In the midst of her devotions she thought of her innumerable indiscretions and adulteries, made an act of contrition, and wept bitterly as she offered an oath of celibacy to the Virgin Mother Mary. Still on her knees, she asked for a scissors and commanded that they shear her head. "Dear Charles . . . ," she wept as she spread her flaxen tresses on his emaciated chest. "Dear, sweet Charles. . . ."

The young officer stepped forward and helped her rise from the velvet cushion. How young and handsome he was! She had noticed him when he came to escort her back to Cap Français. He, too, had addressed her as *Madame la*

Générale. Now he seemed saddened by her shorn head. She turned her tear-stained face toward him and permitted herself a wan smile. "Do not be perturbed, Lieutenant. It is said that cropping makes the hair grow more luxuriantly. Could you obtain a kerchief for me?"

Pauline emptied the Government Palace of all its objets d'art and accompanied Leclerc's body back to France.

20

Command of the French in Saint-Domingue was now in the hands of Lieutenant-General Rochambeau, and he rushed to Cap Français and established himself in the Government Palace. He was astonished to learn that Maurepas, a Black general who had remained loyal to France, refusing to join the defectors, Dessalines and Christophe, was still in command of a brigade. It was *une moquerie!* He was Rochambeau! He intended to replace the entire Negro population with docile slaves and if this included reliable Blacks on the plantations then it must also include Black generals.

He immediately ordered General Maurepas placed under house arrest and taken out, with his family, to the warship *Duguay-Trouin* for execution. The Black general was tied to a mast. His wife and children were forced to watch while the ship's carpenter nailed his epaulets to his shoulders. Then he and his family were bayoneted and cast into the sea.

Rochambeau wrote for 30,000 reinforcements. It was December, the fever had subsided, and with the additional troops he hoped to conquer the island in thirty days. While he awaited their arrival, he began to systematically rid the island of its Blacks. Captured ex-slaves were put to the sword, shot, hanged, buried alive, tortured by sadistic experiments, and drowned by the shiploads. He even tried his hand at the slave trade, and French ships that had *Liberté - Egalité - Fraternité* painted on their prows began to hawk slaves, at "refuse" prices, in the Caribbean. Some ships sailed as far south as the Lesser Antilles and as far east as Guadeloupe and Martinique, without finding buyers. No one wanted rebellious Blacks from Saint-Domingue, and the unsalable human cargoes were jettisoned.

In the meanwhile, Blacks and mulattoes, with Dessalines as their commander in chief, climbed higher into the mountains. There they built camps in the peaks of Valliere and La Mina. Christophe, convinced that the Blacks could not prevail unless they matched the French in discipline, began to fashion a new army. Six years ago his assignment had been an almost impossible one—to create a fighting force from Guinea Coast Senegalese; Slave Coast Wydahs, Nagoes, and Pawpaws; Gold Coast Coromantees; Gambia Mandingoes, Eboes, and Angolese. All had been distrustful of each other and disjoined by the barrier of their dialects. Now his endeavor was quickly rewarded, for all had mastered the patois phrases and while, six years

[169]

ago, they had only rebelled against the insufferable conditions of their enslavement, now they were about to defend their very lives, which had become, somehow, expendable! Six years ago the educated and skilled mulattoes had been their antagonists. Now they, too, had become the hunted and were rushing to the Black camps. Dessalines watched as griffes, quadroons, octoroons, and every gradation of *gens de couleur* clambered up the mountain paths to join them. "Soon all Saint-Domingue will gather in our hills," he cried, "and then we will sweep down and smash the cursed whites into the sea!"

General Rochambeau was not only emptying the towns of Blacks and mulattoes but sweeping the countryside in order to capture them. Having learned that trained dogs were used in Cuba to hunt down runaway slaves, he imported more than a hundred of the brutes. They would not only track Blacks who had hidden in the woods but smell out Dessalines' ambuscades that had begun to plague his sorties.

The training of these hounds became Rochambeau's passion and their employment his favorite diversion. By the middle of summer he decided to exhibit his disciplined animals, for the entertainment of his officers, by having them attack and devour a chained Black. The courtyard of the Jesuit monastery was chosen for the spectacle, and tiers of seats were erected in the shade of the cloister for the officers and their mistresses—mulattresses who had been granted special dispensations as courtesans. Anger tugged at the corners of Rochambeau's mouth as he watched General Boyer escort his mistress Bajéan (who had perversely denied herself to him) to a front row seat. She was not a mulattress. She was a griffone! Tall and slender, with high, outthrust breasts and an unblemished skin, she was supple in repose, languorous in movement, graceful in gesture; and there was an intimation of sexuality in her dark, restless eyes. Boyer introduced her everywhere as Bajéan, *ma zibeline déesse* [my sable goddess.] How did she dare deny herself to him! And Boyer to defend her! He was not a patient man, and it would end by his setting the dogs on her!

General Boyer sensed the tension in his mistress as she seated herself. Could it be that the naked Black, chained to the post, was known to her? He did not think so. He had caught a glance of recognition between her and Rochambeau. Bajéan had turned away, disdainful and unintimidated, her cheekbones glistening in the sun; but Rochambeau's eyes were little wells of cruel malice. He had evidently not forgotten her. Nor absolved her constant and unalterable fidelity to Boyer. She had given herself to Boyer a year ago, when he had arranged the *loiloichi* for Pauline. Some strange, magnetic quality that he had not known he possessed had attracted her to him, and he had permitted her to lead him from the garden. After that night she had attached herself to him with a devoted constancy. His self-assurance, his complacency, even his conceit would dissolve and vanish in her presence. Uninhibited, free of embarrassment or restraint, she drew sexual responses from him that he had not known he possessed and, with the naturalism of an animal, urged him to raptures that left him enervated and hollow as an empty gourd.

At his very first meeting with Bajéan, Rochambeau had been aroused by the erotic sensuality that emanated from her, like some strange animal magnetism. Deviant, voyeur,

[171]

and sadist, he had asked to borrow her for the night. Boyer neither understood Bajéan's deep, unswerving attachment for him nor realized his own involvement with this griffone that he laughingly called *ma zibeline déesse*. She had listened intently as he had spoken of Rochambeau's infatuation and had shed no tear while he had appeased that the Lieutenant-General desired her company for only a single night. She had swept her shift up over her head, exposing her dark form in its unabashed nakedness, had pressed a knife into his hands and urged, "Cut out *moin coiyou!* Carve it out, for only after it has died will your pig-eyed Rochambeau enter it!"

There was a roll of drums, and four large dogs, especially starved for the occasion and now straining at their chains, were led into the courtyard. They scented the Black, burst into frenzied baying as they caught sight of him and rushed toward him with great bounds as they were unleashed. The Negro writhed against his chains. His eyes swept the courtyard beseechingly, while his heavy, smoke-tinted underlip trembled with the anguish of anticipated pain. As the brutes reached him, they stiffened their forelegs, snarled, circled the post to which he was fettered, and sniffed at the terrified, motionless Black. Then one raised a hind leg and pissed on the Negro's naked feet. A suppressed titter rippled among the spectators.

Rochambeau, wild with anger, looked to General Boyer, who had helped him train the dogs. Boyer shrugged. He had not foreseen the fiasco. The hounds had always seemed ferocious. Rochambeau rushed to the post, drew his sword, and slashed open the Negro's belly. Aroused by the sight of the blood that gushed from the wound, the dogs immediately snapped and fought among themselves in order to tear the entrails from the shrieking Black.

Rochambeau's rage was unappeased. The incident did not confirm the ferocity of his hounds. He ordered a fresh pack of dogs and another Negro to be brought in and chained to the post. The guards brought one of Dessalines' scouts who had been captured that very morning near the Morne du Cap ravine. Barefooted and without a shirt, he was dressed in cotton trousers and a tattered French officer's coat which he could not button across his wide chest. His wrists were manacled behind his back and his face was encrusted with blood where the stroke of a saber had laid open a cheek to the very bone. As the baying dogs were released, they rushed to him and sniffed at his dust-caked feet. One snarling hound sprang at his throat, snapped at the injured jaw, and raked his chest with its claws as it slid downward. The Black stood motionless and stared down at the dogs with indifference as though unaware that his reopened cheek was dripping blood onto the flagstones. For a moment the long-eared hounds circled about him, growling ... threatening with deep-throated snarls, and then left him to rip and tear at the exposed organs of the dead Black, who had been cast aside.

Rochambeau was furious. He ordered a pyre of *bagasse* to be built about the chained Negro. The Black knew they intended to burn him alive. Yet he paid no attention to the preparations but looked at the officers and their mistresses, on the tiers of seats, with defiant arrogance. Rochambeau did not realize that the scout was a Coromantee, of the haughty and ferocious Ashanti tribe. They were all born heroes, implacably revengeful, and possessed an insubmissive, self-inured tolerance of pain that was beyond belief. One could hack them to pieces without their emitting a cry or groan.

The edges of the pyre were ignited. As the blaze coiled

toward him the Black lifted his foot, thrust it into the flames, and held it there. The foot and then the leg smoldered, blistered, and dripped spatters of grease into the flames as the flesh curled away from the bone. The smell of burning flesh became more pronounced than the scent of the blazing *bagasse*.

Suddenly the Coromantee cried, *"Zautes, pas connait mouri! Guettez comment yo mouri!"* [You don't know how to die! Watch how I die!] His French coat was smoldering and only his face and neck were now above the flames, yet there was no betrayal of hurt in his eyes nor the escape of a single cry of anguish from his lips.

Boyer felt a warm hand slip into his and clutch it tightly. He glanced at Bajéan. She had averted her face and her lips were trembling. "Come," he whispered. "Come . . . ." He guided her across the courtyard. Others rose from their seats.

"Wait!" cried Rochambeau. "Wait!" But the spectacle was over.

21

*D*essalines' *anger was volcanic when he heard what had* befallen his Coromantee scout. He had learned that betrayed "papa Toussaint," imprisoned in France, had died in a dark dungeon. Nor would Christophe ever see his son again! Little Ferdinand, despite General Boudet's promises, had been thrown into an orphan asylum in Paris where, neglected and abused, he had wasted away.

How much more of deception, betrayal, torture, and death did the white world presume the Blacks would endure! He would wait no longer! His nature rebelled against patience and concealment in the hills. He met with his officers and their aides in a clearing in a mountain forest. His great cockaded hat was shapeless from many rains. The rich blue dye of his gold-braided coat was faded from the fierce sun and stained by dark circles of sweat. His knee boots were unpolished and worn. His scabbard hung carelessly at his side. With his bullet head and his powerful back and chest he seemed indestructible as he cried to his generals, without dismounting, "France is annihilating us while we hide in the hills like frightened goats. Tomorrow we shall leave and take back the plains ... even the very sea itself! But there shall be no *Marseillaise* and no France!" He brought out a tattered French tricolor from beneath his coat, grasped it in his powerful hands, and tore the white stripe from the flag.

There was no sound as he stared about him—at aristocratic Christophe, at cultured Pétion, at impetuous Moyse, who had stuffed his still-weeping empty eye socket with a bole of cotton. "From now on," cried Dessalines, "the whites shall have no share in the destiny of Saint-Domingue. Bastard Rochambeau plans to repopulate the island. Well, then, we shall do it for him. But with our own children!"

They were startled by the unexpected reverberations of a tambour on a mountain peak. The sounds of other drums drifted up from the plains and echoed from the hills. For weeks there had been rumors that war had broken out once again between France and England. Now the drums not only confirmed the reports but advised that a British fleet had arrived to blockade the ports of Saint-Domingue. Without a word, Dessalines spurred his horse and dashed from the clearing. The others followed where he led, and by noon they reached a craggy promontory that overlooked St. Marc. With the aid of Christophe's treasured telescope they could see as far as the island of Gonave. It was true! There they were. British frigates were sealing the bay from Môle St. Nicolas to Port-au-Prince. Rochambeau, like a cat in a bag, was left without supplies or reinforcements. The gods of Africa had not deserted them! They held a hasty council and mapped their strategy. They would lay siege to the towns that were cut off from the sea by the British. Pétion would rush to the South Provinces, Christophe would encircle Cap Français, and Dessalines would bring haughty Port-au-Prince to its knees!

Dessalines assembled his forces and led them southward to Port au-Prince. As his followers marched down from the hills they were no longer Negroes, griffes, or mulattoes but natives of Saint-Domingue—equal inheritors of the land! Dessalines ordered them to shed their shirts so the scars they bore upon their backs and the brands upon their chests would remind them of past cruelties. Forbidden to chant the inspiring *Marseillaise*, they devised their own song, fashioned from phrases that laughed at death, and sang in cadence to their steps:

> *Grenadiers, a l'assaut!*
> *Ca qui mouri zaffaire a yo.*
> *Qu'y a point papa,*
> *Qu'y a point maman.*
> *Grenadiers, a l'assaut!*

> Grenadiers, to the attack!
> Those who die, that's their affair.
> They have no father,
> They have no mother.
> Grenadiers, to the attack!

When they reached Port-au-Prince they found that the French had erected a half dozen small forts and built a palisade about the town. Dessalines ordered a regiment to

[177]

attack each of the forts and marched his main force toward the very gates of the town. The French trained their artillery upon every possible approach. The Blacks laughed in the face of death and marched with unbroken ranks into volleys of shot and bursts of musketry. When the order came to attack they smashed at the gates with the press and weight of their numbers and tore at the timbers of the palisade with their bare hands and the bursting strength of their backs. They became their own battering rams, as Dessalines and his officers no longer clamored for liberty but bellowed for retribution! There was no sound of agony from the dying ... no compassion for the dead ... and finally they smashed through the gates and clambered over the palisade like a tidal wave of vengeance.

As the Blacks overran the town, the French threw down their arms and surrendered. Creoles, remembering that Toussaint had granted them amnesties, rushed from their homes in order to welcome the Blacks and convince them that they bore them no animosity. To their horror, Dessalines spurred his horse through the streets and ordered that no prisoners were to be taken. The Blacks were free to avenge themselves upon the whites ... to satisfy any and all inclinations ... to butcher them! The Blacks began to massacre the French and Creoles; hacking them to pieces in the streets, pursuing them to the quays, and searching every possible hiding place in public buildings and warehouses.

A French officer, his blue coat stained crimson by a dozen bayonet wounds, lay dying in a street. Recognizing Dessalines, he struggled to one knee and cried, "General Dessalines ... General Dessalines. ... Consider what the world will think of you for this massacre!"

Dessalines turned his horse. With his face contorted by unsatiated vengeance he roared, "Why should I care for the opinion of future generations? We are repaying savages crime for crime, outrage for outrage! They tortured me like an animal. I give you the *coup de grace* like a man!" He leaned from the saddle and thrust his saber through the officer's heart.

Dessalines cantered through the streets and watched while Blacks tore into shops and homes in order to rout out hidden French and Creoles. The town was filled with piercing screams and anguished cries as some were shot, others were pricked to death with bayonets, some were bludgeoned, and many were tortured. All the barbaric and sadistic cruelties that the Blacks had been forced to witness and endure, they now perpetrated upon the French. Bloodied, still-palpitating bodies were dragged from their hiding places, and young white children were transfixed upon bayonets. The streets became littered with the hacked remains of victims.

The following day, Dessalines supervised the restoration of order and directed that the mutilated and dismembered bodies be carted beyond the palisade and cast into the bogs and marshes. He was informed that almost fifty Creole women had hidden themselves in a subterranean cellar of the Government Palace. He directed that every white woman left in Port-au-Prince be spared . . . provided that she consented to live with a Black, as his wife . . . and ordered that the Creoles who had concealed themselves in the palace be brought before him. Their faces were tear-smudged, their hair disheveled, and they hugged their breasts with their inadequate arms, for the Blacks, urged by a curiosity to view the blanched and sickly pallor of their naked flesh, had torn away half their clothes. Dessalines watched their expressions of horror with rude indifference, as an aide explained the ultimatum to the Creoles. He was well aware that, before the insurrection, many white women in Saint-Domingue had chosen full-blooded Blacks for clandestine lovers. Why should they, with hypocrisy, refuse to indulge openly in what they had practiced in secret? He caught sight of a pretty face—haughty, unstained by a single tear—and recalled, with an excellent memory, that this was the same Creole who had offered him the bouquet of jasmine when he had come here with Toussaint and Christophe five years ago. He looked directly into her eyes and said, "You have a choice, Madame. To live with a Black or be ravished and cast into a marsh. Since we have met before, I offer you death without dishonor." He stepped to her side and handed her his saber.

Her eyes were wild with anger. She grasped the hilt, and for a moment he thought he would have to elude the sharp blade. With conspicuous impertinence, she studied his bullet-shaped head, the thick neck that supported it, and the gold epaulets that surmounted the shoulders of the powerful Black brute before her. Then, without a break in her voice, she said, "I find myself widowed and bereft of everything I possessed. But I am not a fool. Misfortune makes harlots of us all and so, if you please, I shall attach myself to you."

22

*O*n *March 25th, Dessalines left Cap Français in order to* join forces with Christophe and Pétion. He had plundered Port-au-Prince and sent everything of value to a cache in the mountains, where he had begun to amass a personal treasure. He swept everything before him as he worked his way northward, pillaging the seacoast towns and massacring the whites. Mont Rouis, Anse Rouge, and Jean Rabel were sacked and deserted. He was in no hurry to reach Cap Français. Where could the French go? They were penned between the hills and the sea.

Despite the protestations of Claire Heureuse, he began traveling with a harem of mulattresses and white women. As a consequence, Claire left him. He was advised to sleep lightly, for it was rumored that the Creole who had given herself to him in Port-au-Prince intended to assassinate him.

"Impossible!" he laughed. "What she did not attempt in broad daylight, she will never undertake to accomplish in my bed."

When Dessalines finally reached Pétion's and Christophe's forces, he found them bivouacked on the vast plain between Cap Français and the hills to the south. He joined them and strung his troops toward Pointe Picolet. Christophe, with almost no artillery and an awareness of the heavy casualties his Blacks would suffer in an attempt to storm the French fortifications, had been easily persuaded, by Pétion, to besiege the town. By the time Dessalines arrived, Cap Français was starving! The inhabitants had torn the last fig from its branch and the last coconut from its bole. The French troops had been reduced to eating their horses, their donkeys, and even Rochambeau's imported dogs. They could not abandon the island, for setting out to sea meant capture by the British men-of-war that tacked back and forth, in full sight, across the wide bay.

Adamant in his opinion of the Blacks, Rochambeau decided to ride out of Cap Français and engage them in a pitched battle, despite their entrenchments. He ordered his artillery to cannonade the plain incessantly during the night, and when the first ocherous bands of sunlight appeared on the horizon he led his veterans out through the gates with flags flying and drums beating. If it was his intention to flaunt his inviolability it miscarried, for his columns were immediately surrounded by an undulating sea of frenzied Blacks. With wild shrieks and horrible grimaces, they flung themselves upon the French in such numbers that their own comrades could not effectively use their arms. Many impaled themselves upon French bayonets in order to tear the muskets from the hands that held them. Others smashed their way toward the French officers and the mounted dragoons. The field in front of Cap Français' palisades became a cauldron in which horse and rider bubbled and burst, fell and rose, pitched and scattered, rushed and smashed while morning sunlight glinted from stained machete and dripping bayonet.

Suddenly there was a blinding flash of lightning. A deafening reverberation of thunder rolled from the hills. The sun changed quickly from blood-red . . . to yellow . . . to black. A tempest of wind spiraled across the field, and as it abated rain fell in such a torrent that one could see nothing but water. The sky was an inverted sea. The earth became a quagmire—and between heaven and ground a fantastic waterfall obscured everything from sight. Like animals, the Blacks recognized their enemies by scent and touch and slashed at the haze of their forms. Rochambeau ordered a retreat. Sluices of water muffled the sounds as drums and drummers were smashed and trampled into the bog. Horses floundered as though in quicksand. The French groped their way to the palisade, rushed through the gates, and thrust them shut upon a quarter of their troops, abandoning them to be massacred.

By midmorning the sky cleared and the tropic sun sucked the puddles from the plain in a cumulous fog that drifted seaward. The red-stained field was sown with dead and dying. The Black Generals sought each other in order to estimate their losses. Pétion was weeping, unashamedly. His brigade had been the closest to the palisade. Dessalines looked to Christophe, who sat his horse, imperturbable. He had an irritating fault! One could never tell what he was thinking! Dessalines surveyed the strewn field, turned to Pétion, and cried in anger, "Why do you grieve? We have lost ten Blacks to every one of your bastard, bleached mulattoes!"

Pétion was not intimidated by Dessalines' violence. "My heart cries for Black and mulatto alike. Even for the French. I am distressed by the many dead that are all about us."

"I am touched by your compassion. See that you do not weep for yourself!"

On the morning of November 19th, Rochambeau capitulated to Dessalines. Promising himself that he would return with a fresh force and devastate the entire island, regardless of the cost, he agreed to hand over the forts and the artillery on Pointe Picolet, undamaged, provided he, his troops, and the French inhabitants who chose to follow him would be permitted to embark with their personal possessions. As a token of good faith, he presented his superb horses to Dessalines.

Dessalines smiled as he accepted them. "He is faced with annihilation," he laughed to Christophe, "for he will never evade the British. I give him until sunset. Advise him that I will sink his ships with red-hot shot if they have not left the harbor by then."

As the red sphere of the sun dipped westward, seeming about to extinguish itself in the sea beyond Môle St. Nicolas, Dessalines, Christophe, and Pétion rushed to the abandoned fortress on the promontory of Pointe Picolet. Three French frigates and seventeen smaller ships were drifting toward the open sea.

There was little doubt in Rochambeau's mind that they would all be taken by the British and escorted to Jamaica,

where the vessels would be sold as prizes, personal possessions confiscated, and the men interned. But until then he
was Donatien Marie Joseph de Vimeur, Vicomte de
Rochambeau, Lieutenant-General and Governor of Saint-
Domingue! He ordered the frigates to lower their colors
and fire a broadside. He intended it as a show of strength
rather than a token of surrender. The puffs of smoke lingered over the water and then drifted up into the blue sky.

On Pointe Picolet, Dessalines took the French banner,
from which he had torn the white stripe, and ordered the
red and blue colors to be raised as the new flag of Saint-Domingue. The twelve-year struggle was over. They were a
new nation of Blacks—victors of the greatest slave revolt in
history!

23

Six weeks later, on New Year's Day, 1804, in a field near Gonaïves where Toussaint had been hastened aboard the *Creole* after his treacherous betrayal, the independence of Saint-Domingue was proclaimed at a conclave of all the generals amidst a tremendous assemblage of the army, townspeople, and former slaves, who were now designated as natives.

After Rochambeau's withdrawal, Dessalines had turned at once to the extermination of the French who had been left stranded on the island. Pétion, Christophe, and others refused to participate in his frightful retaliation for Rochambeau's atrocities.

Dessalines would not be placated. "You do not remember Maurepas!" he cried. "Cast into the sea with his epaulets hammered into his shoulders! Well, if you will not avenge him, I shall. I will have my horse walk in blood up to his breastplate in order to avenge him!"

Pétion, Christophe, and their educated aides drafted an *Act of Independence* for Saint-Domingue, deciding that the island should now be called *Haiti,* an old Indian name meaning high place, and that all its citizens, with equal rights, should be known only as *Noirs,* irrespective of their shades of color. Meanwhile, Dessalines, joined by Moyse, massacred the stranded whites, sparing only the lives of priests and foreigners who could prove they were not French. They rushed back to Gonaïves, at a last moment, in order to participate in the creation of the new state.

All night the roads and trails that led to Gonaïves had been pounded by the bare feet of Blacks who had come to witness the dream that Dessalines had fulfilled for them. Some had only loincloths, many wore tattered cotton trousers that had been plantation issue, while a few were dressed in coats and breeches that had been stripped from slain French. They had stuffed themselves with plantains, bananas, and mangoes that they had plucked along the way.

They crowded into the field, rocked in front of a hastily erected platform, and whispered in the slurred singsong of their faulty patois: "Free rum? We now get free rum? *Grand moon li mort!*" They had effaced the evidences of their former condition—had buried the chains and the whips, dismantled the bells that had called them to their arduous toil, razed the factories—and now expected reparations for their enslavement.

Moyse opposed the constitution before he heard a single word of its text. He had his own formula for freedom. He insisted that every former slave be given his own piece of

[187]

land where he could work as he pleased. He tore away the madras kerchief that he had tied across his empty eye socket and cried, "There are to be no more plantations, and I shall never permit whites on this island until they have given me back my eye!"

Dessalines insisted that the *Act of Independence* be read to him before it was disclosed to the multitude in the field. He did not fully approve of it, for he found it too verbose. The drafters were educated mulattoes and griffes, whereas he wanted the full-blooded Blacks to understand its clauses. He glared at Pétion and cried, "The Act must contain a curse against the French and express eternal and inextinguishable hatred for France!"

One of Dessalines' aides, seething with a violence that had been bred and nurtured by his commander, sprang to his feet and cried, in patois, "We did not drive out the French assassins with curses and we will not declare our independence with words alone! To set down an *Act of Independence* we need the skin of a white for parchment, his skull for an inkwell, his blood for ink, and a bayonet for a quill!" The Blacks roared their approval.

The secretaries whispered among themselves and bent to the task of making innumerable changes. Dessalines scowled as first Pétion and then Christophe offered suggestions. He glared at his aide, Dupuy, as the young mulatto agreed with them. The sun reached its zenith and shone mercilessly upon the platform, the gathered troops, and the milling Blacks who sweated in the field. After many deletions, alterations, and additions, the Act was finally agreed upon and it was decided, with unanimity, that it should be presented by Julien Prévost, an elderly and highly educated mulatto. Intelligent, well-informed, sensitive, and temperate, he had always expressed an abhorrence for slavery and professed belief in equality between Black and mulatto. The field burst into a thunder of acclaim as he rose with the *Declaration* in his hands. When all was quiet, he translated its French phrases into patois:

Before posterity, before the entire universe . . . we swear to renounce France forever and to die rather than live under domination. . . .

Prévost's reading ended with a roll of drums and blasts from battered French trumpets. In the presence of the general staff, within sight of the gathered army and those who had tramped for miles to observe them, the generals were asked to affix their signatures to the Act. Pétion dipped the quill into an inkwell and signed the *Declaration* with a flourish. Christophe followed and scribbled the only word that Marie-Louise had as yet taught him: *Henri*. Dessalines looked from Pétion to Christophe. He had never held a slender quill in his hand. He was ferocious, audacious, and cunning, but he had no single intellectual endowment. With an innate sense of the dramatic, with which he had begun to dominate every scene, he turned and bellowed, "I once promised you liberty or death. I now give you liberty. Black liberty! From now on black is the color of life. Never shall a European set foot on this soil with the title of master or owner; and all the citizens of our new state shall be known only as Blacks!" While the crowd cheered and applauded, he passed the quill to a secretary and, as though unobserved, pointed with a broad finger to where he wanted his signature inscribed.

[189]

The sun was about to set. It had been red . . . glorious
. . . and as it slanted its rays into the westward bay, Dessalines was declared Governor-General of the new *Haiti*.

Now that there was peace at last, Haiti had no need for
Dessalines' brute force. He would not admit, even grudgingly, that he possessed no talent for civil administration,
and he refused to be guided by cultured Pétion or talented
Dupuy. Devastated plantations were not restored, burned-
out villages were not rebuilt, and Black citizens, after
twelve years of idleness, were not urged to return to habits
of indutsry. There was no state treasury and no civil
authority.

And yet, when Dessalines learned that the Senate, in
Paris, had "offered" the title of Emperor to Napoleon
Bonaparte, he determined not to be outranked by a
Frenchman, though France was 4,000 miles away. He
ordered the drafting of a proposal that would nominate
him Emperor of Haiti, and circulated it among his Generals for their signatures. Christophe would see to the unani-
mous acceptance of the petition. Now that the hostilities
had ended he found himself jealous of Christophe's handsome figure, his affable personality, and his grace. Still, he
felt that he would not object to the proposal, for he had
appointed Christophe commander in chief of the Haitian
army and bestowed upon him the status of heir apparent.
Nor would Pétion decline his request. Tainted by white
blood, in a Black majority, Pétion owed him his very life!
He could no longer stand the sight of that bastard mulatto
whose French education and knowledge of politics rankled
him . . . whose advice and guidance he would not accept
although the new government of Haiti was in a deplora-
ble, insolvent, and bewildered state.

Elated by the prospect of his coronation, Dessalines initiated a series of lavish balls in the Government Palace. Behind closed doors, he spent hours under the tutelage of a mulatto dance master in preparation for them. He ordered his personal fortune to be brought from its cache in the mountains and, despite the presence of Madame Dessalines, who had returned to his side, began to squander it upon innumerable Black, brown, and tan mistresses. It was as though life had denied him the gratification of his whims and desires and now, at last, he had smashed its barriers and could fulfill, with neither negation nor remorse, any and every inclination. He ordered all his officers and advisers to attend every gala festivity and was unaware that only his mistresses declaimed his attempts at social amenities and lavishly praised his clumsy dance performances. When he would explode on the ballroom floor, in moments of excitement, into wild and abandoned capering, Claire Dessalines would leave as though her presence were needed to supervise the preparation of refreshments. A few very bold mulattoes would snicker behind their hands at his antics. He did not know that Christophe considered his attempts at the cotillion and the quadrille as an affront to the dignity of his race and had tagged him, mentally, as "that jumping jackass." Only Défilée, who now wandered in and out of the rooms of the Government Palace as though she were a member of the family, thought him beautiful and graceful despite his sweating, brutish head and the pronounced limp effected by his once-broken ankles.

One night, with his left hand thrust into the breast of his tight waistcoat, Dessalines led the sweating Blacks through the intricacies of a freshly learned minuet. Urged on by the mendacious applause of his mistresses and the

[191]

misunderstood silence of his officers, he insisted on displaying, with tiresome repetition, a grace he imagined he possessed. Pétion, who would not exhibit the proficiency with which he had mastered the graceful movements of the minuet in France, turned to Christophe and whispered, "Our intended emperor seems to possess a flawless ability to imitate animals. When we were at war he led his followers like a tiger. Now that we are at peace he leads them like a gorilla."

On October 8, 1804, Dessalines was crowned Jean Jacques the First, Emperor of Haiti. His title, at his insistence, included the phrase, "The Avenger and Deliverer of His Fellow Citizens." He had ordered a new capital to be built on a highway that led southwestward to St. Marc. It was to be called Dessalines, in his honor. Too impatient to await its construction, he permitted the coronation to take place in Cap Français, which had been renamed Cap Haitien. Christophe watched the services with a mixture of trepidation and regret. Father Corneille Brelle, a Breton missionary who had been one of Toussaint's chaplains, officiated, and Défilée stood at one side of the throne, dressed in a red robe. The withered remains of a tree snake was wound about her waist, while a feathered *ouanga* snuggled in the cleft between her half-exposed breasts. Dessalines, though he understood no single catechism, had accepted Father Brelle's function in order to give the coronation validity, yet would not withdraw from the voodoo rituals that Toussaint had proscribed.

The mulattoes had gathered on one side of the hall. They appeared as they had when Christophe had observed them on the day Vincent Ogé had been executed. Their faces were filled with doubt and uncertainty. A sense of misgiving moistened their dark eyes. Christophe left Marie-Louise and moved to Pétion's side. "Your face is not a happy one, Alex," he whispered. "Is this day not prophetic? We have achieved not only our freedom but our own government . . . our own kingdom! Does it irk you that, despite your fair skin, you must now call yourself *un Noir*?"

Pétion permitted himself a wry smile. "You know me better than that, Henri. If Dessalines were to offer us a republic, where every man could have a voice in its government, I would not care if I were called red, green, or purple. But look about you, Henri. There is no single unwashed or tattered Black. As though he has not stemmed from them, they are being kept outside, like herded cattle. I shall say it now, before it can be labeled treason. Are we about to accept a domestic tyranny in place of a foreign one . . . to exchange a Black despot for a white?"

Christophe turned to brilliant Dupuy, who now resided in the Government Palace and was constantly at Dessalines' side. "What say you, Dupuy?"

The young mulatto smiled. "I have forgiven our Dessalines many things, but I shall refuse to sanction a single act of despotism. I will abandon Haiti rather than accept in an Emperor what I have tolerated in a General."

Christophe looked toward the new throne. Father Brelle was perspiring profusely, and his hands trembled as he tried to adjust the crown on the emperor's head. The *bijoutier* had fashioned it too small. "Do not be alarmed,"

[193]

laughed Dessalines as he tugged his ermine-trimmed cloak about him. "It will not fall, and no one shall remove it without my consent!"

As though at some prearranged signal, there was a roll of drums and then a boom from cannon that had been lined along the quays. There was to be a parade of freshly uniformed troops. With banners held aloft and drums beating, they were already approaching the coronation hall . . . marching, eight abreast, with perfect and ostentatious pomposity. Dessalines set aside his scepter and rushed outdoors to view the parade. He had leaped from a mud-and-wattle hut in a Guinea swamp to an Emperor's throne on the richest "Sugar Island" in the Antilles; but his ascendance had been so tempestuous and rapid that, for the moment, the reverberant and colorful parade was of more interest to him than the crown.

24

Jean Jacques Dessalines was Emperor of Haiti, but he knew as little of government as when he had been a slave. The island was now so ravaged that some of the most influential families lived like gypsies or slept in derelict hovels. His secretaries suggested amendments, recommended laws, and plagued him with trivia. How soon could the aqueducts be repaired? Would he subsidize the rebuilding of the towns and villages? Should claims to abandoned plantations be considered?

He was impatient with their endless petitions and drove them out. How could he interest himself in civil affairs when he was restless . . . bored? Even his mistresses no longer aroused his jaded appetite. He secluded himself in his elaborate palace, which was nearing completion, and left government matters in the hands of elderly André

Vernet, who had married Toussaint's niece, and reluctantly appointed Pétion, treasurer, for Dupuy, true to his word, had abandoned him.

Dessalines became angry when Pétion, as though spurred by the Creole blood in his veins, insisted upon the resumption of foreign trade. What did Pétion imply when he complained that the people were hungry—had taken to foraging in the woods? Was he reproaching him? He had abolished slavery. He had given them freedom! Must he feed them too?

The southern peninsula of Haiti is a procession of steep mountain ranges that stretch all the way from Port-au-Prince to Dame Marie and stipple the slender finger of land with a hundred precipices. Regarded as untillable by the Creoles, mulattoes had settled in the peninsula and with hard labor and frugality had become prosperous planters, until Rochambeau had driven them from the sloping, fertile valleys. Now that the war was over, survivors drifted back to what was left of their plantations. They scorned the coronation of uncouth and untutored Dessalines, hated him for his insistence that everyone in Haiti should be designated as Black, and refused to accept social equality with the crude, unwashed, and often violent Africans.

When Dessalines was advised that mulattoes, who had lived in northern towns all their lives as shopkeepers, artisans, and *hôteliers,* were leaving to work on the southern plantations, he laughed, "Good riddance! It will save me the trouble of massacring them. They are corrupted by their white blood and still consider themselves French. But I am the law in Haiti. I am the Emperor! When I say sit, they shall sit. When I say stand, they shall stand. Even when I say starve, they shall starve! *Je suis la loi!*"

In October, exactly two years after his coronation, Dessalines learned that Pétion had gathered most of the mulatto officers about him and left for Port-au-Prince. Dessalines roared with a raging fury. The sneaking yellow bastard had betrayed him! For months he had been hinting of the advantages of a republic ... a government in which every citizen would have an interest.

Had Pétion been intimating that Dessalines could not govern because he was illiterate? Because he was Black? Well, no one would strike the crown from his head. They would not dare! He almost welcomed a rebellion. It meant activity again—a temporary activity—for he had but to ride majestically before his subjects, in his finest uniform, and ebony, brown, or tan, they would remember who had attained their liberty. He would not consider that the irascible Blacks blamed him for their tatters and their hunger. There was no bell to call them to work, no whip to drive them, but there was also no molasses and no meat. They were reduced to eating frogs!

He did not alert Christophe, in Cap Haitien, for he was Jean Jacques Dessalines, Emperor of Haiti. He needed no help to nip a yellow rebellion in its bud! He mounted his horse, gathered his bodyguard about him, a troop of blue-uniformed grenadiers, and left for Port-au-Prince. The white-dusted road that led southward toward Petite Rivière was bordered by bowing cacao trees. As he rode under the dry heat of the sun, he found himself snuffling the odor of his horse's sweating flanks and finding it pleasurable. He had permitted himself to grow soft—stuffing himself with food and drink—his only exercise tumbling about in his mistresses' beds. Whores! They were all whores! There was not a fig's taste of affection in a single dry kiss. And the paler their skins the shallower and falser their responses as though they were removed from animal-ism in proportion to the fairness of their sun-shielded flesh!

He found himself thinking of Défilée. There was a woman who truly loved him! Unlike his wife, Claire, whose intellectual attainments and griffone's shading had enveloped her with an aura of aloofness, had he married Défilée she would have snipped the nipples from every Dominicaine with whom he had slept. She would have shriveled the flesh from Claire's bones, with her voodoo, had he not forbidden it.

He approached the little seacoast town of Arcahaie. He was still twenty-seven miles from Port-au-Prince and his grenadiers had begun to lag. He decided to sleep over in Arcahaie. It would rest his horse and he, himself, would be fresh in the morning. He was startled to find the town swarming with mulattoes, like a beehive when the drones are gone. The town had escaped the scars of war, yet its residents seemed in no mood to welcome him. Surely they were aware that he was their Emperor, Dessalines. Yet nei-ther mulatto nor griffe would glance his way. If they must blame someone for their ills ... let them curse the misce-genation that had spawned them!

Dessalines left Arcahaie at five in the morning. The rubescent sun had not yet scaled the green peaks of the hills, and the air was fresh and cool, with a taste of salt in it. The road that wound along the bay, across from the isle of Gonave, was bordered by wind-twisted shrubs and gro-tesque cactuses that thrived in the sandy loam. An almost inaudible reverberation of a tambour disclosed, in an undertone, that there was an awareness of Dessalines' approach. As he neared Port-au-Prince, he rode past cultivated plantations and noticed that Blacks dropped their implements and hid from sight as the cavalcade cantered by.

Unexpectedly, an officer of his guard left the road and dashed into a cane field. Three grenadiers turned and spurred after him. Dessalines reined in his mount, rose in his stirrups. and looked after them. Why? What had they seen? To the east, in the cerulean sky, the sun was like a spherical, igneous furnace. To the south, at the end of the white road, Pont Rouge, the bridge that led into Port-au-Prince, shimmered and danced like a mirage above the shallow water.

Dessalines glanced at his grenadiers. They were silent and imperturbable. The bastards! Did they know something he did not? Was their loyalty so fickle? He kicked his spurs into his mount and raced away from them. A mulatto officer appeared in front of the red bridge. He was scarlet-pantalooned, blue-coated. One pale hand rested on his sword hilt, and Dessalines mistook him for one of Pétion's aides. Dessalines rode toward him, unaware that his grenadiers remained in the road where he had left them. The officer made no move to salute his Emperor, but drew his sword from its scabbard. Suddenly mulatto soldiers sprang from their hiding places in roadside ditches and from behind tall, thorny cactuses. Two mulatto officers galloped across the bridge and cried, "Fire! Fire!"

Dessalines had ridden into an ambush! It was incredible. He was the Emperor!

He wheeled his horse in order to dash back up the road. No one had dared fire at him, but the Arcahaie road was blocked by a hundred rebel troops. In the distance an ascending spiral of dust followed his deserting grenadiers.

The rebels circled about him, dropped their muskets, and grasped his horse's saddle, the bridle, the stirrups—anything their hands could clutch. A roar of volcanic anger burst from Dessalines' throat as he stared down at the sea of mutinous heads and struck at them with his heavy riding crop. The faces that circled his pivoting horse were every color from freckled near-pink to cocoa brown. Hatred overcame their terror as he bludgeoned their heads. A half dozen rushed at him with fixed bayonets, yet hesitated when they reached his side. They sensed the legendary violence of this Black brute who had decimated their kin, no less than Rochambeau, and seemed, for the moment, indestructible.

Taking advantage of their hesitation, Dessalines drew the pistol from his holster and fired, point-blank, into the nearest face. They released the bit and the reins and scattered. He was free! Of course he was free. He was the Emperor. He was Dessalines! In a few weeks he would massacre every mulatto in Haiti just as he had slaughtered every white!

There was a musket report from the roadside. A young mulatto, his face cut open by Dessalines' crop, had turned, taken careful aim at Dessalines, and fired. Dessalines' mount, free of restraining hands, reared, and the bullet struck its chest. The horse fell, trapping Dessalines' leg, and a little cloud of white dust eddied about the Emperor as he struggled, with all his brute strength, to free himself.

The spell of his inviolability was broken as he thrashed about, defenseless, in the road. There were claps of musketry as both fallen horse and trapped rider were riddled with bullets. Dessalines' plumed hat fell from his head. His big hand, with its spatulate fingers, clutched at his throat, and blood gushed from his mouth. The rebels watched as a spasm shook his frame and little geysers of blood stained his coat. His bloody hand fell away from his throat and revealed two gaping wounds. His ugly face, now turned toward the blistering sun, was twisted into a grimace that tugged back his lips and disclosed his blood-stained teeth.

When they felt certain that the great Dessalines was dead, they rushed to where he lay in the dust, thrust their bayonets into his quivering flesh, and smashed at his head with the stocks of their muskets. They hacked off his fingers in order to steal his rings and stripped the gold lace from his coat.

Mulatto field hands rushed from a cane field that bordered the road. They had known of the ambush. The entire countryside had known of it, but no one had warned the sanguinary brute who had slaughtered thousands of their caste. He had reduced them to working side by side with Blacks ... with ignorant Nagoes, stinking Angolese, and thieving Congos!

"*Il fait accompli! Il fait accompli!*" they cried as they dashed to the circle about the dead horse and rider, swinging their machetes with vengeful arcs. They slashed at Dessalines' face, thrust a hundred lacerations into the flesh that now refused to bleed, hewed at his arms and legs, and finally hacked off his head. As though unsatiated, a mulatto whose angular features belied the sadistic violence in his heart, tore away Dessalines' pantaloons, cut off his genitals, and held up the hairy scrotum. From its wrinkled pouch a stallionlike phallus hung, like an elongated brown tumor.

A mounted officer clattered across the Pont Rouge, fired a pistol into the air, and ordered the crowd to disperse. He insisted that Dessalines' remains be gathered and thrust into a heavy burlap sack. A donkey was led across the bridge and the halterless animal was held while the heavily loaded sack was lifted and slung across its back. There were no girth straps and the sack sagged and fell as they tried to secure it. The officer shielded his eyes from the sun and stared over the Arcahaie road. The dust had settled and there was no one to be seen. To the left was the blue arc of the bay; to the right, the low hills. Had Dessalines' grenadiers dashed for reinforcements? Were they about to alert the little town of Cabaret? Impatient with the bungling efforts of the men about the donkey, he ordered them to desist and permitted the animal to drag Dessalines' remains across the bridge and over the highway that led to Port-au-Prince. As they approached the former capital, Blacks rushed from their thatched huts, and mulattoes began to line the highway in order to gape at the blood-stained sack that twisted and thumped as it was dragged by the slow-gaited animal.

In Port-au-Prince, the streets were deserted. But for the splash of water in its fountain and a whisper of sea wind in its trees, every public square was hushed and avoided. When the rebels reached the open square in front of the Government Palace, they flung the sack on a plot of grass and left it.

Pétion would not come out but looked at it from a balcony. He ordered that a cannon in the harbor fire a single salute. Later, he would insist that he had not ordered the assassination of Dessalines. But that single cannon blast was the only tribute he would ever pay to the first Emperor of Haiti, the brutal man who had lived and died by the only passion he understood—*violence*!

Through the droning October afternoon, the drums that echoed from every sun-baked hill informed the entire island that Emperor Dessalines was dead. Black and mulatto children, in tatters, drifted into the government square, poked inquisitive fingers through the holes that had been worn in the heavy burlap sack, and wondered at the red stains above which dozens of flies now buzzed and hovered. Mulattoes who had lost everything but their lives in the years of holocaust and bloodshed wandered into the square to look at what remained of Dessalines—the hated tyrant who had pillaged their homes and massacred their families.

When night came, Pétion ordered Dessalines' hacked remains carted to a cemetery at the outskirts of town. There the sack was dumped unceremoniously into a thicket of tall grass and scrub oleanders. From beneath a liana-tangled tree, a shadowed face watched with the furtive eyes of a hunted animal as the bloodstained sack was abandoned. It was Défilée! Some extrasensory perception had urged her to Arcahaie.

Arriving there too late, she had dashed through the town as though possessed. Tireless, aware of neither hunger nor thirst, her bare feet encrusted with gray road dust, she had followed the throbbing of the single tambour. She had reached Port-au-Prince when the sun set and, as though she truly possessed the voodoo prescience she insisted she had inherited, she had rushed to the cemetery and flung herself into its shadows.

Now, hunched like a feline, she waited until the mulatto foot soldiers left. Springing to the encrusted sack, she tore it open and suppressed a wild animal cry of anguish at the sight of its blood-smeared, mutilated contents. She drew

[203]

out Dessalines, piece by hacked piece—an arm, a leg, the battered head. . . . She laid the sections tenderly on a nearby plot of grass that was chrome-stained with patches of moonlight, struggled with the heavy, half-naked torso, and assembled the parts.

Her inherited theology insisted that only an entire man could return to Guinea after his death and, instinctively, she had brought a heavy needle and cobbler's thread. She groped in the coarse sack and withdrew the thick phallus and its black-wooled, blood-encrusted pouch. A remembrance of the uncontained and ferocious passion with which Dessalines had thrust himself past the carved-away portals of her sex welled up in her, and she brushed the dismembered genitals against her cheek. She spread the severed legs, positioned the phallus into place, tore away her shift, and then, with a wild, demented animal sob that retched up from her very bowels, she threw her gaunt, half-naked body on the horrible cadaver that had been Dessalines.

25

Confirmation of the assassination of Emperor Dessalines was brought by a military messenger to Christophe at Cap Haitien. He dictated a letter to Dessalines' widow, expressed his sympathy, asked if she felt in any danger at Marchand, and offered her the hospitality of his plantation at Milot.

He watched and waited for the next move of Alexander Sabes Pétion. He refused to believe that this cultured mulatto had voluntarily returned from France for the sole purpose of furthering his own ambition. He was mild-tempered, conciliatory . . . and Christophe recalled how he had wept at the slaughter, three years ago, when they had defeated General Rochambeau. Christophe acknowledged Pétion's altruistic desire for equality in Haiti but, with shrewd and innate intelligence, he could not envision a few thousand mulattoes governing, without prejudice, 400,000 illiterate, full-blooded Blacks whom they despised.

In December Pétion, as though he had already grasped the power of government in his hands, ordered an *Assemblée Constituanté*, a constitutional assembly, to convene in Port-au-Prince for the purpose of establishing a republic. He invited Christophe to attend as a representative. A representative! He could neither read nor write. There were few mulattoes, quadroons, or even octoroons who had no schooling! What could he and the few educated Blacks who were faithful to him achieve in a representative assembly when the entire south and west were now dominated by Pétion and the mulattoes? He recognized his limitation and refused to attend.

The Assembly met in Port-au-Prince, where it debated, quarreled, and finally drafted a new constitution. A rumor drifted to Christophe that the Assembly considered appointing him President of the newly established Republic of Haiti. Were the mulattoes tossing him a bone or did they need him to keep under subjection the Blacks who so greatly outnumbered them?

While Christophe awaited the rumor's confirmation, placated and hopeful, he cantered across the northern roads and climbed the tortuous, overgrown trails that led to the peaks of the hills. He carried his brass telescope with him, and when he would reach the summit of a cliff he would turn to study the view below him. The great plains and the once-whitewashed towns were now spectacles of devastation. The plantations were stretches of brambles and weeds, pocked by the charred remains of burnt manor houses. The blackened ruins of fires were everywhere. Every hillside was pitted by cannon balls, and the hamlets that nestled at their feet were confusions of tumbled walls and sagging thatch roofs. If left to themselves, the Blacks would never rebuild them.

He loved his people from whose loins he had sprung full-statured, intelligent, and comely. He also understood them. They needed pride! Pride in a white man's world! Pride of ownership and pride of heritage! They were not ready for a representative republic—a tolerant republic which, though it would not exploit them, would permit them to choose their own destiny. Such a choice would inevitably be influenced by their thousand-year-old love of carefree gaiety. Even if against their will, they must be educated, taught skills and professions. "Papa" Toussaint had called them his children—and so they were; but they must be trained and disciplined! For this, one needed authority. Authority!

Christophe was finally advised that the Assembly had elected him President of Haiti for a term of four years. He was elated and rushed to Milot so Marie-Louise could read the appointment to him without interruption. He intended to commit to memory its every clause and phrase; just as he had memorized entire segments of the constitutions of other nations. He would go to Port-au-Prince and accept the office of President, but would insist that Cap Haitien be designated the capital of Haiti. He would have it rebuilt and the grandeur it had once possessed would be regained. He would restore the plantations! His people welcomed idleness. What better things could there be to do than sleep away the drowsy days and dance through the night, in the moon-drenched fields, to the throbbing of the tambours and the rattle of the tchia-tchia gourds? He

[207]

would teach them respect for accomplishment and an awareness of pride!

In Milot, Christophe listened intently while Marie-Louise read the provisions of his appointment. When she began to enumerate the restrictions of the presidential office, he sprang up and cried, "Alex is wrong! Our people are not ready for self-government! Would you force shoes on a child before it can walk? A President is not a King, Marie-Louise. I realize that a President may only advise whereas a King can command, but I must make the world recognize the rebirth of Haiti! I shall restore its prosperity and rebuild its towns if I have to work, in the heat of the sun, by the side of its masons, with a trowel in my hand! Help me draft my acceptance speech, Marie-Louise. And you must teach me to sign my full name . . . *Henri Christophe.*

The following morning, when Christophe returned to the Government Palace, he was told that a boy had slept on its steps in order to gain an audience with him. The boy had walked all the way from Port-au-Prince and insisted that he would speak with no one but the Governor. When he was admitted to the reception room, Christophe's interest was kindled by his appearance. He was a boy of fourteen—perhaps fifteen—and, although slender, tall for his age. He had the tan coloration of a griffe, curling black hair, thickly lashed dark eyes, a slender mouth, and a sharp nose that was a heritage of his mulatto blood. Something about him was vaguely familiar to Christophe as he held himself stiffly erect and said, in excellent French, "I am Armand-Eugène Mongeon."

Mongeon. . . . Mongeon. . . . Christophe thought he

should know the name. Momentarily it escaped him. "You speak French well."

The boy smiled. "*Oui.* I also speak English and Spanish. And I can read and write all three languages. My mother is Lutétia Mongeon." He groped with two fingers in a drawstring pouch. "She said to give you this and you would remember." He handed Christophe a tiny nautilus shell that was pierced by a gold band.

Lutétia Mongeon. . . . Of course! The years folded back and he recalled the cottage behind the pepper trees. Armand-Eugène. . . . She had said she would name him Eugène. He studied the boy and, despite the mulatto traits, seemed to recognize a part of himself in the youngster's not-quite adolescent features. The small ears and the sturdy neck were surely as his own. The eyebrows ended in a frown at the bridge of the nose. And the ridiculous nautilus shell. . . . It had been years since he had worn an earring. The French despised them on a man, and the English considered them barbaric.

"*Maman* said you would remember her."

"I remember her," said Christophe. "How is she?"

"Well," said the boy, "we live in Port-au-Prince, now. She said to tell you she would have come with me, if she had not grown old and fat."

Old, thought Christophe. She could be no more than forty-five. . . . Forty-seven . . .?

"But it's not true," the boy added. "She is still beautiful. And graceful. She sent me to warn you that the office to which Pétion's followers have elected you is a false one. The office of "President" will be only an honorary title, like a tchia-tchia gourd that makes a noise only when it is shaken."

[209]

Christophe smiled. "You tell Lutétia that I am not a Dessalines. But neither am I a cacao tree that bows whenever a wind blows."

"It is true!" the boy insisted. "I am a page at the Assembly and have attended all its meetings. César Télémaque is a senior representative and, as though he bears you a grudge, has endorsed every request that Monsieur Pétion has made. The government is to consist of a senate of twenty-four members. Led by Monsieur Pétion, they will have the right to appoint ministers, pass laws, and control the army. The presidency will be an honorary distinction without voice and without authority." He hesitated and added, "Monsieur Pétion has slandered you. He has implied that you can neither read nor write."

Christophe sprang from the chair, his face so filled with tempestuous violence that the veins in his dark throat stood out like whipcords. The yellow bastard, Pétion, had cheated him! What would happen to his impatient dream of a flourishing Haiti? Of Black equality? He had not heard the boy's last words but grasped the acceptance speech over which he had labored with Marie-Louise and tore it into shreds. That French bastard, Pétion, was not then the placid, unprejudiced liberal he had presumed him to be; and Dessalines' assassination was actually a mulatto coup d'état to take over the government of the country! It was strange that this young Armand-Eugène, whom he had sired, should know so much and be here at this time.

"Will you stay in Cap Haitien, Eugène? You are welcome in my home."

The boy shook his head. "I must not. *Maman* is still in Port-au-Prince, and it must not be known that I have come to see you."

The boy carried himself like a man. Two years ago Marie-Louise had presented him with a son whom they had named Jacques-Victor, in honor of Jacques Dessalines. Would he grow up as intelligent and comely as Eugène? Or was it the strain of white blood that Eugène had inherited from his mother that made him as he was. He did not believe it! A Black had as much sagacity as a white! He could see it in his home where, because no patois was spoken, little Jacques' phrases were clearly enunciated in grammatical French: "*Bonne nuit, papa. Merci, maman. J'ai faim. . . .*"

"Let me give you some money, Eugène. Allow me. . . ."

"No," the boy interrupted. "I am to tell *maman* only if I was welcome."

"Do you feel welcome?"

"*Oui, papa,*" he whispered. The *papa* almost inaudible. "And now I must rush back to Port-au-Prince."

Christophe decided that he would not permit Black equality to be suffocated in a mulatto-dominated Haiti. Had not these mulattoes been spawned in Black wombs, entombed in Black flesh, nurtured with a Black's milk? The difference, then, was rooted in their upbringing and not in their heritage!

With the exception of an honor guard, almost all of Christophe's troops had been disbanded. He sent riders as far west as Môle St. Nicolas and as far south as St. Marc in order to summon them. He attired himself in his most impressive uniform—a peacock-blue coat that was edged with scarlet and embroidered with gold. Claire Dessalines sent him a huge half-moon hat that was adorned with red and blue ostrich feathers. It had been her husband's, and she insisted that Christophe accept it as a gift; as though

Christophe's appearance alone could stem the civil war toward which Haiti was now drifting.

Christophe's fervor began to wane as he marched his troops toward Port-au-Prince. Two years ago he had dismissed a spiritied and well-disciplined army. Now, as thousands flocked to his banner, he found himself at the head of a disorganized and carefree horde. Just as the untilled fields had reverted to tangles of weeds and uncultivated shrubbery, so the Blacks had become indolent and indifferent. They straggled after him now with flagrant insouciance.

As he rode across the plain. past Petite Rivière, he was joined by influential mulattoes who had left the coastal towns in order to join him. Faithful Lieutenant-General Paul Romain and André Vernet were already with him. And now Julien Prévost and Pompée Valentin Vastey rode into his camp. He did not know if they were grateful for his defense of mulattoes during Dessaline's reign or if they expected to profit by Pétion's defeat. He did not question their motives and welcomed their attachment.

When Christophe reached Port-au-Prince, he was unable to harangue the Blacks into storming its palisades. They were no longer slaves! They had joined Christophe for a lark—for the excitement the excursion offered. He placed the city under siege. Yet how could he enforce a siege when any small boat could easily sail up to Arcahaie, to Mont Rouis, or directly across the bay to the Isle of Gonave. Futilely, he battered the city's defenses, while his unconcerned soldiery bivouacked on both sides of the road and danced, with camp followers, in the moon-drenched fields at night, or watched as a wizened, ebony-black *mamaloi* whirled herself into the frenzy of a *sise de loa*.

[212]

At the end of two months, the mulattoes came in a group to Christophe's tent. Julien Prévost, his graying head indicative of his age, his cultured manner a contrast to his being on a field of battle, was their spokesman. "You must not doubt our loyalty, Henri," he said, "but we have decided that Alex Pétion's ambition is not worth a civil war. Let there be a Republic of Haiti in the south, and a State of Haiti in the north, where we shall give you our support. Alex insists that he accepts Blacks as equals; but we shall help you *make* them equal, Henri. To be accepted and *to be* are not the same. I know Alex well. He will offer the Blacks equality out of charity, compassion, and kindness. How long can such a false equality last? The equality must be earned with skills, knowledge, and dignity! We recognize our common heritage and will help you achieve that equality in Haiti."

Christophe turned to Paul Romain and André Vernet as they stood, side by side. He glanced at slender Pompée Vastey who, with his short-clipped reddish hair, could almost pass for white. "We shall follow wherever you lead, Henri," said Lieutenant-General Romain. "But our sentiments are with Julien."

In the morning, Christophe abandoned the siege and withdrew from Port-au-Prince.

26

Christophe watched, with mute despair, as his troops deserted him on the long march back to Cap Haitien. Julien Prévost insisted that he assume the title *Henri Christophe—Commander in Chief of the Empire of Haiti,* and Pompée Vastey drew up a document to attest the validity of the assertion. It was a vague and hollow title, for he now found himself a commander without an army and the head of the north provinces without a government.

He took a good look at Cap Haitien when he returned, and was conscience-stricken by what he saw. He had spent too much of his time on his prized plantation, behind Milot, and left everything in care of the disinterested Dessalines. The Rue d'Anjou and la Carenage were still cluttered with rubble. All along the Rue du Conseil, where stately buildings had crumbled, looters had stolen what the fires had not consumed. Rains had swept through great gaps where tiled roofs had once been, and the debris was now overgrown with weeds and overrun by vermin. Along the Rue Avine, parts of burned and gutted buildings were still standing—gaunt walls, blind windows, smashed balconies, and rusted garden gates that led nowhere and were filigreed with wild vines. Goats wandered among the ruins, and scrawny hens scratched at weeds in untended gardens.

Their belief in zombies still deeply rooted, the Blacks insisted that the ghosts of former inhabitants haunted the blackened and tumbled blocks of masonry and refused to disturb them. Nor had the Rue Notre Dame escaped the great fire. Though the walls of the church had remained standing, its burned roof had fallen in and its nave was open to the sky.

He had secluded himself too long! First in the converted Auberge de la Couronne and then in the Government Palace, while he had commuted to the serenity of his plantation. Now, as a seed of empire began to sprout within his dreams, he realized that Cap Haitien, the hub of his fantasy, had become a stinking carrion that was desiccated by the tropic sun. Had the Blacks no pride?

One morning he wandered on foot outside the town and noticed that where the Rue Espagnole ended, there had sprung up a camp of filthy shacks that had been erected with salvaged boards and charred timbers. Beyond the settlement, the road led through a scrub jungle of untended coffee shrubs, wild sugar cane, plantains, and banana trees grown ragged and unfruitful from neglect. He drifted back into town, and his footsteps led him to the refuse-filled Rue d'Anjou, not far from the Place d'Armes. A woman and a youngster were clearing the debris from a charred cottage. A row of broken pepper trees, with green shoots thrusting themselves insistently from their trunks, reminded Christophe where he was. The boy looked up and recognized him instantly.

"*C'est moin papa!*" he cried. "*Regarde ici, Maman. C'est moin papa!*"

"Eugène! You must not call him *papa*. Forgive him," the woman said. "I have kept him aware of all your accomplishments and, though he has been taught not to speak of it, he is proud that you sired him."

"How are you, Lutétia?" Christophe said, smiling. It was as the boy had said on their first meeting. Though no longer slender, she had not grown obese as his Marie-Louise had done. Her straight black hair was untouched by gray, her unblemished skin was a much lighter tan than the boy's, and she held herself erect with dignity and poise. The boy stepped to her side and put an arm about her waist. The gesture emphasized his slender height, and in that instant Christophe thought of little Ferdinand, whom he had unwittingly sent to his death in France. For what! For the sake of a schooling and a *bienséance* that this youngster seemed to have acquired here, among the mulattoes.

"You need not trouble yourself with the cottage, Lutétia. I have renovated the Auberge de la Couronne and I give it back to you. As a gift."

She smiled, and he recalled how she had once loved him, passionately, grateful for a young man's strong loins that had heedlessly hurdled the years between them. "I shall take the boy with me, Lutétia. To my home. I said I would take him one day."

She unwound the boy's arm from about her waist. "*Allez-vous?*"

"*Oui, Maman.*"

"You do not mind, Lutétia?"

She studied Christophe. He had grown heavier. He seemed to carry himself with pride rather than arrogance and, though his features now seemed stamped with an indomitable will she had not known he possessed, his smile was reassuring. "No . . . I do not mind, Henri. It is why I have returned to Le Cap."

27

Christophe threw himself into the rebuilding of Haiti with a tempestuous and consuming passion. He had learned that the changing world had no use for sloth, ignorance, or poverty. Animals could live their contented lives in the shade of a banana tree, but the inquisitive nature of man was fashioning a new destiny, and the Juggernaut of transformation would crush beneath its wheels those who did not clamber aboard as it moved toward its unpredictable destination. He would show the world that Blacks could, in a single lifetime, create an empire that would equal in pomp and splendor what the courts of Europe had achieved.

He often awakened Eugène at sunrise and, with a detachment of grenadiers, before the heat of the day became oppressive, they would clatter across every road and path that led from Cap Haitien. They would descend on a cluster of huts like a storm cloud, and Christophe would hurtle from the saddle while his mount still careened to a stop. The fruit of the gourd vine was hung to dry from the walls of every wattle and daub hut. To Christophe, the gourds had become the emblems of accepted poverty, for the Blacks had neither bowls nor spoons, and when the gourds were scraped clean of seeds, they would be cut into the shapes of utensils. Utensils! They had no tables, no chairs, no beds . . . and were not even aware of the need for them! Dried calabashes were their only sign of domesticity, and behind every hut the trodden grass was always littered with broken shells. Christophe would burst into the huts, drive out the half-naked Blacks, and order his grenadiers to tear down the walls and set fire to the thatched roofs. Only by making them homeless could he resettle them on plantations. Haiti was bankrupt! She had no currency and no credit, but he would see that she had crops!

He dictated letters to the English and American governments, proclaiming Haiti's return to peace and tranquillity, forecasting her restoration, and offering trade agreements and protection for their merchants. In anticipation of the return of trade, he forced the Blacks into labor units and rebuilt an entire range of warehouses along the quays in Cap Haitien. He kept watch over the masons and carpenters, as they sweltered in the tropic sun, and drove them unmercifully. Time and again he would remove his coat, grasp a trowel, and show them how mortar should be applied.

Before the sun would set he would walk to the quays and stare out over the wide bay. To the north of him were the British-dominated Bahamas; to the northwest, the tip of Florida. Why did they refuse to recognize him? Why did

[219]

they consider him a usurper? With the slanting rays of the sun on his face, he promised himself that he would lure them with the corrupting smell of profit. He had learned that the white world would exploit anything for gain!

Christophe arose early, worked late, and drove everyone with impatient urgency—the Blacks as though he owned them, his advisers as though he were their sovereign. Since he rarely went to Milot, Marie-Louise moved back from the plantation and established herself in the Government Palace. She was disturbed by the compulsion which now possessed him completely. When he would return, after dark, she would exhort him, "You are killing yourself, Henri. It's not worth it."

"Not worth it? Look at yourself, Marie-Louise. Look at me. What are we? Thoroughbreds are created by breeding, but we have no time for breeding, Marie-Louise. I must create Black thoroughbreds in Haiti in one generation. One generation! Rub my back, Marie-Louise; and my shoulders. With that cottonseed oil and pimento. And read to me. Have you some new book on the courts of Europe? Some new pamphlets?"

She pattered back with the liniment, but did not bring the new pamphlets that Vastey had given her that day. She knew Christophe would fall asleep before she had finished massaging his tired back.

Christophe spent four years in rebuilding the towns, restoring the plantations, and designating work for Blacks according to their abilities. He was elated when England finally accepted a commercial treaty, and he welcomed the English merchants who opened trading posts in Cap Haitien. He had known that, with the restoration of the plantations, the wealth of Haiti's sugar, coffee, cotton, and indigo would become once more irresistible to foreign trade. He wanted Black-dominated Cap Haitien to be recognized as a great port, and he restored the public parks and supervised the construction of a majestic palace, on the west side of the Place d'Armes, where he decorated the main hall with portraits of famous British statesmen. He had bought what vessels he could, and by April, 1809, the State of Haiti owned seven ships of 112 guns and a navy of over a thousand sailors. It was not formidable but it was a nucleus. It patroled Haiti's harbors and bays and was comprised entirely of Blacks!

To Christophe's pleasant surprise, mulattoes, who had won their freedom in America, began to migrate to Haiti. They came from as far north as the New England states and as far south as the Louisiana delta that had been purchased from France by the United States. He welcomed back Dupuy, who had just turned thirty. When he had resigned as Dessalines' secretary, he had emigrated to Philadelphia where, with shrewd investments, he had amassed a small fortune. Haunted by his love for the tropic island where the foliage was always green and the winters were free of snow, he had sold his business interests and returned. He brought a friend, a freed Negro by the name of Saunders, who had been born in New England and had attended Moore's Charity School at Dartmouth College. English abolitionists had suggested that Saunders go to Haiti. Now that it was free of French domination, he could organize schools and further the cause of Protestantism. Catholicism, with its Trinity and its innumerable saints, was too complicated for the untutored, and the Blacks must become Christian converts!

Christophe insisted that Dupuy and Saunders accompany him over the mountain trails in order to visit the outposts of the new state. One morning they rested their horses on a ledge, after a long and arduous climb. While the horses nibbled at tufts of grass, they looked down at the island that was spread beneath their feet. The sun was a huge brazen gong, infrared, in a faultless blue sky. Down in the green valleys the villages were like clusters of toy cottages, and the plantations were patchwork quilts of yellows and browns and vermilion. In the distance a Negro cultivator, unseen, was chanting a low, monotone song of Africa. Somewhere a goat bleated, and its cry echoed from the warm rocks while humid mists hung motionless in the distant hilltops.

"You have done a great deal since I left, Henri," said Dupuy.

"No! I have not done enough! I want the world to see what Blacks can accomplish! I must not let them rest until they have taken a giant step in the white man's world. I want the cultivators bound to the plantations and not allowed to leave their work without permission. Now they shirk or wander away, led by any whim that urges them. I shall give them fixed hours of work and rest. And I must discourage promiscuity. I have seen that family ties encourage pride and personal ambitions. I want them to rear the greatest number of children in a reputable manner. I will see to their care and education. But I must have authority. Authority! A president can only suggest but a king could command! I want Haiti to have a king!"

Dupuy was silent, but Saunders seemed startled. "We have no king in the United States. It is true that my brothers are still enslaved, but they look forward to freedom because there is no king who will own them once they have gained their liberty. I am free."

"Exactly!" cried Christophe. "Exactly! You are free but you are also cultured and educated. There lies the key to the white man's world. Culture and education! Would even a fool attempt to harness a thoroughbred to the shafts of a dray? We have a republic to the south of us, Mr. Saunders. Complacent with its illusion of freedom, Pétion's government has not rebuilt a single town, repaved a single road, or rearmed a single fortress—in the event of a new invasion by France, by Spain . . . even by England! The plantations are as devastated as when Pétion first assumed office, and its citizens are as unconstrained by regulations as the republic that permits them to fritter away their lives in the sun.

"My Blacks are like children, Mr. Saunders. For their own good, until they have grown into manhood, I shall shape their destiny. Dupuy will help me fashion laws for them. I hope that you, Mr. Saunders, will help me destroy the voodoo cults and the *hungans* that perpetuate their African superstitions. The world is watching us. Come, I have work to do."

They followed Christophe down to the plain. He tied his big-brimmed hat to the pommel of his saddle, and his round head was bare to the blazing sun. They watched him as he sat his horse, his long legs thrust out, his broad back erect. He allowed his reins to hang slack so the horse could pick his way carefully over the loose stones in the narrow trail.

"This is my native land," whispered Dupuy. "I am constrained to remain here."

"Nor shall I leave," breathed Saunders. "These are my people. I shall stay and watch how Henri Christophe shapes their destiny."

28

*S*hrewd and foresighted, though his education consisted only of what Marie-Louise read to him of the history of other nations and the important journals of the day, Christophe gathered about him only those who could best help him with the administration of his new government. Not influenced by color, judging men only by their abilities, he carefully formed a state council that recognized the thorny task of framing a code of laws suitable to the heterogeneous Haitians—statutes that would be welcomed by the knowledgeable *sang-mêlés,* and ordinances that would, without too great resentment, transform illiterate Blacks into hard-working, law-abiding citizens.

Recognizing Christophe's ambition and the need for indisputable authority in a government that was supported neither by precedent nor representation, the Council of

[224]

State met privately in March, 1811. It subscribed unanimously a motion that would offer Christophe a crown; and voted that Saunders, who was influenced by his knowledge of American democracy, prepare a draft for a Royal Constitution.

Christophe was elated. "I shall dedicate my life to the welfare of my people," he cried to Marie-Louise, "and not be a despot such as Dessalines permitted himself to become. It is too soon to replace the language of Haiti—it will still be French—but I shall change all else! I shall lift the people from ignorance to industry, and the Kingdom of Haiti, with a complete disregard for the color of a man's skin, shall take its place among the nations of the world!"

Remembering the paucity of Dessalines' coronation, Christophe determined that his own would be effected with pomp and splendor. Recalling that the tattered Blacks had milled about outside closed doors when Dessalines was crowned, he decided that his ceremony would be open to all. He sent for books on heraldry and accounts of coronations in the kindoms of Europe. The church of Notre Dame now had a new roof but, rather than regild an old structure, Christophe decided to build a pretentious cathedral. He urged Father Corneille Brelle to leave Port-au-Prince, where he had attached himself to Pétion after Dessalines' assassination. Marie-Louise doubted that Father Brelle would come, but she was wrong. He deserted Pétion with alacrity, for Christophe offered him the title of Grand Almoner to the King and promised to appoint him Archbishop of Haiti.

While Christophe waited impatiently for the completion of the cathedral, he met with his advisers and established a hereditary nobility. They decided upon four Princes—two of royal blood—and two Princesses. There would be eight Dukes, twenty-two Counts, thirty-seven Barons, and forty Knights Chevaliers. Christophe's head swam as his advisers suggested appointments for the royal household . . . chamberlains, masters of ceremonies, heralds at arms, pages. A neoteric aristocracy was being established in the Caribbean.

On April 12th, Christophe issued dress regulations for the new nobility. He wished his court, patterned after that of England, to be as lavish and formal as any in Europe and the minutest detail of etiquette to be strictly observed. He invited foreign representatives to attend. He wanted them to observe what Blacks could achieve if given the springboard of initiative; and on April 20th, he created his order of chivalry: the Royal and Military Order of Saint Henri, which would be the Haitian equivalent to England's Order of the Garter.

Indefatigable, obsessed by his ambition to achieve greatness for himself and his people, he arose early and worked until long after dark. No far-flung plantation was too small for him to visit and no misdemeanor too petty to warrant his personal castigation. His charm became magnetic, his physical endurance inexhaustible, and his aspirations more expansive as the day of his coronation approached.

One night Christophe asked Eugène to accompany him to the Champ de Mars in order to inspect the new cathedral. He had learned that Eugène, now nineteen, had been baptized, and he speculated upon how deeply the roots of the church had embedded themselves within him. A deep affection had sprung up between them and Marie-Louise had not protested when Christophe had recognized him, titled him a Prince, and established him as le Duc du Môle.

They left the Place d'Armes and took a shortcut across the rebuilt Place Montarcher. The coronation was to take place in three weeks and, in order to ensure the completion of the cathedral, Christophe had ordered every mason, carpenter, and craftsman within a hundred miles to assemble in the Champ de Mars. The artisans now worked through the night in rotating squads, while the tropic moon's yellow light was augmented by smoking flambeaux. The immense walls of the cathedral were finished, and above its roof rose a towering belfry in which a set of chimes would be hung. As they entered the unfinished nave, brightened by dozens of little blue flames whose wicks floated in gourds of coconut oil, Christophe noticed three Blacks, curled in a corner, fast asleep. He rushed to them and kicked at them with his boot. They were big-chested Congos who had been brought from the jetties of Port-de-Paix. They rose to their feet with the indolent grace of slow-moving animals.

One of them folded his heavily muscled arms and challenged: "Moé pas esclave! Moé pas travayé!" [I am not a slave! I don't want to work!]

Christophe glared at him in anger. He was addressing Henri Christophe, who would soon be the King! "Free whites work everywhere in the world," he appeased. "And so shall the Blacks, in Haiti!"

"Blanc travayé, li mangé pain." [The white man has to work, he eats bread.] "Li Noir pas bessoin, Li mangé patate. Li managé banane." [The Black doesn't need to. He eats sweet potatoes. He eats bananas.]

[227]

Christophe pivoted. His arm shot out, and his big fist smashed into the Black's jaw without warning. The blow would have felled a young ox. The Black staggered but remained on his feet. "Je suis le roi!" bellowed Christophe. "Je sui le roi! Everyone works in Haiti! Or starves in the military stockades!"

Cowed, the Blacks turned and climbed the ladders that led to the unfinished belfry.

"Louable. Out, très louable," said a voice in the shadows.

Christophe turned and recognized Father Brelle. He had learned that the priest came here often on cool nights, to observe the progress. "I am impressed by its architecture," said Brell, "but I still maintain that you should have built the cathedral in the Place d'Armes. A church as imposing as this one should be located in the central court of a town."

Christophe, irritated by the incident Father Brelle had witnessed, answered, "Notre Dame is already within sight of my balcony! Must I fill the sky with reminders of my obligations to your God? I have built you a new cathedral, and you are still not pleased!"

The lean and sallow Breton smiled. He had exiled himself from France, to Saint-Domingue, where everything had gone wrong. Now he had left the company of learned and gracious Pétion for the dominance of an untutored Black. And yet, what could Pétion give him in his impoverished Republic where everything was decaying? Even the church! This shrewd Black, with his magnetic personality, had offered him unlimited funds and the office of chaplain to a King . . . perhaps an Emperor!

He was aware that Christophe, unlike Toussaint,

scorned the church and called its God a plaster image with which it intimidated the Blacks. Well, he would do more than frighten the Africans. He intended to subjugate them with tales of hellfire.

"I would like you to know my son," said Christophe with a trace of pride in his voice. "Prince Armand-Eugéne. . . ."

The priest did not quite hear Christophe. He was thinking of his title: *His Grace, Monseigneur Corneille Brelle, Duc de l'Anse. Archbishop of Haiti.* A white Archbishop in a Black land! But what did that matter, as long as he was the Duc de l'Anse? There would be enough whites and mulattoes to make life interesting.

───── 29 ─────

*O*n *June 2nd, the citizens of Cap Haitien filled the Place* d'Armes and lined themselves, shoulder to shoulder, along the coronation route. They had been told that members of the coronation ceremony would gather in the palace, proceed along the former Rue d'Anjou that had been renamed Cours de la Reine, and then along la Rue Avine to the new cathedral in the Champ de Mars. Mulattoes and full-blooded Blacks, griffes, quadroons, and octoroons sweated uncomplaining in the congested Place d'Armes for two hours, until finally, with an impressive roll of English drums and trumpet blasts from four heralds at arms, Henri Christophe appeared, stately and majestic. His heavy legs were in white silk stockings and his small feet in high-heeled, black leather pumps whose burnished gold buckles reflected the morning sunlight. Despite the torrid heat he had dressed himself in a quilted satin vest, adorned his heavy shoulders with golden epaulets, and buttoned a gold-embroidered, peacock-blue jacket almost to his throat.

He glanced down to where the royal carriage waited patiently at the foot of the steps. An honor guard of grenadiers, with drawn swords, was at full attention behind it. Marie-Louise reached Christophe's side, and as she lifted the train of her satin gown with one gloved hand she placed the other, with delicate grace, upon Christophe's extended arm. The elegance of their descent was not lost upon the quiet watchers, who withdrew to make way for the approaching members of the court, so that they could assemble at the foot of the palace steps, with proper protocol, in order to follow on foot behind the royal carriage and its honor guard.

The crowd was awed and hushed. They had never seen such a display of pomp and ceremony. As the members of the new nobility gathered behind the carriage, they formed an assemblage of red morocco shoes, gold-hilted swords, black-and-red plumes, satin gowns, and embroidered coats—stiffly postured beings with alert eyes, lifted chins, and proud mouths. Not until the carriage moved forward and the procession followed it was the spell broken. The crowd broke into a thunderous applause and, after a moment's hesitation, followed the ostentatious cortege through the Cours de la Reine.

In the Champ de Mars, the new royal arms of Haiti had been hung above the cathedral's entrance, flanked on either side by a black-and-red national flag (the blue and red having been usurped by Pétion's republic) and a banner that proclaimed: *Liberty! Independence! Honor!*

Christophe glared at the newly created nobles as some of

them rushed to take their places on the cathedral steps. A rehearsal had instructed them to form a double line and remain there until after their majesties had entered. Christophe had invited a number of Americans and Englishmen to attend the ceremony. Affluent merchants and ships' captains were now in Cap Haitien, and he wanted them to observe that his coronation was as well regulated and impressive as that of any European monarch; and the nobility that he had created as aristocratic as that of any worldly court!

Slender Julien Prévost sidled up and down the line of nobles, whispered last-minute instructions, and led them into the cathedral, where they seated themselves with studied decorum. They had been instructed to stand or sit rigidly at attention; and, though they did not turn their heads, they could not keep their dark, restless eyes from observing the niches that held freshly painted plaster saints. Motes danced and tumbled in a wide beam of brilliant sunlight that thrust itself through an aperture which had been left open to the blue sky, for a stained-glass window, ordered from abroad, had not yet arrived. Black aristocrats glanced about with diffidence. Yet a constrained, newborn arrogance tugged at their mouths, for Christophe had ordered erected a tremendous cupola that rose almost to the very beams of the Gothic ceiling. Above a carved and majestic throne was stretched a magnificent, crimson baldachin—gold-fringed, gold-embroidered, sprinkled with stars, and emblazened with gold phoenixes—perhaps to signify the rebuilding of Cap Haitien from its ashes. Toussaint had once refused a simple baldachin to shield him from the sun, reserving its right to God, but Henri Christophe's pretensions accepted no limitation. The unfinished walls were draped with blue silk, spattered with gold stars; and the path to be taken by the King was carpeted with an Aubusson runner into which the newly designed royal arms had been woven.

The nobility sweated in the hushed cathedral and wondered at the delay. The doors had been left open to any and all observers. The nave and the narthex were packed with onlookers, and the heat became oppressive. Finally, preceded by heralds at arms, Christophe and Marie-Louise entered from a sacristy. Marie-Louise turned with grace, despite her heavy figure, and approached the crimson-hung tribune that had been reserved for her and the members of her household. Her white satin gown was richly embroidered with gold sunflowers, and its train was looped on each side with gold tassels. A gold net fell from her left shoulder. Gold combs, studded with precious stones, held her headdress of gilded feathers in place. Her broad face beamed with good nature and seemed to express, without articulate words, *Do you see? Do you see what Christophe has achieved?*

Christophe stepped to the altar and glanced to his right, where the Archbishop's purple-canopied chair was strangely unoccupied. Behind it, he could see the children's choir that had been rehearsed to sing a motet. Their scrubbed faces were like little brown pumpkins above their white tunics. Had Corneille Brelle deserted him? He would flay him alive!

The newly appointed Archbishop rushed in, slightly disheveled and out of breath. A maniple dangled precariously from his left wrist, while his right hand clutched the chasuble to his heart, as though he were in distress. Stifling with the heat of the crowded cathedral, for the press of the onlookers had now sealed every doorway, he inaugurated the coronation with as much haste as would not incur a reprimand, for he had begun secretly to fear Henri Christophe. With simulated devotion, he anointed Christophe's forehead, carefully placed a golden crown on his head, a jeweled scepter in his hand, and intoned: "Henri—by the Grace of God and the Constitutional Law of the State, King of Haiti; Sovereign of Tortuga and Gonave; Destroyer of Tyranny; Benefactor of the Haitian Nation; Defender of the Faith...."

Christophe ascended the throne and surveyed his subjects with unassuming dignity, as though he had been born to rule. A messenger was rushed to the quay where an English frigate, the *Reindeer*, had escorted three English merchant vessels to Cap Haitien. It flew the Union Jack at the poop and the black-and-red of the State of Haiti at the main—a recognition of its new government. A salute of twenty-one guns burst across the bay, thundered and echoed from the hills that shouldered Cap Haitien. An English regimental band thrust its way to the cathedral steps, struck up *God Save the King*, and followed the rendition with *Rule Britannia*, so that one could not tell if they were honoring the newly crowned King Henri or their own King George. Within the cathedral, the music sobered the Blacks, filled Christophe's chest with pride, and discomfited Archbishop Brelle, the only Frenchman within its sound. Outside, exuberant cries of *Vive le Roi! Majesté! Majesté! Vive le Roi!* seemed to fill all Cap Haitien. Rada drums burst into sound, and full-blooded Blacks shouldered themselves into space for twisting, turning, and stamping their unshod feet. Now that Christophe was King, they would never have to work again! Their lives would be one continuous round of feasting, dancing, and love-making!

From where he sat on his gilded throne, Christophe surveyed the pomp and splendor of the court that he had created. The nobles, Black and mulatto alike, were dressed in magnificent tunics. Their white silk hose and their gold-buckled shoes were lost to sight, but the light glinted from the polished hilts of their swords. The Princes and Dukes were attired in gold-embroidered black coats with scarlet facings, the Counts and Barons were in cardinal red, and the Knights in bright blue. The four Princes were seated together. Christophe had given André Vernet the title Prince des Gonaïves, and placed him in charge of finance, for he was considered above suspicion or corruption. He was past seventy and sat with his veined hands in his lap. His gray head lent an emphasis to his fine-featured, aristocratic face. He had held the office of Treasurer, under Dessalines, after Dupuy had left, but had not been able to keep that dissolute despot from tottering on the brink of insolvency.

Lieutenant-General Paul Romain sat at Vernet's side. Christophe had established him as Prince du Limbe, his birthplace, and appointed him Minister of War. He had been with Christophe through all the campaigns, and he felt assured of his loyalty and devotion.

Prince Armand-Eugène and Prince Jacques-Victor Henri were seated side by side. Little Prince Jacques-Victor, plump, with a round unsmiling face that pouted with disinterest, was a sharp contrast to his slender half brother.

Christophe glanced toward Joseph Rouanez, whom he had titled Duc de Morne and appointed Minister of State. Was he ill at ease? Uncomfortable? Three weeks ago he had overridden protests that Rouanez was neither Black nor Haitian, but Spanish with a family in Santo Domingo, where slavery was still permitted. Christophe had pivoted about the council room and cried to his advisers, "And what were you? And you? And you? I have no interest in what a man was. Only in what he can accomplish! And whether or not Haiti needs him."

He studied expatriate Rouanez now, for a fleeting moment. He was young, handsome, and patrician in his bearing. He was a linguist, well educated, shrewd . . . and with his olive skin, could easily be mistaken for a quadroon. Yes, he had made a good choice.

As he had made in elderly Julien Prévost, his private secretary, whom he had elevated to the important post of Secretary of State and Minister of Foreign Affairs, with the title of Comte de Limonade. Educated in France, Christophe considered him the most cultured and distinguished of his associates and was grateful for his attachment. Any other woman but Marie-Louise would have accused Christophe of being influenced by Prévost's young wife, an astonishingly beautiful mulattress but, if Marie-Louise had such a thought, she kept it to herself.

He caught a glimpse of Pompée Valentin's round head with its thick, crinkly red hair. Christophe recalled, with a smile, that Dessalines had always referred to him as "the white nigger." Educated in France, he had accepted Prévost's vacated post of private secretary and, after much deliberation, Christophe had granted him the title of Baron de Vastey and appointed him to the Privy Council.

Christophe glanced to the left of the altar where Queen Marie-Louise was seated on the tribune. She was perspiring from the weight of her headdress, but her round, sable face was placid and serene. Little eleven-year-old Princess Athénaire was seated to one side of her and thirteen-year-old Princess Améthiste on the other. Unlike their insipient brother, they had already mastered their lessons in French grammar and were studying a history of the European courts. He must take little Jacques-Victor in hand. Perhaps if he imported a private tutor....

Christophe's thoughts were interrupted by the sound of a staff on the marble flooring. Names were being called; nobles sidled into the nave and pressed forward in order to receive the *Royal and Military Order of Saint Henri.*

"Julien, le Comte de Limonade...."

"Richard, le Duc de Marmelade...."

The titles were taken from townships that had been named, long ago, by the French. One by one the nobles approached the throne, bowed, and then stood at attention while Christophe pinned the Order of Saint-Henri onto their tunics—a black-and-red ribbon that was looped through a medallion, set with brilliants and enameled with lapis lazuli. On one side, under a royal seal of two gilded lions embracing a crown, was a casting of Christophe's head and the inscription, *Henri, fondateur, 1811*; and on the other a crown of laurels, a star, and the words *Prix de Valeur*, a phrase endorsed by Christophe, who could read neither English nor French.

As Christophe pinned the Order of Saint-Henri on tunic after tunic, he acknowledged to himself that his dream of empire was coming true. First Haiti, then Jamaica! He would extend the dominion of his Blacks as far north as the Bahamas and as far east as the Windward Islands. The whites had uprooted them from their coastal homelands in Africa. He would educate them and make the entire Caribbean their new *Guinea!*

That night the entire Place d'Armes was illumined with torches, and a grand ball was given at the palace. By Chris-

[237]

tophe's order, no social distinctions were to be recognized, and gaping citizens, their Black skins burnished by fastidious scrubbing, filtered into the ballroom and watched fascinated, as mulatto Barons payed their respects to newly created Black Duchesses. Masons, carpenters, and cultivators, in stiff white shirts and short pantaloons, drifted past clusters of English sea captains, American traders, and Black generals in dress uniforms and polished knee boots. Members of an English military band and native drummers sat side by side and, between renditions of cotillions, minuets, and chicas, the immense candle-lighted ballroom was filled with uninhibited laughter of the Blacks, clipped English phrases, nasal French chatter, and a babble of patois repartee. Servant girls with trays of tarts and glasses of wine passed and repassed deftly among them. Commander Douglas, of the frigate *Reindeer*, asked for a moment of silence and proposed the health of the new monarch. The officers of his vessel rushed to his side, raised their glasses, and cried, "Hear! Hear!"

Christophe lifted his glass to them. He had spoken only French in every public gathering. Now, to their astonishment, he proposed in precise English: "A toast to my brother, George the Third. May he always be a constant friend of Haiti!"

"Hear! Hear!"

The military band struck up a fresh cotillion. White traders and mulattresses approached the dance floor, while the Blacks, citizens and nobles alike, drifted to the sanctuary of the chair-lined walls. Their retreat was not lost upon observant Christophe. Equality seemed to have a hundred unacknowledged facets. There was so much to strive for and so little time in which to achieve it!

Christophe sipped from every glass that was offered to him—native rum and *tafia*, Bordeaux wine, red Burgundy, English sherry. He was unaccustomed to drinking, and the stiffling heat of the room was making his head swim. He decided to steal away from his guests and lave his head and face. He entered a bedroom at the head of the stairs, and caught sight of a young mulattress. She had lifted her gown and was adjusting a drooping stocking. As she glanced up, he recognized her and was startled by her beauty. She was the young bride of Richard, the new Duc de Marmelade. He had not been aware of her enchanting loveliness but now ... now his heart beat within him like a yearling's hooves. Marie-Louise, never comely, never really graceful, had grown obese. One could say of her only that she had accepted the white man's God, practiced the virtues with fidelity, and expected him to do the same.

He unbuttoned his tunic, approached the young Duchess, and encircled her with his arms. She was all crumply satin and soft contours, her little breasts like bursting buds that had not yet flowered into womanhood, her skin like rubbed rosewood. She reminded him of Lutétia, when they had both been young, and he kissed her hungrily. He gathered her gown so that he could lift it and thrust his hand under it. To his amazement she thwarted his effort by turning away, and he was left with a fistful of bunched satin. Her dark eyes widened with anger and, as he tugged her toward the bed, she thrust her fingers into his thickly curled hair and pulled with all her strength. He thought it a gesture of foreplay and kissed her averted face with an awakened passion that had smoldered within him through all the war years. As she opened her mouth to protest, his tongue darted in and, instantly, she bit it. Despite the torpid fuzziness of his mind and his aroused passion, he felt the hurt and was aware of the trickle of blood on his lips. He tossed her onto the bed and cried, "Je sui le roi. Je sui le roi!"

"And I am not a whore!" She sprang from the bed and faced him, enraged and defiant. "You are drunk! I shall not tell Richard for, King or no, he would cut out your entrails and feed them to the fishes!"

He dabbed at his lip and chin as she dashed from the room. The incident sobered him and he was saddened by awareness of the passage of time. *No!* he told himself as he turned to the mirror and surveyed his reflection. *No. . . . Not yet!* His crisply curling hair was turning gray at the temples, but he was strong and vigorous. He had grown heavy, but he was tall and well proportioned. There were many who considered him handsome. Both Toussaint and Dessalines had enjoyed many mistresses—Blacks, mulattresses, even whites—and Toussaint had been wizened and puny, Dessalines brutish and ugly. He had been faithful to Marie-Louise! For eighteen years he had slept with no one else. And now a young Duchess had audaciously spurned a King and taught him that everything was a matter of time and place . . . and courtship.

He saw Marie-Louise in the mirror as she entered the room. Heavy, perspiring, unsmiling. "Are you ill, Henri? Our guests are asking for you. There are a Dr. Duncan Stewart, of Edinburgh, and a Mr. M. J. Moor, of London, who have just arrived and wish to be presented."

Nothing seemed to arouse the suspicion or disturb the tranquillity of Marie-Louise.

30

Disturbed by the occurrence in the bedroom, Christophe found himself concerned with time. He was forty-four years old, more than half his life was gone, and there was so much to do! He wanted every devastated plantation restored and the irrigation system rebuilt. He divided state lands and leased them to members of the nobility. He met with members of his privy council—Vastey, Prévost, Rouanez, André Vernet—and drew up a *Code Rural* that would regulate the lives of Haitians from Prince to vagrant. One-quarter of the crop on every plantation was to be paid to the state, and one-quarter to the workers as wages. Every adult man and woman in the kingdom would be required to work from daylight to 8 o'clock, given an hour for breakfast, work from 9 to 12 noon, given two hours in the heat of the day for their rest, and then work from 2 p.m. until nightfall. Later, he would grant them privileges. Now he wanted the cultivators bound to the soil and no one permitted to change residence.

André Vernet demurred, "Haiti will become rich, but in Pétion's republic it will be said that you have returned the people to modified slavery."

"It is true," said Dupuy. "The citizen will no longer have his freedom."

"Freedom!" cried Christophe. "I shall give them whatever freedom they can understand. They will not be required to work on Saturday afternoons or Sundays, and they can go to the villages and spend their money as they please. I shall build hospitals for the sick and require landlords to support the aged and infirm. This alone will give them freedom—freedom from want and freedom from care. Would you maintain that I encroach upon freedom when I insist that begging and female licentiousness should be severely censured? Prostitutes and stragglers shall be arrested and forced to labor for their livelihood. Every child must attend a school where he will be taught reading, writing, and simple arithmetic." He smiled, glanced about him, and laughed, "The children of Haiti will become better educated than their King. Would you call that slavery, André?"

Because of Christophe's driving and relentless compulsion, Haiti became richer than she had been under French dominion. In one year, Christophe's plantation alone produced more than ten million pounds of sugar; and the single port of Cap Haitien, whose name he changed to Cap Henri, exported, besides sugar, twenty million pounds of coffee, five million pounds of cocoa, and four million pounds of cotton.

In his rush to become self-sufficient, Christophe induced

experts to come from England and build a weaving mill in Cap Henri so Haiti could cease to import cotton cloth. His heart burst with pride as he watched full-blooded Blacks tend the spindles and shuttles. They were taking a giant stride from the soil to industry . . . stepping into the white man's world with true equality!

More and more Englishmen came and settled in Haiti because of her munificent and profitable trade. Cap Henri lay on the way to Jamaica and was a convenient shelter during the hurricane months. Visits of full-rigged British men-of-war put heart into the Britons who bought Haiti's produce and sold Birmingham pots, lanterns, and bracelets in the markets along the quays.

Christophe built a handsome clubhouse for the English, on a coastal strip beyond which he would allow no European to go without his special permission. He frowned upon miscegenation. What Haitians accomplished must not be attributed to the white blood in their veins, nor should their acceptability by whites be in proportion to their Caucasoid physiognomies!

Unsettled and indefatigable, Christophe began the construction of seven chateaux and a half dozen castles close to the principal towns of his kingdom; and gave them such fanciful and evocative names as The Cloak, The Scepter, The Necklace, The Embuscade, Victoire, and Belle-vue-le-Roi. As though he intended to surround himself with majesty wherever he might be, he dashed about the countryside, supervising and hastening the work, dressed in a severely plain jacket with no decoration other than the gold medallion of the Order of Saint-Henri, and carrying a stout, silver-knobbed cane in imitation of his model monarch, George III.

In the midst of this driving work, this compulsion to erect enduring symbols of his reign within sight of Le Limbé, Cap Henri, Port-de-Paix, Gonaïves, St. Raphael, and a dozen other towns, he was tortured by the remembrance of the young Duchesse de Marmelade. She had aroused in him a restless and insatiable passion. During his visits to the construction sites of the chateaux and castles, he took a continual round of mistresses, paid them with gifts, and abandoned them. So casual were these dalliances that he could not remember from one day to the next with whom he had slept the night before. He had presented them to the world as Baronesses, Duchesses, and Countesses—the elite of a new nobility—and they presented themselves to him as whores!

Restless, his dream of grandeur still unfulfilled, he returned to his plantation and began to build a palace at the edge of the pleasant little town of Milot. This was the spot he loved best. This would be his home! A wide valley stretched itself between the hills and, if one climbed the slope of a precipitous mountain that thrust its head and shoulders just behind Milot, one commanded a view of his plantation that stretched toward Plaisance to the west, the Plaine du Nord to the north, and beyond it Cap Henri, the harbor, and the sea. He erected his palace with its back against the foothill of this mountain and decided to call it Sans Souci [without care]. He insisted that the palace must become a showplace of the West Indies—the symbol of a Black man's pomposity, taste, and interests. While the building was going on he stayed at Milot and rushed each morning to direct architects, masons, carpenters, glaziers, and decorators. He strode about tirelessly amidst the clatter and confusion. Meanwhile his secretaries, his Minister of State, his Minister of Foreign Affairs, and members of his Privy Council pattered at his heels, for there were commercial agencies to be established, diplomatic treaties to be sought; and correspondence was the only contact with the outside world. A hundred letters were dictated and signed amidst the acrid smell of plaster, the resinous scent of freshly chipped pine wood, and the sounds of tapping hammers and rasping saws. Epistles to foreign governments were interspersed with orders for paintings, crystal chandeliers, Gobelin tapestries, and *objets d'art*. He wanted the rooms floored with marble and paneled with polished hardwoods. He wanted emphasis placed upon spaciousness, everything built on a scale of grandeur—yet insisted that he must endorse the selection of every chair, every candlestick, and even the books for an extensive library though he would read no single word that they contained.

Christophe was at peace. The restless, driving energy that had impelled him to erect his monuments, his chateaux and castles within sight of drowsy villages, now found an open sluice gate in the completion of magnificent Sans Souci. It rose four stories above its highest terrace and dominated the entire countryside—a testimonial to a Black King's prestigious affluence. It was a gaudy bouquet of color in the tropic sun, for its roof was of red tile and its walls of bricks plastered over with bright yellow stucco. In order to keep its great Hall of State cool, a mountain stream was conducted under its floor, and the diverted water gushed out from a marble arch in front of the palace, spilled for twenty feet over a bright blue wall—a simulated sky—and cascaded down a channel that was painted a rich Pompeian red. Christophe had considered every extraneous detail of Sans Souci, and its formal garden was filled with statuary, while the majestic staircase that led to its terrace was flanked by stone sentry boxes. He had built stables, a special barracks for the palace guard, a small arsenal, a completely equipped printing shop and a royal chapel—for Marie-Louise had become devoutly religious. And yet, if one were to ask Christophe what he admired most in Sans Souci, he would have replied, without hesitation, its façade. For beneath the fretted iron gates of its main entrance, under a white portico flanked by tall French windows, was a central arch surmounted by a great, gilded sun and the bombastic legend: *Je vois tout et tout voit par moi dans l'univers.* [I see all, and all in the universe see by me.]

When the palace was completed, Christophe made a final tour of inspection alone. If there were faults to be found, changes to be made, he would rely on his excellent memory. He wandered through the banquet hall, the audience chamber, and examined the rich tapestries and the carefully chosen paintings. He sauntered through the exquisitely furnished suite of rooms that he had chosen for himself and Marie-Louise. He glanced into private rooms that had been prepared for guests. In the library, knowing he was unobserved, he fondled the gilt-embossed covers of the books and wished that he had taken the time to become literate so he could assimilate, perhaps utilize, the knowledge they contained. He wandered out onto the terrace, and as he approached the staircase he could hear the splashing of the diverted mountain stream. He descended to the gardens and made his way to the royal stable. Horses were in their stalls, and harnesses, embossed with the gilded coat of arms of Haiti, hung from pegs on the whitewashed walls. He had groomed horses once, in the stables

[246]

of the Auberge de la Couronne, and had been owned as one owned a dog or an ox. He was enough of an altruist to realize that he had not accomplished all this by himself . . . but Boukmann was dead, as were Maurepas, Toussaint, Dessalines, and thousands of others whose bones were rotting in the marshes and in the fields.

Christophe opened Sans Souci on a Thursday and declared that public audiences would be held in his Throne Room every Thursday afternoon. There, for one hour, his subjects could come, witness the pomp and ceremony of the Kingdom of Haiti, see for themselves the proud heritage that their King was founding for them, air their grievances, or address their monarch on any matter directly.

He insisted on the strictest court etiquette. The nobles were required to appear in especially prescribed dress, immaculate and correct to the last button. The position of each chair was assigned according to rank, designated by pages. The new *haut monde* of Haiti, the nobles, took their places with their consorts in a semicircle that faced the dais on which the King and Queen were seated. There were no vacant chairs, for Christophe had made it plain that he would forgive no absence on a Thursday. They were all there, seated beside their wives . . . Princes, Dukes, Counts, Barons, and Knights Chevaliers. Many a man among them was a full-blooded Black who had been born on an earthen floor where an exhausted slave woman had writhed in lonely pain and squeezed him forth like an animal. Such men could not break themselves of sleeping on a palm-fiber pallet, a lifelong habit, or preferring boiled plantain and rum to grouse and white wine, but they cherished the dignity of their titles and the magnificence of their court costumes. Their coats were so embroidered with gold lace that one could not tell the color of the cloth, and their shoulders were so burdered with enormous and ostentatious epaulets that the vast audience chamber seemed filled with gilded tassels. Nature had separated them by physical differences, society had segregated them by their abilities and endowments, but he, Christophe, had united them with pomp and ostentation. He glanced from proud face to constrained countenance. Among the Dukes and Duchesses, he caught site of the young Duchess of Marmelade, and could look no further. He had not seen her since the coronation . . . and yet he could feel a vein begin to throb in his temple. To his surprise, she smiled at him as though the incident in the bedroom had never happened. He averted his face and gave his attention to the barefooted cultivators and artisans who began to drift into the Throne Room and wandered about in order to study its magnificence. A chamberlain tapped on the marble flooring with his staff and informed any who had a grievance to come forward and express it to His Majesty. The visitors were either without wrongs to be righted or intimidated by the grandeur of the audience chamber and the pageantry of the assembled nobles; for they retreated and pressed their backs to the walls in silence.

As Christophe waited for some criticism to be presented, he glanced again at the young Duchess. She seemed as slender as a sunflower stalk and as supple as a kitten. Her husband Richard sat beside her with apparent indifference. Had he grown tired of her, or was he taking her youth and beauty for granted—as though it would last forever? She had parted her hair in the middle and combed it to each side so that, from beneath her tiara, the dark tresses fell to

[248]

her slender shoulders in a graceful cascade. She had the burnished skin of a mulattress and the prominent cheekbones of a griffone. Her mouth was full and sensuous. Her dark, intelligent eyes wandered about the Throne Room and studied the imported paintings and tapestries on its walls. Two years ago she had been offended by the impetuous advance of a newly crowned and inebriated King. Now she seemed impressed by the pomp and splendor that Henri Christophe had created.

No one appeared restless as Julien Prévost, Comte de Limonade and Secretary of State, read new regulations:

Workers are not to go into town unless properly dressed.

The cart whip, the symbol of slavery, has been abolished; but punishment for misdemeanors will still be inflicted by canes and lianas.

Every boy shall be compelled to learn a trade. The government will supply both the masters and the tools.

From now on, the study of English shall be required in the schools. The more advanced students shall be urged to learn Spanish.

Etc. Etc.

When the audience hour was up, a page sounded a trumpet that was hung with blue-and-gold tassels. The assemblage rose to attention as Christophe adjusted a great cocked hat, offered his arm to his consort, and left the Throne Room, his gilded scabbard swinging with his stride while Marie-Louise, warm and perspiring, hurried her mincing steps in order to keep pace with him.

[249]

31

Four white men, out of curiosity, adventure, or profit, gravitated to Christophe's court at Sans Souci: Dr. Duncan Stewart of Edinburgh, Mr. M. J. Moor of London, Señor Domingo Torres of Madrid, and Father Juan de Dieu Gonzales of Santo Domingo. Christophe had met Dr. Stewart, a tall dour Scotsman, and Moor, mathematician and *bon vivant,* on the night of the coronation. He had engaged Dr. Stewart as "private physician to the King," appointed him the director of the Royal Hospital, which was nearing completion, and established a chair of anatomy and surgery for him in a College of Medicine that was as yet on paper. Had Moor no engineering skill to recommend him, Christophe would still have found quarters for him in the palace, for he was widely traveled and possessed a carefree, infectious laugh and an inexhaustible fund of fascinating anecdotes. Nor would he part with the company of Señor Torres, for his knowledge of the customs, history, and political intrigues of the Spanish court was expansive. Christophe insisted that Father Gonzales remain and officiate at the Royal Chapel, for the Cuban had confessed, to Christophe's delight, that he had atheistic tendencies and could not determine, in his mind, whether or not to completely abandon the church, for it was steeped in mythology. Was not the same snake that the Africans worshiped, coiled under the naked feet of the Virgin Mary in almost all the statuary?

Rouanez, le Duc de Morne and Minister of State, himself of Spanish ancestry, welcomed the newcomers effusively. André Vernet and worldly Julien Prévost accepted them with reservation; while impetuous Pompée Valentin mistrusted the sincerity of their attachment. Whether they were opportunists or not, their travels and erudition became a leavening rapport among them. As their mistrust of each other dissipated, their communal evenings on the terrace, filled with tropic starlight, where Saunders and Dupuy would join them, evolved into fast friendships, despite their diversity of backgrounds, attainments, and ambitions.

Christophe would be the first to leave the gatherings, although reluctantly, for now that Sans Souci was completed he set himself a timetable for the further growth of Haiti. With a true perspective of the world about him, he forced himself to remember that, despite the cosmopolitan and unprejudiced atmosphere on the terrace, in Jamaica, in St. Croix, in Guadeloupe, in Barbados, in Grenada ... in a hundred far-flung islands ... even in the Republic of the United States ... white men owned Blacks!

He would awaken early, descend the grand staircase

[251]

accompanied by a sleepy-eyed page who carried his battered telescope, stride across the Sans Souci gardens, saddle a horse without disturbing the grooms, and disappear into the concealing overgrown paths that spiraled upward into the hills. Every cultivator and artisan, from Milot to Cap Henri, knew that Christophe might appear at his elbow if found idle! From the rocky eminences of the hills, Christophe could look into the scattered villages and, with the aid of his telescope, into almost every hut. He dashed from building site to building site—in Plaisance, in Limbé, in Port Margot—applied his silver-knobbed cane vigorously to idle heads and shoulders; and issued stockade sentences to rebellious workers and dissenters. There was no time. No time! The Blacks were tortoises in a race with white hares! The gangs of masons and carpenters might doubt the benefits he was bestowing upon them, but in order to instruct their children Haiti must have schools! He was importing English educators, and so that he could do away with uncivilized drums and supplant them with a postal service, he galloped about and gave his personal attention to roads and bridges.

At midday, before returning to Sans Souci, he would stop at a secluded chateau that he had built on a hillside at the edge of L'Acul—a halfway mark between Cap Henri and Milot. There he would refresh himself and rest awhile. He admitted, to himself, that he was aging, that he was no longer inexhaustible; but he refused to return to Sans Souci while he showed evidence of fatigue. One afternoon, to his amazement, he found the Duchess of Marmelade in the sheltered chateau. She had dismissed the servants, filled a slipper bath with tepid water, and prepared a lunch for him on a shaded balcony that overlooked the chateau's garden. To his further astonishment she entered where he was laving himself, knelt unabashedly beside the tub, and proceeded to rinse his back. The fatigue of the morning left him and he swept a hesitant indecision from his mind. He reached behind him, grasped her wrist, and tugged her to him. Two years ago when he had cried, "I am the King!" she had protested that she was not a harlot. Yet she had remained in his thoughts as though she had conjured a concupiscent spell on him. After Sans Souci was completed he had seen her every Thursday in the Throne Room, seated beside her husband. Lately, their glances had met more often and had been held much longer. Each seemed to relinquish the sight of the other with apparent reluctance.

Two weeks ago he had appointed Richard Military Governor of Cap Henri. Was the presence of the Duchess a payment for the appointment? Was this encounter with or without Richard's knowledge or consent? Did every female, from slave to aristocrat, barter her most essential being for material things?

He rose from the slipper bath and, as though the sight of his nakedness was more natural to her than the elegance of his court dress, she began to towel him. When his sable phallus rose, its crimson bud bursting from its prepuce, she said, "Richard does not know. He would disembowel me. And I have neither been seduced by the splendor of your palace nor the nobility of its court. You have aroused an insatiable curiosity within me. It has made me dissatisfied with Richard and torments my nights. I have seen how you look at me, and I give myself to you without reservation—but not because you are my King. You may call me Mariée. Come." She led him from the slipper bath with one hand. With the other, she tugged at the fastenings of her gown.

32

G reat Britain's Foreign Office, overwhelmed by curiosity as well as the fabulous growth of Haiti's profitable trade, for England had become the island's best customer and most valued friend, suggested that Sir Home Riggs Popham, Commander in Chief of the British West Indies fleet, call at Haiti.

It was to be Christophe's first official visit from a foreign power. He relied upon Moor, who claimed to be a specialist in world politics, and Dr. Stewart, who was familiar with London, to guide him and instruct the members of his court in the proper amenities and protocol.

When Sir Home arrived in Cap Henri, Christophe dressed himself in a uniform of white satin trimmed with gold, chose the apparel for the entire royal family, and sent

Baron Dupuy, whose English and courtly manners were impeccable, to escort Sir Home to Sans Souci.

Popham, expecting to find a still-devastated Cap Henri, despite its bustling trade, was astounded to see a freshly rebuilt city with a seemingly carefree and integrated populace. Prepared to accept the hospitality of illiterate and temporarily flourishing Blacks, he was as much impressed by Dupuy's knowledgeableness and elegance as he was by the royal, London-built carriage that was sent for him. Drawn by four matched grays, the interior was lined with rich velvet and its cornice, supported by figures of liberty, was surmounted with a royal crown and a profusion of gilded lions. As they drove along the wide, stone-paved royal road that ran straight from the gates of Cap Henri to the palace of Sans Souci, Sir Home found himself listening to Dupuy's informed discourse on politics, books, and personalities. It was almost impossible to believe that this was a country being governed by and established for the Black savages that his countrymen had bartered and helped to uproot from the shores of Africa, as one tore useless weeds from a field. He was impressed by the beauty and freshness of the countryside, the cultivated fields on either side of the road, the drowsy, pastoral simplicity of Milot; and he was astounded by the majestic elegance of Sans Souci. Sir Home was tall and distinguished, with an unsmiling mouth and a slightly tilted head that minimized the angular sharpness of his features. He had attired himself in a full-dress uniform and chosen his aides with care in order to impress Christophe. To his amazement, when he was ushered into the Throne Room, he found the elegance of his staff eclipsed by the splendor of Christophe's courtiers; and he was pleasantly surprised by the presence

of whites—Mr. Moor, Dr. Stewart, Señor Torres, and
Father Gonzales, who had dressed himself in the vestments
of the church. He could not deny that he was in the presence of royalty—no matter how recent or bizarre its gene-
sis—and when the presentations were made he said clearly,
"I am honored, Your Majesty," and bowed.

They retired to the informality of the library, where tea
was served, and the conversation shuttled first between
Moor and Dr. Stewart, who was well versed in English lit-
erature; then between Dupuy and Saunders, who spoke of
Thomas Clarkson, the English abolitionist who, with Wil-
berforce, had helped to abolish the British slave trade.

Sir Home permitted himself a wry smile and darted at
Saunders, "Americans were so anxious to gain their own
freedom, yet I find them reluctant to bestow it upon
others. Every race should have the right to fashion its own
destiny." He glanced about the room, at André Vernet, at
Julien Prévost, at Pompée Valentin Vastey, and added,
"Or be assimilated."

Christophe sat and listened to them in silence. He was
no orator and seldom took part in contentions, but now he
said, "My race is as old as yours, Sir Home. In Africa there
are as many Blacks as there are white men in Europe.
Here, before we drove out the French, there were a
hundred Negroes to every master. The world is beginning
to insist that governments should be instituted for majori-
ties. Yet here, where we were a majority, we were slaves.
Except in Haiti, nowhere in the world have we resisted
you *en masse*. We have suffered, grown dull; and, like
cattle under a whip, we have obeyed you. Why? Because
we were diversified and had no pride! And we had no

pride because we had no material possessions—the goods that have become the Damballa, the god, of the white man's world."

Christophe paused as he noticed Sir Home Popham listening to a reverberation of sound whose resonance filtered through the open windows. "They are drums, Sir Home," he said. "Somewhere my people are dancing. It was all they once had—the drums, laughter, love for one another, and courage. But white men could not understand what we had. You despised our primitive culture, killed our snakes, and broke the stones you thought were our gods. If we had had wealth—monuments, towers, palaces—you would have respected us. I shall try to accumulate that wealth. I shall give my people a reason for pride if I have to break every back in my kingdom!"

That night, at a state banquet, Sir Home drank vintage wine from a golden goblet, wiped his lips with a damask napkin embroidered with the coat of arms of Haiti, and accepted the actuality that he was in the presence of regal splendor. What would have astonished him would have been the disclosure that the King was illiterate, for at one point, slightly tipsy, Christophe leaned toward him and said, bombastically, "I intend to confound the calumniators of our race by proving to the world that we are in no respect inferior to other inhabitants of the globe. We shall demonstrate that we are capable of acquiring and practicing the sciences, the arts, and attaining civilization to an equal degree with Europeans. To the National Schools, one of which can be viewed from my terrace, I am adding Royal Academies and intend to found two Royal Colleges. Every child in Haiti shall be educated, and moral virtues

[257]

will replace ignorance and dissoluteness. France still plots to return us to slavery, but we have become citizens of the world. Should the universe conspire to return us to slavery, the last Haitian will resign his last breath rather than cease to live free and independent!"

33

If Marie-Louise was aware of the reason for Christophe's protracted visits to the little chateau at the edge of L'Acul, she gave no intimation of that knowledge. Her round face remained serene and, though their physical intimacies had eroded, she appeared secure in the depth of his marital obligations and his attachment to their daughters—to precocious Améthiste and comely Athénaire.

Christophe dashed on every free afternoon to the secluded chateau that was shaded by tall palms; filled with the scent of hibiscuses, oleanders, and jasmine; and hushed, but for the distant, wind-born chant of cultivators in the fields, the echo of a rada-tambour in the hills, and an untiring choir of frogs in a nearby marsh. He was morose and impatient when Mariée was late . . . brooding and angered when she did not come. It was not her youth alone to which he had been first attracted, then attached as though she had spun a web about him. Unfettered by the taboos of the Christian church and untouched by the hypocrisies of the white man's moral ethics, she was part woman—with a façade of guile, promises, and deceptions; and part animal—curious, sensuous, responsive, and passionately fulfilling. He found himself wondering what life would have been like with her, when he was young, and conjectured a large brood of children, unlike fat and sluggish Victor-Henri, but cast rather in the mold of Armand-Eugène.

One afternoon, as she stepped from the slipper bath, a golden goddess with her dark hair curled into a *Chinois* bun, she said to Christophe, "Richard says you are a tyrant; that no matter how benevolent your intentions, your heavy hand is often resented."

He never tired of looking at her long-waisted form and the supple grace of its every movement.

"Richard says that Pétion is favoring mulattoes, restoring estates that Dessalines confiscated, and has abolished the annual tax on crops."

"Pétion is a fool," Christophe said. "If one does not tax a country's crops, one is forced to tax its labor. His republic, with its worthless tin currency, is bankrupt. He has grown soft, like an old woman sitting in the sun."

"Richard says Pétion is giving land to the Blacks."

Suddenly he lost his patience with her and cried, "Richard says. Richard says! What does your Richard know? Your Richard is Military Governor of Cap Henri only because I appointed him so. Does he think I have no knowledge of what goes on in Pétion's Republic? A Republic with an empty treasury? The Blacks have freedom there, but they live in ignorance and poverty. Blacks are unprepared for absolute freedom. They have not yet acquired habits of industry and possess no self-direction. Pétion is permitting them to acquire land by simply squatting on it. But what will they do with it! The entire Republic is a prey to indolence, disorders, thefts, and crimes!"

She turned away from him as though she did not want to see his face distorted by wrath or acknowledge the irascibility with which his words were enveloped.

"You drive too hard, Henri, and you are losing the support of the army that no longer sees you."

He drew himself up to his full height. "The army? I am the army. *Je sui le Roi!*"

She was thrusting her hands through the armholes of her shift, and her voice was muffled by the cotton cloth as she informed him, "You are to be assassinated, Henri. Assassinated!"

He grasped her by the arms and shook her. "Who told you this? Has Richard told you this?"

"No. Not Richard. I have heard it from others. Corneille Brelle is in constant secret correspondence with Pétion. The Archbishop has been unable to tame you with his God and you have not compelled the Blacks to kill their snakes, discard their thunderstones, or break their rada drums. Marie-Louise worships the Trinity, but you merely permit the existence of the Church."

"That French bastard!"

They had not heard the clatter of the horses and were unaware that they had visitors until Richard burst into the room. He was booted and spurred and, as he looked from Mariée to Christophe, the fury and rage that his face expressed softened to resentment as though he had expected to discover someone else. He was disconcerted for a moment and then, a portion of the anger returning, he asserted, "Sire, you are being flattered as 'Papa Christophe,' the father of all the children of Haiti—but I have no desire to become the parent of your son!" He offered his arm to his wife. "Are you coming, Mariée, or must this day end in violence?"

She turned to him as though his appearance were long overdue. Their leaving was interrupted by Christophe's matter-of-fact voice: "One moment, Richard. One moment. When you return to Cap Henri, I want you to place Corneille Brelle under arrest."

"Monseigneur Brelle? The Archbishop?" His voice decried knowledge of any plot against Christophe.

"The Archbishop. And if it were the Pope himself, it would still be an order!"

The following Saturday, Christophe rode to Cap Henri at the head of the *Chasseurs de la Garde*. Father Juan de Dieu Gonzales rode on one side and Prince Armand-Eugène on the other. Directly behind them rode Gaffie, a big-chested Black who had been appointed the state executioner. Gaffie's mount was caparisoned in black and, as though to display the insignia of his office, he rode with a drawn saber across his saddle. Richard, prompted by perversity, had not carried out the order to arrest Archbishop Brelle, and Christophe had authenticated the rumor that there was actually a plot against him being fomented, by mulattoes, in Port-au-Prince.

Did they hate the Blacks so much? Why? It was true that most Blacks were still unwashed, unkempt, untutored, and unskilled, while the mulatto, that bastard issue from miscegenation, whether by consent or rape had hurdled into the white man's world and even embraced his senseless inhibitions and religious myths. Well, he would change the image of the Blacks if he had to smash every *hounfour* in Haiti! He had no fear of the dark cults and did not believe the mysteries of their *vaudou*. He would build more schools! More factories! He would make Blacks as acceptable as mulattoes!

They reached the Champ de Mars and clattered across the square, to the cathedral where Christophe had been crowned four years ago. The *chasseurs* formed a double line in front of the impressive structure. Christophe, Prince Eugène, and Gaffie dismounted and entered while Father Gonzales waited at its steps. His broad-brimmed hat shielded his face from the tropic sun, but he was uncomfortably warm and suddenly felt ill at ease. He was two hundred miles from his birthplace. The new Haiti with its declaration of tolerance for all had attracted him, but now the land, despite its affluence and nobility, seemed beneath its surface, as violent as the eruptions that had once created its mountains.

Flanked by Prince Eugène and powerful Gaffie, Christophe strode through the nave of the deserted cathedral and burst into its sacristy. Archbishop Brelle was seated at an escritoire, engaged in writing. He turned, saw them, and sprang to his feet. Christophe motioned to the desk and, as Brelle shuffled backward, Eugène began to rummage through its drawers and scatter papers on the floor. He hesitated and said, "A letter from Jean Pierre Boyer . . . This one is from Pétion. It requests a listing of our garrisons."

Christophe's face was suffused with anger. Brelle had

backed against a wall, speechless, his lower lip trembling.

"Gaffie!" roared Christophe and pointed an inflexible finger of accusation at Brelle.

"*Sanctuaire! Sanctuaire!*" cried the Archbishop as he extended a crucifix toward the Black, who hesitated to strike him. Gaffie feared all gods, whether known Damballa or unknown Christ.

Christophe rushed to Brelle and, impelled by violence at the thought of this imposter whose false blessings he had accepted, he tore from him both the crucifix and his tunic. As the superstitious Gaffie still hestitated, Christophe wrenched the saber from his hand and thrust it through the Breton with such ferocity that he impaled him to the wall. Followed by Eugène, he strode from the sacristy without a backward glance.

Outside, the square was filled with bright sunlight and citizens who had been attracted by the elegance of the *Chasseurs de la Garde.* Christophe strode to Gonzales and looked up into the Cuban's face. "You are now the Archbishop of Haiti," he informed him. "I assure you that religion and government shall never drink from the same gourd in my kingdom; yet I will be kinder to traitor Brelle than he would have been to me. You may give him the last rites before Gaffie beheads him and carts him away."

As though nothing had happened, Christophe led the *chasseurs* over the Cours de la Reine and turned in the direction of the quays. They cantered to one side to permit a number of gendarmes to pass by. They were escorting three Dominicaines from the town. Christophe had revived an old punishment for prostitutes, and the gendarmes were parading them through the streets, each astride an ass, naked and facing its tail. The girls were young; one a quarteronné, the others mulattresses with regular features and outthrust breasts. They were unabashed, and their arms hung listlessly at their sides. The townspeople were unimpressed by their familiar nudity and one of the gendarmes, a young Black, held their rolled shifts under one arm so he could toss them at the prostitutes when they reached the gates of Cap Henri.

Christophe dismounted when they reached the Place Royale and, with Eugène at his side, climbed the promontory where the mansion that the Leclercs had occupied was a mottled shadow behind the shelter of its palms. Sir Homel's flagship was still anchored in the bay. On the quay, at the foot of the Rue du Conseil, a platoon of soldiers was guarding a number of iron chests, each one secured by a heavy lock and the royal seal. An officer and a detachment of British sailors were transporting them to the flagship, for Christophe had entrusted Sir Home with four million pounds in gold, to be deposited in the Bank of England, in the name of Marie-Louise Christophe.

The sight of the departing gold and the thought of Brelle's treachery touched Christophe, for the first time, with a sense of insecurity. He turned and said, "I am not a tyrant, Eugène, but I insist upon making my people ambitious and knowledgeable. When I see red coffee berries rotting, neglected, I am angered by the waste. And when I see a Black, sleeping in the sun, I think of him reading a book or acquiring a trade. They say that all Henri Christophe understands is work, power, and pomposity; but in the time that remains to me I must accomplish what I have planned. My subjects do not love me but, if they obey me, that is enough! When death opens this fist, my work will be done. Haiti will be strong, rich, proud! Then the

Blacks will not forget Henri Christophe, who not only gave them equality but acceptability. Until that time, if I am not loved as a man, at least I must be obeyed as a King!

"Le Duc de Marmelade has not carried out my order. You must go now and place him under arrest. He is to be confined until I determine his sentence . . . and I suggest you take Gaffie with you."

34

The assassination plot sobered Christophe and awakened
a realization that he was ringed by enemies. Nearby America, fearing the effect a Negro state might have on her slave
system, refused to acknowledge his authority. France, once
again a monarchy, plotted a fresh invasion of the island.
She planned to return Negroes to slavery (their "natural
lot"); but she would be magnanimous to mulattoes and
permit whites to assimilate them. Assimilate them! Is that
what Pétion now desired? Damn Pétion! Christophe
wanted Blacks to retain their identity and dictated an open
letter:

> "To all the Sovereigns of the world . . . to mankind
> at large, to the whole universe: look upon us and
> witness the determination of Haitians to remain free!"

Aware of France's intention to invade, Christophe organized, once again, a large standing army. He imposed the harshest discipline and held formal reviews on parade grounds, where he gave the most meticulous attention to details of dress and drill. The uniforms of the officers were extravagantly colorful, the skill of the soldiers above reproach. Yet he sensed that something was lacking. They were no longer slaves, looking forward to freedom; but well-fed, unambitious Blacks who were being kept from their pleasures and their beloved life of indolence!

Sensing that he could no longer entrust the preservation of his government to troops who were fickle or rely upon the disaffected loyalty of officers such as Richard, who once would have followed him anywhere and executed any given order, Christophe decided to import mercenaries. Had not Great Britain always used them? He chose them from the warlike kingdom of Dahomey, which had conquered both Wydah and Ardra—powerful, full-blooded Blacks. Refusing to buy them as slaves, he arranged to hire them and imported an initial 4,000 carefully selected Dahomans. He gave his full attention to their training and paid little regard to indications that the Haitian regulars resented the imported Africans. He did not deny that they were paid more and better treated. Why not? The Royal Dahomets, as he called them, were quickly disciplined and responsible to him alone! He formed one hundred and fifty of the youngest and most powerful into a *corps d'élite*, a personal bodyguard under the name of the Royal Bon-Bons, dressed them in magnificent elegance, and was assured of their immediate loyalty.

Louis XVIII, having been placed upon the French throne, concluded that he could succeed where Napoleon had failed. He promptly sent two envoys to Haiti to nego-

tiate a return of the island to the status of a French colony
. . . a French colony and slavery. There it was—after
twelve years—the eruption of the boil that had festered
and never completely drained! But the island was no
longer Saint-Domingue, as the French still called her, not
Hispaniola as America termed her . . . but Haiti! She was
free and self-sufficient! A quarter of her natives had
become skilled in crafts. Many had become literate and
knowledgeable. Would the French revert them to the
status of animals while the Caribbean, from the Bahamas
to the Windward Islands, watched and waited? Christophe
refused any veiled or overt gesture of appeasement but,
with a ruthlessness that he had learned from Dessalines, he
executed one envoy as a spy and sent the other ignomin-
ously home.

Dessalines had begun and abandoned the construction
of a great fortress that straddled a mountain peak, 3,000
feet above the sea. Haunted by the nightmare of an immi-
nent French invasion, Christophe rushed to complete his
fortress. He intended to build an impregnable stronghold
—a citadel—to which he could retreat with his family, his
personal bodyguard, most of his army . . . and continue to
battle against whatever the white world would hurl against
him. The difficulties seemed insurmountable! Thick, tropical foliage barred most of the way to the mountain top
and even mules could not climb up the precipitous paths
that led to its summit. A mulatto engineer by the name of
Henri Bassé evolved a design for the citadel, under Christophe's direction. Its proportions and ramifications
equaled the ambitious endeavor of a Pharaoh! Christophe
assembled hordes of laborers, put them to work under the
tropic sun, and made virtual slaves of them. The cart whip
—the symbol of slavery—had been abolished, but he did

not hesitate to order his drivers to lash the sweating Blacks with thick liana stems, in order to enforce discipline and submission. Bricks for the inner walls were molded on the mountain peak, but enormous blocks of stone were dragged, pushed, and pulled up the winding mountain paths with ropes, rollers, pulleys, and the exertions of straining muscles and breaking backs. Exhausted Blacks were permitted brief periods of rest on platforms cleared for that purpose. From these resting places, panting and sweating, they would look down into green valleys, wish they were once again in the sun-drenched cane fields, and curse Christophe. Beyond a final resting stage the liana-tangled trees, bushes, and creepers were left behind. From here it was almost impossible to proceed, so treacherous were the smooth surfaces of the rocks. There were now no scrub saplings to grasp and, when one turned and looked down, one could see only the sharp facets of precipices and deeply-scored gullies in which streams trickled and shone like shards of glass.

Not since the construction of Sans Souci had Christophe's time been so taken up with a single project. He spent entire days on the mountain summit as the completion of the citadel became an obsession. He envisioned it as a gesture of defiance against the white world, and lives became expendable as huge slabs of stone and scores of cannon were hauled to the mountain peak. Self-assured, recognizing only the motivation for the fortress, he did not realize that the forced labor he was exacting was planting the seeds of rebellion.

Slowly the citadel emerged, breathtaking and awesome in its immensity. It seemed to grow out of the very mountain cone on which it rested! A maze of passages and galleries wound and twisted beyond its iron-studded gates, while deep within the bowels, murky dungeons now confined those who dared to defy Christophe.

On October 1st, 1814, Christophe received a letter from France. Dupuy broke the Bourbon seal and read its contents to the impatient Christophe. He was offered French citizenship, the island of Tortuga, and a title—in return for his acknowledgment of the sovereignty of Louis XVIII. Christophe's resistance, the letter said, would only end in his own death and the annihilation of all Haitians!

Christophe's anger was volcanic as derision and retaliative threat struggled to erupt from his throat at one and the same time. A title when he was already King! Tortuga! An islet that he already owned and could gallop across in an hour! And the letter made no mention of either freedom or equality for Blacks! He thrust a quill into Dupuy's hand and cried, "I refuse to negotiate with France on any other footing than that of power with power and sovereign with sovereign!"

Christophe increased the size of his army, with feverish haste, and impressed enlisted men into toting military supplies to the fortress. Their grumbling protestations fell on deaf ears. Six miles of serpentine mountain paths led from Milot to the citadel, and up those paths, cleared of loose stones, the sweating Blacks, like a column of gargantuan ants, lugged casks of gunpowder and heavy cannonballs. Now and again a careless or clumsy shifting would drop a thirty-pounder and it would instantly skitter downward, gather momentum, crash down the mountainside and carry with it three or four screaming Blacks.

As it neared completion, the citadel became the most titanic fortress that had ever been constructed in the western world. Its massive walls, twenty to thirty feet thick, rose in some sections to a height of one hundred and forty feet. The very rock of the mountain was tunneled and casemated to provide shelters for battery positions. A stone staircase led to four galleries where the snouts of cannon were thrust through embrasures . . . three hundred and sixty-five cannon . . . cannon that had been cast in England, in Spain, even in France! The citadel could house a garrison of 10,000 men. Vast cisterns could store rain water, and there would be enough supplies to withstand a year's seige. A miniature palace was erected for Christophe at one corner of an immense parade ground, and a larger one, named after his favorite bird, the *ramier* (wood pigeon), was constructed on a neighboring slope.

Distressed by Christophe's abandonment of the secluded chateau at L'Acul, Mariée packed a few belongings in two donkey pouches and made her way to the unfinished citadel. Christophe roared with astonished delight as he saw her approach. He swept her into his arms and immediately wondered how much of his irascibility and drive for the citadel's completion had been goaded by the denial of his sexual hunger for her. They planned the furnishings for the miniature palace, as though they were newlyweds, and plotted to send Richard to the Marcassi River, across from Dajabon, for which Christophe would offer him the rank of General. Later he would order him to patrol the coast from Gonaïves to St. Marc. Even as far south as Cabaret.

Mariée's visits to the citadel became protracted and extended, upon occasion, to a fortnight. Her name, Mariée (bride), had once been titilating and appropriate. Now Christophe thought of her as *éspouse*. On cloudless nights they would leave their bed and saunter to the larger palace. From the flat roof of Le Ramier, open to the trade winds, they could see the islet of Tortuga across a stretch of dark-blue sea. Nearer at hand, below the foothills of the mountains, past a stretch of cactuses, they could see the moon-drenched plains ... a countryside dotted with plantations that were bounded by hedges of citron and lime. This was Haiti. Fruitful, prolific Haiti! The free Haiti of which Toussaint had dreamed, for which Dessalines had fought, and that he, Henri Christophe, had rebuilt. Time was a fleet runner. Boukmann's uprising had erupted a quarter century ago and more than half the Blacks now on the island had never known slavery ... had never seen any other land. He would never relinquish this cherished Haiti to the enslavement of France!

One night, on the roof of Le Ramier, Mariée startled Christophe by declaring: "I would like to bear a child, Henri. A son."

A child! He was past fifty! It was years since he had given any thought to offspring. He was still vigorous but there were times when the presence of Marie-Louise and his daughters made him feel as though his loins were now a superfluity.

"But what of Richard?" he parried.

She watched a shooting star arc across the sky and vanish into the distant sea.

"He no longer comes to my bed. Do you still sleep with Marie-Louise?"

He recalled that she had once promised: "I give myself to you without reservation." Had she changed?

"You are my love, Mariée," he said. "You are the spirit that soothes my mind and the flesh that satiates my hunger ... but Marie-Louise is the Queen."

Determined to eradicate vestiges of French dominion, Christophe announced his intention to declare English the official language of Haiti and to change the state religion from Roman Catholic to Protestant. De Dieu Gonzales, with his unorthodox attachment to the Church, should not mind; and Saunders would be elated. He advised Saunders, who was in constant touch with American abolitionists, that he would subsidize the emigration of freed Negroes from the United States to Haiti. They would assist in introducing the English language and should welcome Haiti's freedom from discrimination.

Despite his recognition by England, there was a constant thorn in Christophe's pride. Periodicals and pamphlets that reached Dr. Stewart, Mr. Moor, and Señor Torres attested that the white world watched and waited for Haiti to collapse. They still considered the Blacks an anthropological link between animal and man and refused to believe that Negroes were capable of maintaining a stable and efficient government or establishing a moral and cultured society. French journals influenced by exiled Creoles, began a campaign of slander and mockery directed at Haiti. They lampooned pretentious Christophe as a crass, despotic savage and ridiculed the elaborate court that he had established at Sans Souci. No one knew better than Christophe the contempt with which Negroes were regarded by all but a few whites. He had observed their scorn and indifference, years ago, in the Auberge de la Couronne. Enraged because his people seemed to understand neither his pride nor his ambition, he grew savagely impatient; and attempted to plow under, in a single generation, the heritage of a thousand years!

As he had boasted to Sir Home, Christophe founded a Royal College and lured schoolmasters from England. But it would take at least two generations to educate enough

Blacks! He had frowned upon miscegenation. His ambition had been to have full-blooded Blacks help him achieve an enviable position in a white man's world. But now, impatient with the inherent languor of the Blacks, admitting his country's need for white men . . . for their skills, their knowledge, and their energies that even a tropic climate could not seduce, he issued an edict under which a white man who married a Haitian woman would qualify for full citizenship after one year, and a white man who married a Negress, anywhere in the world, might settle in Haiti. He must make the world acknowledge that Blacks were an acceptable facet of humanity! In a great vault, under the dungeons of the citadel, he stored millions of gold coins with which he hoped to purchase the Dominican section of the island from Spain. It would be a stepping stone to his dream of empire in the Caribbean.

On many nights, unable to sleep, he would leave Sans Souci and clamber up the twisting mountain paths that led to the citadel. When Mariée was not there he would be provoked by her absence, aroused by the scents in her boudoir and storm through the small palace in a fit of tempestuous anger. In a private chamber of the fortress, he would change into a ragged coat, torn knee breeches, and a pair of lime-caked boots. He would climb a ladder to an unfinished point on the highest rampart, and in a little while the night watch of the garrison, gathered about their fires. would be attracted to the heavy slap of wet mortar and the sound of bricks being tapped into place. Cold fear would touch the hearts of the sentinels as their eyes were drawn to the sounds of the trowel. Mists scudded up from the sea and obscured the moon but, when the heavy, low-hanging clouds parted, one could see, silhouetted against the sky, a

[275]

lonely figure . . . bending, lifting, tapping . . . indifferent to the bats that darted through the embrasures and skimmed about on spread wings. It could be no other than a living dead—a zombie! The startled sentries listened for the sound of other trowels and accepted the rumor that Christophe had resorted to the use of zombies in order to complete his citadel. It was a fate which might become their own—to be dug up from their graves!

Hounfours, where forbidden rites were exercised, sprang up on every hillside, and the nights were filled with the ceaseless throbbing of rada-tambours. The Blacks now buried their dead in deep pits. They drove wooden stakes into the chest cavities and rolled huge boulders on top of the graves so that the dead could not be exhumed to join Christophe's night workers—to become zombies with expressionless faces and no human light in their eyes.

35

In August, Marie-Louise attended her patronal festival,
the fete of the Assumption, in the little village of Limonade. A cortege of carriages bearing Duchesses, Countesses,
and Baronesses had assembled at Sans Souci early in the
morning, paid their respects to the Queen and left, preceded by the King's Light Horse and the Queen's magnificently uniformed corps of Royal Amazons.

It was Sunday. Despite the clatter, Christophe had slept
late, an unusual indulgence, and awakened in a seemingly
deserted palace. He had been having fitful, recurring, half-
remembered dreams of Dessalines and Défilée, whom he
had not seen in years—and was disturbed by them. Not
quite refreshed, he entered the terrace through a studded
oaken door that led from his private bedchamber. Below
him, shimmering in the sun, were the royal stables; west of

them, the Petit Palais and the barracks of the household troops. Behind him, where he could not help but see it if he turned, towered the completed fortress, like a massive gray ship that thrust its prow into the clouds—a strange mirage in the blue sky. Obsessed by his dream of greatness, tortured by how much remained to be accomplished for Haiti, angered by the spread of dark cults and the return of the superstitious Blacks to the sinister mysteries of *vaudou*, he wondered what else he could do to hasten the civilization of the island. He would debate the matter with lax de Dieu Gonzales and concerned Saunders.

As the day progressed, Christophe became restless. Marie-Louise would be attending Mass now, encircled by the family and the ladies of the court. Prince Eugène would be there. He was a devout Catholic, and Marie-Louise had accepted him as though he were her own son.

He wondered if Mariée would be at the Queen's fête. He had not seen her since he had learned that she was with child. Did Richard abuse her? Richard had never forgiven his arrest at the time of Brelle's treason and was embittered by his sentence of a month's hard labor in the citadel . . . as though he were a common Black!

At a last moment, Christophe decided to go to Limonade. He informed his *corps d'élite*, and gave orders for his horse to be saddled. It was high noon, and most of Haiti rested in the shade. The vertical rays of the torrid sun burned relentlessly on his perspiring back as he galloped over the empty, white-dusted road. Thoughtlessly, he whipped his sweating mount so that he soon outdistanced his bodyguard of Royal Bon-Bons.

He found Marie-Louise and her entourage in the parish church, a diminutive copy of the Notre Dame in Cap

Henri. It had been months since Christophe had attended a service. He could not tolerate the foreign-tongued Mass and loathed the confessional. It was absurd for a King to disclose his venial sins to an unprepossessing white who fed scrounging chickens on a sun-scorched plot of ground, before his morning ablutions.

The shaded church was dim and cool. The Royal Bon-Bons dismounted but did not enter. As Christophe's presence was noticed by Princess Améthiste, she stepped from a little prayer stand and advanced to his side. No one had expected Christophe to come. He had said that he would not attend. She noticed that circles of perspiration were spreading from under his armpits and staining his coat. His smooth cheeks were tinted with a rose blush beneath their sable color. Christophe paused, slightly out of breath, as though to recover before he knelt. He looked up at the Breton priest who was conducting the service, one of the few who had not abandoned Haiti.

The priest interrupted the Mass as though to give His Majesty a moment to adjust himself and, as he stepped back from the altar, a burst of pain erupted in Christophe's left temple. It was as if he had been struck by a bludgeon. He stared at the priest with glazed eyes and imagined he was looking, once again, at Corneille Brelle as he had last seen him ... impaled against a wall by a still-quivering saber. Christophe's face lost its blush, and a grayish pallor diffused itself beneath its sepia tone. In his fantasy, suddenly Défilée seemed to spring, barefooted, to the priest's side. She had grown gaunt, with shriveled breasts and a toothless, wizened face. One could not believe that a *grand blanc* had once been jealous of her beauty. She thrust a gnarled hand toward Christophe and shrieked, as

[279]

though blind, "Qui bo' li? Qui bo' li?" [Where is the traitor hiding?]

"No!" replied Christophe. "No! I did not plot Dessalines' assassination!" But no sound came from his trembling lips, though the words fashioned themselves in his mind. Little flecks of foam gathered at the corners of his mouth as his eyes stared in terror at the imaginary Défilée who danced toward him. He clutched the *prie-Dieu*, and the dry wood cracked noisily as he struggled to rise to his feet. Suddenly, with a groan that gurgled and erupted from his massive chest he crashed to the stone floor.

Four Royal Bon-Bons carried Christophe's unconscious body to the nearby Belle-vue-le Roi chateau, and Dr. Stewart was immediately sent for. Within two hours the physician, Vastey, and Dupuy joined the Queen at Christophe's bedside.

Drums began to reverberate and echo from every hill. Crowds pattered to the little village of Limonade and gathered in front of the chateau. Dr. Stewart, aided by Dupuy, stripped Christophe and immediately diagnosed the ailment as a stroke ... apoplexy. He ordered the drums sought out and silenced; and insisted that every dog, goat, cock, and child be removed from within the sound of the chateau. A grief-stricken Marie-Louise watched as he opened a vein in Christophe's arm and bled him.

Christophe lay on his back, immobile, his respiration shallow, his breathing labored and stertorous. The concerned faces of Améthiste, Athénaire, and Prince Eugène peeped from an open doorway. The dour Scotsman who had settled himself within the Christophe household, as personal physician to the Royal Family, put his arm about the weeping Queen. "The King has a strong constitution,

Your Majesty," he comforted. "There may be paralysis for awhile, but he will recover."

Duncan Stewart canceled his lectures at the Royal College, where Christophe had appointed him professor of anatomy, remaining on call night and day, and Marie-Louise insisted on sitting constantly at the King's bedside. On the third day, when Christophe's eyelids fluttered, she immediately sent for Dr. Stewart. He ordered everyone from the room while he examined the King. He spoke to Christophe, whose eyes were now wide open, but a slight flutter of the lids was the only reply. The right side of Christophe's body would not react to the stimulus of pain, but he seemed aware of what was going on.

Stewart announced that the King was out of danger, made no mention of the paralysis, and suggested his removal to Sans Souci. It could be arranged by leveling the floor of the royal carriage with mounds of cushions. He met with Vastey, Dupuy, and Julien Prévost. They were aware of the unrest in the kingdom and feared the dissipation of Christophe's authority. The Royal Bon-Bons were sworn to secrecy and yet, as the carriage left the chateau's drive, drums began to inform the countryside that the King was not only sick but powerless . . . dying. Those who feared Christophe or nurtured personal animosities listened to the drums with suppressed impatience.

36

Christophe recovered slowly. Using the cessation of the Thursday public audiences as an excuse, many nobles no longer came to Sans Souci. They had always felt insecure under Christophe . . . for he had placed the welfare of the island above sinecures and their own aggrandizement. They wished for his death and at Cap Henri, Richard, Duke of Marmelade, whom Christophe had publicly humiliated, met with army officers and plotted the destruction of the monarchy.

Baron Dupuy and Gene Romain, Minister of War, were aware of the intrigues and machinations but were reluctant to act without Christophe's direction. There would be no coup d'état. The country owed Christophe too much. He had been tireless and ruthless, but he had advanced public education, insisted upon habits of industry and temperance, and opened opportunities for fertile minds. Dupuy and Romain were educated mulattoes who did not realize that the full-blooded Blacks still loved boundless liberty and licentiousness more than personal achievements; and while they waited the army grew disaffected and rebelled against heavy fatigue duty. The men of the 8th Regiment of Foot, stationed at St. Marc, had been charged with bringing loads of timber down from the hills for the further work of reconstruction—forced to carry the logs on their backs where the paths were too narrow for carts. The rada-tambours reminded them that their former slavery was a thing of the past . . . they were a new generation . . . entitled to equality . . . and they became noisily discontented.

The entire country waited for Christophe to die. During the heat of the day the drums called from hillside to valley, across the ranges, over the great central plain and into the dry, brown hills of the south. At night the rada-tambours of *hungans* sounded the news that the King was slowly dying—dramatizing it weirdly, as though their curse had effected it. The coded reverberations echoed over the marshes where frogs rip-ped, and vibrated across the Morne du Cap ravine, where they disturbed the nocturnal venery of the bats.

Christophe heard the drums and interpreted their messages as he lay beneath the gold-tasseled tester of his bed, his big hands resting motionless on the silken sheets. His hair had been graying. Now the crisply curled ringlets almost matched the white of the pillow as his mind sifted unexpressed thoughts. He had tried to accomplish so much for his people. Where had he failed? Had he turned despot for his vanity alone?

[283]

One morning, Dr. Stewart and Dupuy entered Christophe's bedchamber together. The leaded windows had been thrown open to a blue sky in which a skein of fleecy clouds drifted toward the mountains. A cool breeze from the sea fluttered the curtains, and one could hear the King's horses whinnying in the stables. Christophe was awake, and suddenly he startled them by speaking. He said only three words but, though his voice was thickened, they were loud and clear: "I am hungry!"

"You must lie still!" cried Stewart. "You must not exert yourself."

Christophe laughed at them. The laughter was deep in his throat as though his mouth refused to open widely. He raised his head, thrust downward with his arms, and slowly his great bulk came out from under the covers. "What's wrong with my legs, Duncan? And my right arm?"

The Scotsman was calm, imperturbable. He had acquired an attachment for this Black who was being misunderstood by his own people and who was more regal than many Kings who ruled by "divine right." "You know as well as I, Henri. You have had a stroke, and paralysis has affected your right side."

"For how long, Duncan? For how long?" One could see that his eyes were clouded by concern.

"Two months," said Stewart. "Perhaps three. Your arm and leg will recover. Later we will exercise them, but now you must rest."

That night, hidden drums reverberated the exciting news that the King was powerless . . . could not ride the countryside . . . could not even leave his bed! Christophe's heart wept within him as he listened.

In St. Marc and Cap Henri, mulatto Chevaliers and

[284]

Barons, now that they would not have to face Christophe, refused to shave. Recognizing the pride the *gens de couleur* still attached to white blood in their veins, Christophe had forbidden his aristocrats to grow beards. Now the mulattoes intended to flaunt their unshaven faces in imitation of the English and the French!

In the hot sweat of the cane fields thick-lipped, dull-eyed Blacks listened to the incessant drums. They arched their backs, looked up into the inviting blue sky, laughed, and stretched their heavily muscled arms. It would be good to sit in the shade and rest. There was too much sugar. Where was the need for so much sugar?

In Port-de-Paix and Môle St. Nicolas, students left their classrooms and rioted in the streets. The more venturesome looted the shops and warehouses along the quays.

Disaffected army officers rode openly from St. Marc to Arcahaie in order to meet with representatives from Port-au-Prince who promised them their support. The treachery at Pont Rouge was forgotten. They wished only to rid themselves of Christophe—the tyrant who forced them to sweat in the sun and intruded upon their pleasures. They would welcome a republican government such as the southern peninsula of Haiti enjoyed.

As Christophe made an impatient recovery, four of the most powerful Blacks of his household regiment, his Royal Bon-Bons, were assigned to his person. Every morning after he had breakfasted, they carried him to the balcony that adjoined his bedchamber. From its height, with the aid of his telescope, he could view his kingdom spread beneath him. The roads and aqueducts twisted through a woods and ran across the green plains to where the tiled roofs of L'Acul glinted in the sun.

While he tried to determine what had incited the unrest

[285]

in the fields, the disaffection of the troops and the student riots that had spread to Gonaïves and Poteau, messengers galloped as far north as Port-de-Paix, as far south as Terre Rouge, and brought reports to Sans Souci. When he was informed of the treasonous action of the officers at St. Marc, Christophe called upon Jean Claude, a full-blooded Black whom he had raised to the rank of General. He now had more faith in the newly appointed than in the jealous and disgruntled officers who had fought with him under Toussaint. No longer trusting even his old servants, Christophe met with Jean Claude on the sunlit balcony and instructed him to take a full company of regulars to the rebellious town of St. Marc and place it under martial law. All who had been tempted by the fruits of revolt were to be brought to him in chains! Mulatto as well as Black, student as well as cultivator, and officer as well as enlisted man. They would learn that Henri Christophe was still sovereign of Haiti!

37

General Jean Claude never reached St. Marc. Aware of his mission, Major Antoine, a ringleader of the revolt, prepared an ambush in the hills that fronted the little town of Petite Rivière. The newly appointed General was shot through the throat with the first volley, and the men in his company threw down their arms and surrendered when they saw him topple from his horse.

The Blacks of the 8th Regiment of Foot rushed down from the hills and welcomed the Sans Souci regulars as though they had come to reinforce their sparse ranks. "No work! No slave's work in the sun!" they cried. "We shall carry no stones . . . tote no beams on our backs. This land belongs to all and not to one man! There will be free rum and rich spoils for all who join us."

As the Sans Souci regulars watched, the Blacks of the 8th

Regiment tore away Jean Claude's gilded epaulets, hacked off his head, and sent it to Port-au-Prince as a symbol of their first victory. They shouldered their arms and grouped themselves for their march to Sans Souci. Major Antoine intended to skirt the town of St. Michel and reach the outskirts of Marmelade by nightfall. As they sauntered over the sun-scorched roads, the Blacks of the 8th Regiment with their tunics unbuttoned, the Sans Souci regulars uncomfortable, yet strangely elated by the prospect of change, first one cried, "*A bas le Roi!*" then another joined him and soon all were shouting, in their full-mouthed, deep-chested, guttural French: "*A bas le Roi! Vive l'indépendance!*"

When they approached plantations, workers raced across the fields, elated to find that the soldiers accepted them. They did not ask where they were going or what they would be told to do. They welcomed any interruption of discipline or labor. The drums had advised them that Christophe was dying, and this would be *s'amuser beaucoup*.

Late the next morning, Christophe met with Prévost, Pompée Vastey, and Joachim, whom he had elevated to the title of Prince. Dr. Stewart watched, on the sunlit balcony, as two Royal Bon-Bons lifted Christophe and settled him into a more comfortable position in his chair. Above it the Bons-Bons had erected a blue silk canopy to protect him from the full force of the sun. Not wishing to meet Christophe's eyes, Stewart looked away. He knew what it must cost Christophe to watch his kingdom topple about him while his massive hands lay idly in his lap. The little gathering waited, in silence, and then Christophe said, his voice strong and touched by anger, "My message to Duke Richard was to be marked most urgent. He was to report to me at once! Was it marked urgent, Pompée?"

Baron Vastey nodded. Trickles of sweat were running down from the edges of his thick, wiry red hair and staining the blue collar of his tunic.

As though intentionally tardy, Richard, Duke of Marmelade, did not present himself on the balcony until high noon. He had dressed himself in his court uniform, and only the perspiration that ran from his temples gave any evidence of his mount's dilatory canter across the twelve miles from Cap Henri to Sans Souci.

Christophe would not turn in his chair but waited until Richard stood directly in front of him, outlined against the haze-filled sky and the green fields in the distance. Then he said, "I was beginning to wonder whether or not you'd come, Richard. I am flattered that you are still afraid of me. I am not yet dead—as you can see. And I have no intention of dying in order to fulfill someone's ambition. The St. Marc garrison and rebels who have joined them have reached Ennery. You have my orders to take a full regiment and march against them." Christophe waited a moment and then said, as though apologetically, "I could have sent you the order, Richard. I wanted to see you accept it."

Richard saluted leisurely, smirked, and turned on his heel.

Suddenly Christophe thrust out his left arm and cried, "Hold! Before you go, damn your traitorous yellow hide, get to your knees and kiss your sovereign's hand!"

The blood drained from Richard's sepia face while his lips trembled with anger. He glanced from Prévost to

Vastey and from Vastey to the alert and watching Bon-Bons behind Christophe's chair. He averted his face and sank slowly to one knee. He hesitated for a single instant, leaned forward, and touched his lips to Christophe's outstretched, heavy hand, and rose and dashed from the balcony.

"You have made an enemy," cried Vastey. "You have humiliated him."

Christophe smiled. "I made an enemy of Richard long before this. Let him go and join the rebels. It will give me an excuse to execute him. It is a sound policy to have all your traitors in one camp. And now we have no time to lose. Send word that I shall review the army, personally, tomorrow morning. Dress parade!"

"No!" cried Dr. Stewart, stepping from the shadow of the balcony wall. "You must not, Henri. There is always the. . . ."

"Must?" said Christophe as he turned his heavy head toward Stewart with apparent ease. "You forget that I am the King, Duncan. Nothing will happen to me. And while there is breath in my body . . . *Je sui le Roi!*"

Early the next morning, a wizened old Black was led, in secrecy, to Sans Souci. Years ago, he had been brought from Africa in chains and he claimed to have béen the witch doctor to a King who had openly wept at his disappearance. For two hours, aided by a valet, since he insisted that no white hand should touch the King, the witch doctor massaged Christophe's right arm and leg with a mixture of red pepper, dried bay leaves, and raw rum. At nine o'clock, after Dr. Stewart, had impatiently watched the witch doctor sprinkle a circle of powered snake bones around the bed, they dressed Christophe in his most

[290]

resplendent blue-and-white uniform, ornamented with gold piping that matched the gilt of his epaulets. At ten o'clock, four Bon-Bons propped him in a thronelike chair and, followed by Prince Eugéne, Pompée Vastey, and Dr. Stewart, carried him down the stairs and out into the main terrace of the palace. Below, filling the roadway and stretching into the village of Milot, were the assembled regiments of the army of Haiti, their uniforms bright in the morning sun. Certain companies were missing, but they had closed ranks. A murmur, first of incredulity then of acclamation, rippled through the regiments as they saw the King being carried to the terrace. They were awed and silenced when he roared, "Bring me my horse!"

Christophe's favorite charger, a magnificent roan that he had named *Bois-Rouge*, its saddlecloth decorated with a crowned phoenix and the motto "*I rise again from my ashes*," had been kept waiting behind a wall. Now the powerful animal was led across the terrace. A tremendous shouting smashed the morning silence and the troops cheered, in unison, "*Vive le Roi! Vive l'homme Chrisophe!*" The rumors had been a lie! The King was alive and well! Regimental drummers pounded wildly and the din beat against the mountains and rolled back in thundering echoes.

The Royal Bon-Bons turned toward Christophe. He motioned them aside and tore away the robe that covered his lap. From a corner of his eye he could see Dr. Stewart about to step toward him, his face solemn and filled with concern. With the aid of his powerful left arm, Christophe thrust himself from the chair and stood erect. The rubefacient warmth from the red pepper and rum had not yet left him. He felt rested . . . strong. He glanced about him, smiled, and to Stewart's amazement reached the big roan with four confident, headlong strides. His left hand grasped the charger's mane, while his right arm lifted itself, a little slowly, toward the saddle. Despite his weight, he had always ignored the stirrup. He bent a little now, in order to leap up, and suddenly his legs gave way. Slowly, like an empty hack, he slumped under the horse as the animal pivoted away from him. Dr. Stewart and the Bon-Bons rushed to his side, but Christophe insisted on rising, unassisted. He struggled to his knees, his head and chest supported by his one good arm. His face was suffused with sweat and he shut his eyes against the sting of the salt. Suddenly his arm trembled, gave way, and he fell face down upon the flagstones.

They rushed to pick him up ... Stewart, Eugène, the Bon-Bons, Vastey ... and carried him to his chair. It had rained during the night, and the morning sun had not yet dried the shaded flagstones so that his uniform was stained. Stewart tried to arrange the robe about him in order to cover the smears. Christophe's lips trembled. One could the wrath rising in his throat, and suddenly he tore away the robe and bellowed, "No! Duncan. By the god Damballa, no! They must accept me as I am!"

The regiments were stunned and silenced. Joachim raced down from the terrace, his scabbard thudding against his thigh, and ordered the dress parade to begin. The first demi-brigade of the Royal Haitian Guard saluted smartly as they passed the terrace; but, as each company of infantry marched by, their salutes became constrained and careless. They had been impressed by Christophe's failure to mount his horse and broke ranks the moment they turned behind the high garden wall. One could hear them shouting, "*A bas le Roi! Vive l'indépendance!*"

Christophe motioned to his Bon-Bons. He would not watch the rest of his ungrateful troops march by. He noticed that the sentries had deserted their boxes, and as he was carried through the palace he was disquieted by its strange silence. Where were the pages ... the servants ... the gentlemen-at-arms and the ladies-in-waiting? Had they slipped quietly away? So soon?

His bedchamber was filled with intimates and the members of his family. Corpulent Victor-Henri seemed unconcerned, as though what was happening would not affect him. Frances-Améthiste and Ann-Athénaire were weeping. Marie-Louise, though bewildered by the unexpected turn of events, tried to comfort her daughters. Christophe insisted that everyone but Dupuy and Dr. Stewart should leave him. In a corner of the bedchamber, hidden by the voluminous folds of a crest-embroidered drape, the witch doctor speculated on his punishment for having failed the King.

Christophe turned to Dupuy. "You must leave me." he said. "Go back to America. And take Saunders with you. It is inevitable that Blacks will gain their freedom in the United States, and they may adapt themselves to a white man's world better than we have here. I dreamed of an empire for Blacks in the Caribbean. I had hoped to erect it in one lifetime, but I have learned that man is a single species and must not segregate himself."

He looked toward the lean and angular Scottish doctor. "You, too, must leave me, Duncan. You have been a good friend; but my time is finished. And now carry me out to the balcony and leave me. I wish to be alone. See what you can do for the girls, Duncan. And tell Marie-Louise not to disturb me. I shall sit in the sun for a little while ... alone."

Christophe sat on the balcony and looked out over his beloved countryside. The sun was strong. It was Friday, October 6th, and the rains were late. The fields were a deep reflectionless green, and along the borders of the road the earth was dry and brown. Suddenly he heard whispering and the shuffling of feet behind him. *I am about to be assassinated!* was his first thought. *No! Not like Dessalines!* his mind shouted, and his left hand grasped the arm of his heavy chair.

It was the young Duchess of Marmelade. She had bribed the witch doctor to lead her secretly to Christophe. She sank to her knees and placed a bundle on Christophe's lap. "See what I have brought you, Henri. Do you see what I have brought?" She unfolded a lace scarf and disclosed an infant in swaddling clothes. It had the features and burnished skin of a griffe. "It's a boy, Henri. Richard has not yet named him."

"Nor shall I," Christophe said. "I have nothing to leave him, for the dynasty will die with me. I predict it. After I am gone the forests will reclaim the hills, weeds will spring up in the plantations, and the carcasses of dead dogs will pollute the aqueducts. Shunned and betrayed by mulattoes, the Blacks will find themselves once more herded like goats and driven in the fields like oxen. Violence will not help them as long as they remain unschooled in a white man's world. Did I drive them too hard, Mariée? Was the time too soon?"

"Why do you speak of death, Henri? You are *un vieillard*. Richard is nothing! I know. I have lived with him. *Vous êtes un grand homme.*" She lifted the infant from his lap. "I have brought you the proof. You will get well, Henri. You must!"

[294]

He permitted himself a smile. "You will not mind if I make you a widow?"

She flung an arm about him and burst into laughter. She knew the vigor of his body and refused to believe he would not recover.

"Then you may name the child *Henri*," Christophe said. "Guard him carefully, for he has royal blood in his veins."

Christophe remained on the balcony. Dr. Stewart and Saunders finally joined him there. Saunders had spent the day in Cap Henri, where a vessel, in its harbor, was about to depart for Philadelphia in order to bring the first batch of Negro immigrants to Haiti. The men sat in silence until the mists settled in the valleys and the sun began to sink below the faraway rim of sea. For a few brief moments, sunlight gilded the mountain peaks and then was gone. As though a blanket had dropped about them, the plain of Milot became instantly dark and murmurous. The sudden transition from day to night made Christophe aware of his own changing fortune and he said quietly, "Marie-Louise once read to me that to be great is to be lonely. I would add my own observation: Not to achieve a dream is to drown in self-despair."

Suddenly the sky was red from the reflection of a spreading fire. The King's beloved chateau, at the edge of L'Acul, had been set to the torch. The memories that the chateau contained sent a burst of adrenalin coursing through Christophe's veins, as a sound of distant cheering and the throbbing of a rada-tambour drifted up to them. Other fires burst skyward and became red lances that illumined the countryside. Before the night was over The Cloak, The Scepter, The Necklace, and The Embuscade would most likely be set to the torch. They might even burn his prized plantation, Ennery. The Black animals would destroy what they coveted! Christophe was spurred by such violent anger that he sprang from his chair. As Stewart watched, amazed, he strode across the balcony, in a limping gait, and bellowed, "No! By all the gods of Guinea and the hell of Christ, no! I will not let them destroy what I have created. They have starved on jackal meat for a thousand years! Now they wish to live like lions. Well, then, let them first become lions!"

38

Friday night, October 6th, was a night of rioting and dancing in Cap Henri. Richard reviewed the troops in the Champ de Mars, appointed himself their General, and harangued them with wild gestures and reckless promises: Under his leadership there would be no exploitation of labor. Their parents had been brought to the island as slaves, and Christophe still treated them as slaves! Surrounded by whites, he acted as though he owned Haiti. The Blacks were entitled to both freedom and reparations! Reparations for their suffering and indignities! He tore the medallion of the Order of Saint-Henri from his tunic and trampled it into the cobblestones of the drill ground. Le Comte de Gros Morne did the same. There was a spontaneous roar from every throat: "Down with the King! *A bas le Roi, Christophe!*"

A cask of rum was tapped. Too impatient to wait, the troops smashed other casks, while many of them rushed away to join the dancers in the Place Montarcher or the looters in the Rue Espagnole. They were met there by malefactors who had been liberated from the stockades. Students marched through the streets, rebelled against the confinement of their classrooms, tore their books, and shouted: "*A bas le Tyran! A bas Christophe! Vive la liberté!*"

Shops along the quays were hastily boarded, doors to every home were closed, lights were extinguished. No one slept in Cap Henri. Haiti had been free of insurrection and violence for sixteen years. Now, once again, there was rioting in the streets.

In the morning, as though the coup d'état was a *fait accompli*, Richard ordered drummers to parade through the streets and inform the troops to assemble in their barracks. When they were drawn up on the drill ground, officers rushed up and down and exhorted them to revolt. The tyrant was to be deposed! Liberty would be returned to the people. Liberty and true independence! Their words of turbulence and rage filled the troops with a sense of excitement. They looked forward to change . . . even to violence! They brandished their muskets and cried: "*A bas le Tyran!*" Sixteen years ago they had known no more than two dozen words of bastard patois. Now they cried, in excellent French: "*A bas Christophe!*"

As the red sun slanted its rays over Pointe Picolet, Richard, Lebrun, and Prophète, Commander of the King's Light Horse, led the assembled troops from the Champ de Mars and marched them to Haut-du-Cap, a village nine miles from Milot, where they entrenched and threw up hasty defenses. Every rada-tambour insisted that Christophe was dying; but while there was breath in his body, they feared him.

All day Saturday, Christophe kept to his private quarters and would see no one. Even Dr. Stewart was refused admittance while the witch doctor continued to massage Christophe's leg and arm with a mixture of red pepper and raw rum. He had now improved the formula with portions of coconut oil. At two o'clock Mariée came to him and informed him of what was happening in Haut-du-Cap.

"They are *ivre imbéciles!* And Richard is the biggest fool of all. They have only four cannon that they have trundled from the Champ de Mars and no one has thought to bring the shot. This morning the St. Marc regulars joined forces with them, and already Antoine and others are disputing Richard's and Lebrun's authority. They are snarling at each other like a pack of dogs about a bitch in heat."

"Come here!" cried Christophe. "You have brought me great news. I feel fully recovered." He reached from the bed, drew her to his side, and tore away the sheet that half covered him. His phallus was like a mangrove root that had shot up from a tangle of black moss. Impatient with her fumbling, he thrust his left arm under her shift and caressed her breast. Suddenly, with a little cry of pain, she sprang from the bed. In contrast to the other, the nipple of her right breast was as distended as the teat of a wet nurse. He looked at his hand. "Forgive me, Marièe," he said laughing. "I forgot about the pepper and the rum."

After Mariée left, Christophe ordered the Royal Dahomans to pass in review before him. Knowing only too well how much his power depended upon his personal bearing, he had himself attired in the full-dress uniform of the Haitian Guard: a long red coat with black revers, red epaulets, white knee breeches, and a shako trimmed with red braid. To the left of his tunic he pinned a gold badge bearing the royal arms and the motto: *"My God, my Cause, and my Sword."*

Leaning heavily on Stewart's arm, he supported himself on his powerful left leg and stood at attention as though fully recovered. A clerk was seated at a table, and as each member of the palace guard passed him on the terrace, he was given four gourdes as a cash gift.

Later that day, Christophe ordered a platoon of Dahomans under command of Joachim, Grand Maréchal du Palais, to sortie toward Haut-du-Cap in search of fresh information. Christophe watched them from his balcony, with the aid of his telescope, as they sallied northward from Sans Souci. Joachim rode proudly up the white-dusted road, as though a great and invincible army rode behind him.

When the brief twilight settled over the countryside, the Grand Maréchal came back . . . alone. A sniper had shot away his cocked hat, he had lost his banner, and the Dahomans had deserted him.

That night, Christophe could not sleep. Awake and restless, he left his bedchamber, limped down the dark staircase clinging to the banister, and wandered out into the moonlit terrace. The servants were stealing out of the palace! He could see their furtive forms as they merged into the shadows of the garden foliage. Grooms were dashing from the stables, and sentinels were deserting their

posts at the arsenal. Elegantly attired Bon-Bons were saun-
tering away with proud and unhurried strides. If only his
leg were well, he would dash after them and smash at them
with his fists. The Black bastards! He could have bought
them as slaves! Instead, he had hired them as men. Where
was their gratitude? Their paid-for loyalty?

He glanced up into the inverted bowl of the star-stud-
ded sky that seemed supported by the dark crags of the
mountains. Behind him, obscured by a drift of clouds, his
citadel brooded—immense and impregnable. Below him,
he heard the splash of water as it spilled over the edges of
the fountain. The night was strangely quiet. Even the
rustle of the palm fronds seemed hushed. He listened to
the throaty rib-bed . . . rib-bed . . . of a single frog in the
distance and was startled by the explosive rumble of
drums. They grew exultant, bombastic, and ominous as
their reverberations echoed and reechoed from the hills.
They routed the murmurous brooding of the night with
their insistent undulations; and Christophe returned to his
bedchamber to wait until dawn.

In the morning, Christophe learned that the grooms had
not only abandoned the stables but had stolen most of the
trappings and some of the saddles. He sent for his citadel
garrison and watched the remnants of his military force
assemble—1,200 infantry and twenty small cannons.
Joachim attempted to form them into companies, but they
were indifferent, indolent, and unresponsive. Dessalines
would have thwacked off a few heads to alert them! Christophe watched as they marched off, without the sound of
fife and drum to which they had become accustomed.

The day was interminable. Milot was as quiet as though

[301]

all Haiti had been struck by a plague. In the morning a single church bell had sounded from across the fields . . . a timorous call to Sunday Mass. Now there was nothing. Nothing but the hot sun, the green fields, and the white-dusted road. Christophe secluded himself in his rooms and brooded on his failure. The Blacks were impatient! Impatient! He had dressed them in gilt trappings and vested them with nobility, but he had not paid enough attention to the presumed aristocracy of their minds—had ignored the core of violence that seethed and erupted with their smallest frustration. If only he could ride as far as Haut-du-Cap! Could he trust himself to be strapped to the saddle? Should he risk the same ignominious dismember-ment with which they had butchered Dessalines?

Joachim was back after dark. He had returned on foot, crossing deserted plantations, secreting himself behind bushes and trees, and avoiding every habitation. The troops had laughed at his order to attack the insurgents. They had overturned the cannons, thrown down their muskets, waved their cartouche pouches aloft as signals of surrender, and cried, *"Vive la liberté! Brisons les chaines de l'esclavage!"* and clambered over the Haut-du-Cap defenses in order to join the rebels.

Christophe sent for Dr. Stewart, who arrived disheveled and slightly out of breath. The Prince Royal was with him. As though unconcerned, he was dressed in a green tunic with pink facings and green satin breeches. His plump face showed little emotion. Stewart had been attending the two princesses, who were distraught and would not be consoled by composed Marie-Louise.

Christophe had abused his right leg, limping about the

balcony, watching for a sign of Joachim. Now it would no longer support him, and he had taken to his bed. He turned to Dr. Stewart and said, "In a few hours, the traitors will be here. I have masked the tempestuous violence of my people with a civilized façade, but I have not torn the snakes and thunderstones from their minds; nor improbity from their chameleonic hearts. You must leave me, Duncan. Immediately! I can no longer ensure your safety. There are still horses in the stables. Take whatever you wish and go, by back trails, to Cap Henri. You will be safe with the British consul. And now send Marie-Louise and my daughters to me. I shall express my good-bys. I have instructed Vastey and Dupuy to escort them to Cap Henri and place them under the protection of English friends."

"Don't be a damned fool, Henri! We will never abandon you!"

Christophe sidled from the bed and, as he limped toward the balcony, Stewart rushed to him in order to support his right side. Impatient with the recalcitrant latch, Christophe flung his great bulk against the French doors and smashed them from their hinges. Starlight glittered on the scattered shards of glass. Down in the valley, at the edge of Haut-du-Cap, a thousand flickering torch flames danced in the night. The reverberations of the drums echoed from every hill, and the night wind carried the sounds of the howling, clamoring, screeching mob that now spilled over the road toward Milot.

Alarmed by the crash of the doors and the shattered glass, Vastey, Dupuy, and the royal family rushed into the bedchamber. Christophe struggled to a chair, and his daughters immediately flung themselves at his feet and laid their wet cheeks against his knees. Stewart motioned Vastey and Dupuy from the room. Christophe glanced at Victor-Henri ... squat, obstinate, unprepossessing. He was fourteen but looked twice his age. Had he really sired him? Even Baron Vastey, who had attempted to tutor him, had taught him nothing. He looked down at his beloved Athénaire and Améthiste. One was twenty, the other was twenty-two; yet they had never married. Had they secret lovers? Surely they were not like the tight-waisted, white maiden ladies who had come, years ago, from the States, to educate them and polish their manners. He glanced up at Marie-Louise. She was like a rock! An ebony, inscrutable sculpture in granite. Never angered ... never truly aroused. Had she known about Mariée? Did she know that Mariée had shared his bed but yesterday? In this very room? He recalled that she had accompanied him, in the early years of the war, with the infants on her back, without food other than wild fruit and berries, exposed to the weather, often half-clothed. And he knew that, as long as there was breath in his body, she would never leave him.

There was the sound of running feet and then a great crash of broken glass. Looters had reached the palace. "You must leave!" cried Christophe. "Hurry!"

They rushed out and found the witch doctor, Prévost, Dupuy, and Vastey gathered outside the door. They stared at each other, alarmed and incredulous. In Christophe's magnificent Throne Room, tapestries were being torn from the walls and rolled like worthless rugs, portraits were being pulled down, and the throne itself was being smashed.

Suddenly there was a loud report from within the bedchamber. They hurried back into it and found Christophe

[304]

lying on the floor, in a spreading pool of blood, the silver butt of his pistol clutched tightly in his left hand. With deadly accuracy, Christophe had shot himself through the heart!

The sounds below them grew in violence. Jabbering and howling spoilers had reached the impressive library with its statuary, its carvings, and its bronze candelabra. They could hear books being flung against the walls and vases being smashed against the marble floor.

"We must hurry!" Dr. Stewart urged. His knees were wet with blood where he had knelt beside Christophe.

"No!" answered Marie-Louise. "I will not abandon Henri to the jackals."

"But Your Majesty . . . ."

"No!" she insisted with a firmness Stewart had not known she possessed. "Save yourselves. Victor and the girls will help me carry him to the citadel."

"Mais non, maman!" cried Victor-Henri. "Non! maman. I shall not go to the citadel with you. They will butcher me!" His lips quivered and he began to cry, looking first to Vastey and then to Dupuy for comfort.

Suddenly Marie-Louise, for the first time, struck him. A little trickle of blood dripped from one dark, wide nostril where her thick hand had slapped him. She turned immediately and began to strip the bed. They helped her tie the sheets to two poles, to form an improvised hammock and load Christophe's body on it, and followed with their burden as she led them from the palace by a secret door. The sound of pillaging was all about them as they reached the dark garden. Dr. Stewart and Dupuy intended to secure horses and rush to Cap Henri. Trembling, Victor-Henri pleaded to be taken along. Marie-Louise, adamant, insisted

[305]

on having the body of the King carried to the citadel, and her daughters would not leave her. Nor would Pompée Vastey, whose fierceness had not been blunted by the peaceful years. With some strange foresight, Marie-Louise had pried the gems from her tiara, and she offered a few to the witch doctor and an old Negress, perhaps his wife, who had silently appeared at his side. They shook their heads, refusing them, and the witch doctor began to dance about the hammock with strange incantations.

"He claims he knows an unused path to the citadel," interpreted Vastey. "Come! We must hurry!"

Christophe's body was a heavy load for aging Vastey, Marie-Louise, and the two slender girls. The witch doctor led the way, barefooted, mouthing alien supplications in the semidarkness. Their first resting place was at the foothills, where they were hidden by dense foliage. They heard the thud and clatter of dislodged stones all about them. Dark shadows raced by . . . obscure forms of masons and sentries who were abandoning the citadel. They could hear the reverberations of drums echoing from all the hills— wild, incessant, exultant. Above them the somber fortress appeared, in a placenta of gray clouds, as though the mountain had just thrust it up out of its very bowels. The mouths of its cannons, lipped with moonlight, grimaced from every embrasure. Marie-Louise urged them on. As they climbed higher, the air grew cold and there was a threat of rain in the dark sky. She would not let them linger at any resting place, for below them the bobbing torches now filled the road all the way from Milot to the steps of Sans Souci; and she remembered what Claire Heureuse had told her of how they had dismembered Dessalines.

It had been midnight when they had approached the foothill of the mountain; it was morning by the time they reached the Martello towers that Christophe had built on the slopes below the citadel. The sun was hidden by the mountain peak upon which the fortress squatted—grotesque and massive—but the mists were rising in the valley. The paths below them became alive with released prisoners who had been too timorous to risk a descent in the dark. Now they rushed downward, dislodging stones and broken branches. One could hear their exultant cries: *"Le Roi est mort! Le Roi est mort!"* as though they had been freed from tyranny.

Exhausted by their burden, leaving a little train of muddied blood, for knife-edged flints has slashed the women's thin-soled shoes to ribbons, the little group finally reached the central court of the deserted citadel. But for a few green parrots that flew cawing overhead, there was no sound. It was as though they had reached the top of the world. Below them was the green, tropic splendor of Haiti. The crags of its mountains jutted into the sky, and the shimmering sea lapped at its beaches.

A huge trough of freshly mixed builder's lime lay open in the center of the courtyard, and Marie-Louise led them to it, as though she had seen it in a vision and knew it was there. She took the crucifix from her neck and wound it about Christophe's stiffened fingers. "Hail Mary, full of grace . . ." she intoned. Suddenly the witch doctor sprang toward Christophe's rigid face and began to brush it, in a circular motion, with an *ounga* bag. Marie-Louise slapped it from his hand. It spiraled above the trough, held aloft by the red-dyed cock feathers with which it was bound. Then it fell and sank into the lime.

"The Lord is with thee . . .," Marie-Louise continued, as though she had not been interrupted. "Blessed art thou among women and blessed is the fruit of thy womb . . ." Tears were ensnared by her lashes and overflowed her lids. She struggled to lift the hammock higher, and Vastey, surmising her intention, helped her. They tilted the hammock, with a tremendous effort, and Christophe's body slid . . . pitched toward the trough and struck the lime with a sucking splash. The girls voiced suppressed screams as it sank quickly below the surface. One arm struck a submerged board and a stiff, gray-coated hand emerged from the lime and pointed toward the tropical blue sky.

Postscript

*The insurgents permitted Marie-Louise and her daugh-
ters to escape to England; but faithful Joachim, violent
Pompée Vastey, proud Armand-Eugène, and terrified Victor-Henri were thrown into the Champ de Mars stockade
where, at Richard's order, they were brutally bayoneted.*

*Dr. Duncan Stewart remained for some time in Haiti,
under the protection of the British flag. Two months after
Sans Souci was pillaged, he wrote to Thomas Clarkson, the
English abolitionist:*

> *December 8, 1820*
> *King Henri shot himself through the heart. He
> seemed sensible that he had used his people harshly—
> a necessary severity. In the latter part of his life he
> became—what is uncommon in a man of his age—li-
> centious, and prostituted the wives of most of the
> nobility. Indeed, the last years of his life, although*

marked by liberality, were sadly stained by acts of oppressive cruelty. . . .

This was the letter that was sent to the outside world by the white man who had lived under Christophe's roof and enjoyed his hospitality and magnanimity for more than ten years.

Three retired Generals had a greater love for their dead monarch. They clambered up to the citadel, built a little hut over the lime trough, and did sentry duty upon the walls as though they were defending an immediate legend.

The conspirators soon learned that it is simpler to overthrow a government than to establish a new order. No sooner was Christophe's monarchy abolished than Jean Pierre Boyer, who had succeeded Pétion, marched a mulatto-dominated army of 20,000 northward and proclaimed the former Kingdom of Haiti incorporated into the southern Republic. Schools were closed, academies were abolished, and all of Christophe's cherished projects were aborted. The name of Cap Haitien was restored to Cap Henri, and many of its streets were renamed. The Blacks, offered a fresh emancipation, mistook permissiveness for freedom, and the "new" Haiti was overrun by licentiousness and misdemeanors.

The neglected citadel, buffeted by wind and rain, looked down as though it brooded over what was happening to Haiti. The island's tropic beauty became scarred by neglect and decay. The towns were now filled with the garrulous patois and the uninhibited laughter of their barefoot citizenry. The sunlit streets buzzed with the incessant droning of flies in the untended kennels. Orange lichens and green mold settled in the unpatched plaster and eroded stucco of the structures whose walls had once reflected the tropic sunlight with freshly calcimined shades of blue, flamingo pink, and brilliant yellow.

Beyond the towns, mangroves and scrub forests reclaimed the plains, while clusters of shacks sprouted along pitted roadways. Filth-caked swine, starved curs, scrawny hens, and naked children scrambled about on the hard-packed earth. Black wenches lazed and prattled while untutored, dull-eyed men dozed in the breathless shade . . . waiting, perhaps, for another Christophe . . . and the dream of Black empire.

Glossary

affranchis   freed slaves
ateliers   plantation slave drivers
auberge   inn or tavern
Auberge de la Couronne   The Crown Tavern
bagasse   dry cane haulms
bijoutier   jeweler
bougies   prayer candles the size of birthday candles
cailles   straw-thatched huts
chigoe   a small flea of tropical America and Africa
coiyou   the vulva of an animal in heat
dengue   an infectious fever of the tropics
Dominicaine   a fancy prostitute
fou!   attack!
gens de couleur   people of part Negro ancestry
gourde   a coin used as currency

grands blancs   wealthy whites

griffe, griffone (f.)   offspring of a Negro and a mulatto

Guinea   Negro name for all Africa and/or the spiritual abode

hôtelier   innkeeper

hounfour   voodoo temple

hungan   voodoo priest

loiloichi   stomach dance

mamaloi   a priestess

mamelouc   offspring of a white and an Indian

mustee   offspring of a white and an octoroon

mustefino   offspring of a white and a mustee

mystère   a spirit

papaloi   a priest

sang-mêlés   a people of mixed blood

sise de loa   the cataleptic seizure of a body by a spirit

/